OWARE MOSAIC

By

Nzondi

Omnium Gatherum
Los Angeles

Oware Mosaic
Copyright© 2019 Ace Antonio Hall

ISBN-13: 9781949054163
ISBN-10: 1949054160

Library of Congress Control Number:2019943601

First Edition

To my real-life superheroes, my sons, Derrick and Bryce, fellow author, Ken Hughes, the ScHoFan critique group, Robert J. Sawyer, Tony N. Todaro, Charlie Franco, Kate Jonez, and librarians, Neil Citrin and Maggie Johnson. Good luck on your retirement, Maggie. We're going to miss you.

PRAISE FOR OWARE MOSAIC

"Once again, Nzondi creates a rich and vibrant world crackling with life. He is a brilliant writer, one readers and critics should be watching."

—Pete Nowalk, creator of
How To Get Away With Murder

"If you're looking for a story that's daringly imaginative, *Oware Mosiac* will scratch that itch."

—Alma Katsu, author of *The Hunger*

"Nzondi's *Oware Mosaic* is real Afrofuturism, speculative fiction actually set on the continent itself. This is the future of SF, and the future is looking good."

—Steven Barnes, author of *Lion's Blood*

"I loved, loved, loved this novel by Nzondi! Breath-taking SF adventure!!"

—Linda Addison, author of
How To Recognize A Demon Has Become Your Friend

LISTENING TO A NEW SONG

By Linda D. Addison

I've said how deeply I love words, real and made-up. Every thing I write, especially poetry, is a way to discover new words, how to use known words in new ways, to give shape to the songs I hear in my head. One day, years ago, I meet this person Nzondi (Ace Antonio Hall) and his warm personality and sense of humor made me want to know more.

He attended my poetry reading and I could see in his eyes that he hears the song, gets the words, the images. Afterwards, we talk and it's clear: we acknowledge the magic of words.

Curious about his writing, I bought his book, The Confessions of Sylva Slasher (about a teenage zombie slasher who also raises the dead for police investigations), and discovered he is a superb story teller. Over time I've found that he has a deep background with writing, as well as other talents (acting, fitness maven, and passionate motivator of life).

Every time our paths cross: laughter and ah-ha moments transpire. It's 2019 and I get a copy of his new science-fiction novel, Oware Mosaic. And there it is, words, real and made-up, the first line: "I was born in a dead man's city."

Damn. That's good. I could write poems to that one line.

The story unfolds, like multi-dimensional origami, far in the future: family, friends, beings, technology, virtual and real worlds built from the intricately imaginative mind of Nzondi.

While I look forward to Nzondi and I meeting again, laughing and more, you get to delve into this wonderful collection of words, the enticing tale waiting for you to turn the page.

—Linda D. Addison, award-winning author of *How to Recognize a Demon Has Become Your Friend* and HWA Lifetime Achievement Award recipient.

1

GHANA AFRICA 2025

01010100 01100001 01110100 01110101

I was born in a dead man's city. My first taste of how bitter life was, came when my parents died on my eighth birthday. I ended up springing from foster home to foster home but spent the majority of my useless childhood playing role-playing games online, to flee from the sting of the African streets. I never played with dolls, wore makeup nor had a boyfriend. Why? The world had fallen ill due to a virus called hate, and that was one disease that led to wars so brutal, it crippled the planet. So there wasn't much to do in an insufferable wasteland but play virtual reality games, get wasted and berate myself for still wanting to make a difference on a planet where the word hope had become obsolete in all languages.

On the last day of spring, at three o'clock in the morning, I sped down the road in one of the last working piece-of-crap vehicles in Ghana, except, of course, military vehicles. The party was on the outskirts of the village of Liati Wote, near Lake Volta, and I had just left. I'd been drinking and hadn't slept in over twenty hours. Needless to say, the world was spinning on its axis just a wee bit, but I'd always managed before. At that time of night, no one was on the road, and it had started to rain a little. I put on the windshield wipers.

They were also one hundred percent crapper material and screeched loudly with every wipe. I received an alert on the temporal transmitter of my neural implant, or in simple terms, a mind-phone, and recognized the identification number.

"Why are you calling me at three something in the morning, big brother?" I asked.

"You have my car, you know? You were supposed to be home, already!"

"Sorry. I got held up."

"Is that your way of saying you met somebody and the two of you drank way too much blood vodka to notice the time?"

"Meet someone? I wish. There were only humans, there. And no, I haven't had one drink, tonight."

"Yeah, right, Feeni. Tell that to someone who doesn't know you."

"I swear, I haven't."

"Are you're home? The twins are sleep, right?"

"Um, yeah. I guess."

"Okay, that's a bit ambiguous. Where are you?"

"In Liati Wote, working on a case."

Liati Wote? I thought. I didn't want to tell him I was there, too. He would have made me turn around and pick him up, and then he'd known for sure I was wasted, and driving his car. I didn't believe for one minute he was working on a case, but decided to change the subject, altogether.

"You need to get new wipers, though. I can't see crap with these shitty dirt scrapers."

"I'll remember how you trash-talk my ride, next time you ask to borrow it."

Laughing, I said, "Don't get butt-hurt, big brother, I'll make it up to you."

"Starting with ironing my clothes every day for a week."

"You're pure evil."

He laughed. "Speaking of evil. I meant to ask you, can

the body produce antibodies to fight any disease, if given antiviral drugs?"

"Good question. It actually depends on—"

The car hit something, and I swerved, trying to gain control of it. It did a full three-sixty before I managed to skid to a stop. Everything happened fast. It took me a few to get my bearings. My head hurt. Blood was on the steering wheel, and I touched my forehead and the crimson substance on my fingers told me it was my own.

"Hey! Hey! Feeni!" Kofi said. "What the hell was that?"

"Nothing—nothing. I think the tire blew."

"Are you okay?"

"I'm fine, just a little bump to the head." The passenger side of the car seemed higher than the driver's. "Great."

"What?"

"I think I have a flat, now."

"You jacked up my tires?"

"Relax, you should be more worried about me."

I got out of the car and groaned. My abs bruised, slamming into the bottom of the steering wheel, although I had no recollection if it had. The rain started pouring down harder, but it felt good in the sweltering summer morning.

"You didn't dent my car, did you?" Kofi asked.

I didn't answer him. There was a child-size sandal covered in blood, lodged under the front tire.

"Hey, Feeni. I know you hear me. Just tell me. Did you wreck my car?"

I took a slow few steps toward the back of the car and gasped.

"What is it?" Kofi asked.

"Oh, no, no, no, no, no," I said, and fell to my knees.

At first, I saw her mangled toes, and then her legs, before I got to the back of the vehicle and saw her small lifeless body on the pavement. Half of her face was gone, leaving flesh and blood on the pavement, a stream of it leaked from out of her ears.

I screamed.

Kofi had to call me back on the mind-celly three times

before I collected myself enough to tell him what happened. By the time he got to me, the time had stretched itself into eternity, and the only living thing that passed me on the road that night was a lone pup mountain wolf, or what the locals called a dhole. Like the people of our country, many of them were affected over the years from nuclear radiation. Usually, they traveled in packs and scared the villagers because of the many-reported vicious attacks.

The driver's side door was still open, and I had one leg out. The pup came up to me and smelled my trembling hand and licked it before he went on his way up the street. He hadn't any deformations or tumorous lumps like most of them did, so I didn't kill it. To be honest, I don't think I was in the right mind to harm it, had it been one of the radiation-mutated dholes.

I didn't even hear Kofi when he approached me.

"Feeni?" he said, shaking me. "Feeni, do you know who that is?"

I looked up at him through glassy eyes and shook my head.

He smacked the heel of his hand to his forehead. "Oh, man. What did you do? What did you do?" He placed his hands behind his neck, pointing his elbows up and outward and walked away from me, mumbling.

I glanced at him, dazed. Not knowing, at the time, if I was awake or sleeping.

He let out a long breath and walked back toward the car, pounding a fist in his other hand.

"Okay, okay, okay. Look, um. You can't be here. You'd be in prison for life and Auntie Yajna would surely lose her job, not to mention, would die of a heart attack if she knew you were drinking and driving."

"What are you saying?"

The rain poured down and dripped from his face, his chin. "Just sit tight. I'll take care of this."

"She's...dead?"

"What do you think, Feeni?" Kofi asked, his clothes drenched. "She's definitely not breathing after having a

Volvo roll over her. What was she doing out here, this time of night?"

"I didn't see her. Believe me, Kofi. It was an accident."

"Right, right. Look, you're a good person, and you've never been in trouble before. I'm going to call Grunt."

"Major Grunt? He—He's with GAF."

The Inspector General of Police, Bete Sibaya, had merged the police force with the Ghana Armed Forces and created the Ghana Allied Forces. Major Grunt had trained with the army branch of the force.

"You just said they'll arrest me. You can't call him!"

"Yeah, I can. He owes me one. He'll pick you up, no questions. I can trust him not to say anything with what I got on him."

I shook my head. "I—I don't know. No. No, it's not right."

"What's not right is what you did to this young girl. She's thirteen years old.

"How do you know that?"

"That doesn't matter. What matters is how everyone is going to judge you for this."

He placed his hand on my shoulder. "You have to do this."

"No," I said, and tugged away.

"Do you want to go to prison for the rest of your life? Bring shame on our entire family, and even our village when this gets out? That girl is dead, Feeni! She's dead! And she's not coming back. You screwed up, but believe me, if you turn yourself in, you're never going to recover from this one. You hear me? Never!"

Thunder boomed, and the rain came down even harder. Kofi called Major Grunt, and just like he said, Grunt didn't ask any questions. When Kofi came back to the car, the rain had slowed up a bit, but he was dripping wet. He sat on the passenger's side and flicked on the old radio. Some young boy or girl, it was hard to tell, was ranting about how people should stand up and not be weak. I was out of it. I didn't listen to much. I just remember wondering who gave them access to speak so freely on the radio like that.

In a tough rasped voice, this is what that person said:

"I had ten brothers and sisters, and when I was nine years old my grandmother trafficked me to a stranger who came to my village looking for kids to enslave in the fishing communities along the Lake Volta. No one did anything to stop her. My parents died when I was an infant and we were impoverished. I promise that citizens of Ghana will have to pay for not standing up to the tyranny of the GFA while children are made labor and sex slaves."

It was sad what she went through, and I couldn't believe such a thing was still allowed in our country. My brother turned off the radio in disgust and got out of the car.

"He's here," Kofi said.

I didn't say anything, just stared forward at the raindrops on the windshield. Wearing gloves, Kofi and Grunt cleaned out the inside and outside of the car. They even put gloves on me and told me not to take them off until I got home.

"Don't worry, sister," he said, cleaning the inside windshield. "We're family. Nothing's more important than that."

Turning to face him, I did my best to smile but didn't believe him. Not after all I'd been through growing up in foster homes. Grunt got in the back and started wiping down the seats. Unlike many of the men of the Ghana Allied Forces, Major Grunt had become friendly with the civilians of our community, including me.

Like the height of a professional basketball forward, he was two hundred and four cm, cut like a bodybuilder and had tattoos of Egyptian hieroglyphs covering his neck. There were tribal scarification marks on his cheekbones. Rain fell on his face, dripped off of his lips.

"I messed up," I said, and broke down again, crying.

"No one needs to know," Grunt said, "It would destroy your family. No, it's better this way."

The two of them took care of the body while I waited

in Grunt's car. I was so out of it, I stayed in the car and shivered, either from being in shock or from the coolness of wearing cold wet clothes. Either way, I waited until they finished doing whatever it was they did. The next morning I woke up with one helluva hangover and wondered had the tragic experience happened at all or if it was just some wild dream.

When I awakened, Auntie Yajna and the twins were home. That was a big relief, but that didn't stop my stomach from being queasy after what I did. All I kept seeing in my mind was the girl's mangled feet beneath the car.

That morning, Auntie Yajna stuck her head in my room with a face full of anger.

"I taught you better than that!" she said. "Coming home in the wee hours of the morning like you don't have any damn sense!"

I didn't want to leave my room, ever. That afternoon, when I went to the bathroom, I overheard Kofi telling Auntie Yajna that he no longer had his car—that it died on him—I stopped listening when he said he had it towed to a junkyard in Accra. Now, he had no way to take her to work, and she'd have to leave extra early and take a tro-tro bus. She was not happy about that at all, and said this killed her chances of asking for a few days off to take the twins for vaccination shots.

When she used the word killed, all I thought of was the teenage girl I ran over. I stayed in bed all day and cried. It was one of the many times that I wished my father was still alive. He'd known how to fix me, make me feel better. Mom always fussed at me, but Dad, he always spoiled me. I needed his love. Just to be held in his big arms would help me get through such an unspeakable incident.

I acted recklessly. Dad used to tell me that desperation brought out the worst in people. He said that when people were faced with the realization that someone or something they loved more than anything was in jeopardy, they'd do just about anything, even kill. He was right.

There were many reports about missing persons on the corneal stream search engines, but I didn't see anything about a body being found in Liati Wote within the last twenty-four hours and was a little relieved. Corneal streaming was a Japanese invention that had put libraries and newspapers out of business in one fell swoop like a hawk capturing its prey.

Kofi knocked on my bedroom door three different times, and each time I screamed at him to go away. I just wanted to escape having to always cope with how hard things were. Life had never been fair, and after that tragic night, it just got worse. Locking my door, I did the only thing left for me to do. I played the House of Oware virtual reality RPG.

2

01010100 01100001 01110100 01110101

I activated the VR mode in my neural implant. A flock of crows scattered into the air, leaving behind their road kill when I passed by them. I didn't know how much longer I'd keep up the pace along the shore of Lake Volta. I ran hard, and breathed harder, as sweat slung from my face. The implant tapped into my nerves and heightened all my neural sensations. My clothes were drenched from exhaustion and my feet were aching for a rest, but I kept going...until...

The stench of the dead rotting drifted my way. I stopped, and bent over, gasping for breath with my hands clasping my knees, perspiration dripping from my chin to my breasts. The odor was unmistakable; a fluid known as civet musk hung its pungency in the air. Her lifeless body was almost hidden in the brush. Black bands around her eyes reminded me of a raccoon. I glanced over my shoulder, took in my surroundings, and then looked back down at the poor creature. It was an African civet, black and white stripes covering her fur like a leopard. Her pupils were eaten out, and maggots were crawling throughout her insides. My guess was that a snake had gotten the best of her.

Two white-bibbed swallows flew by me, one chasing the other. One of them slammed into a tree and startled me.

My mind-phone rang.

"Yeah, Xo, here," I said, answering, still out of breath.

"It's me," the voice said. It was Samora Lamp.

"I know, Lamp—can see your number. Can't talk right now—"

"I need your assistance, Examiner."

"What's going on, eh?

"You heard about the threats?"

"No, what?"

"Some kid in a Xhosa spirit mask keeps hacking into radio and neural streaming broadcasts warning the people of Kumasi that they will be punished for not standing up to the government."

"Instead of going after the powerful Ghanaian government, the kid preys on the weak and oppressed? That doesn't sound like a psychopath, does it?"

"Anyway, I think this victim we found this morning is connected."

"What makes you think that?"

"Well, I haven't gotten there yet, but responding officers said that the victim smells of fish."

"Yeah, and that's is significant because?"

"Boy, you really need to tune in more to neural news, you're totally out of the loop."

"Just cut the crap, Lamp. Why do you like this hacker-kid as a suspect?"

"I didn't say the kid's a suspect, but I do think there's a connection. He, or she, I can't really tell the difference, goes on and on about how the villagers stand around and do nothing while the GAF abducts children right in front of their faces and then traffics them to work in slave labor for the fishing industry."

"Wait, I do remember hearing something like that. And this victim fits the profile of having been one of the child slaves."

"Now, you're cooking with peas and rice! You can meet me, yes?"

"Um...Yeah, yeah. Neural-text me the address."

~

Besides me being able to play a thirty-something-year-old, what I loved about playing the House of Oware game was that many of the cases Lamp and I had were based on cold cases in real life, but this one was, unbeknownst to us at the time, being investigated in real-time. It gave me such a rush to know that we had potentially solved crimes that real investigators hadn't the wits to accomplish.

Lamp wanted to go to the GAF to tell them what we'd discovered but I had a gut feeling that if we did, it would expose to the world that someone mistakenly programmed the game in our neural implants and we'd be forced to delete the most comprehensive virtual reality RPG that was ever made. He thought that bringing slave traffickers to justice was more important than us playing the game. For every trafficker GAF officers imprisoned, it seemed two more came up the ranks, he always said. He was right.

It was a good thing I wore my black jogging suit. Dark clothes were the best at crime scenes in case of blood spatter. There was a lot of it on the ground, too. Not human blood, though. Enhuman blood. The enhumans, a word derived from enhanced humans, weren't bloodsuckers as told in the urban legends. However, we did gain our sustenance from feeding off blood, but we did it within the confines of the law.

There are many old wives tales about how we came into existence. Some of our ancestors said we were borne from a curse through the magic of ancient Egyptians, others say we were born in a laboratory, centuries ago. The truth is, no one really knows since all documentation about it was lost or destroyed.

Scanning the area with curious eyes, I stood in the center of the abandoned water and sanitation plant, not far from a fishing community along the Lake Volta. There was a sea of men and women from the forensic science unit collecting evidence, GAF officers fielding the area and a neural photographer placing yellow markers around the crime scene.

Unused water pipes, some painted blue, others white, most tainted with rust, ran through the plant like tentacles of some great dead beast. There were massive water tanks and rusted metal storage units standing beside the steep hills and brown tufts of weeds that poked out of the cracked pavement.

Patches of dust and dirt had gotten on me from when, I brushed up against the pipes or something, I wasn't sure. Over my jogging suit hooded top, a shoulder holster held my Kahr CW9, 9mm Luger, or what I'd nicknamed *Chucky*. I'd put it on when I got back to my car after my jog.

I'd tried other guns, the Glock 43, Sig Sauer P238, but found my Chucky to be more accurate. Lamp once asked me why I called my gun that. Well, it was a little thing but dangerous as all hell, like Chucky from the horror films. Yeah, it had a stiff recoil spring, but unlike some concealed weapons, it wasn't bulky under my clothes. A brown leather medical satchel with evidence bags, bioswabs, lifting tape, and other forensic tools, completed my outfit.

Samora Lamp, the Detective Chief Inspector (DCI) and head of Ghana's Anti-species Trafficking Unit, was standing over the dead body when I spotted him. Lamp's charcoal gray suit gleamed under the warm sunlight. His black silk tie flew over his shoulder from the breath of the mild wind, and his expensive shoes had collected dust as they crunched over the gravel on the uneven pavement. He had a peculiar gray streak of hair going from his widow's peak to the right side of his head. I thought it gave him a lot of character.

There was a black sheet covering the corpse. The forensic photographer, also wearing gloves, lifted up the cover and twisted his face as he took neural pictures of it. He placed the cover back over the still body and shook his head. There were several yellow photo evidence markers placed around the body.

Lamp was short but a little taller than me. His jawline was strong. His skin was yellowish-brown like honey butter and he could use a little Ghanaian sunburn to bring his complexion a little more color. His hair was cut short, and the tips of his sideburns revealed a bit of gray, typical of a man in his mid-forties. In real life, I had no idea how he looked. Just like if he passed me on the streets of Kumasi, he'd pass me by without knowing who I was. However, I did use an avatar that looked like me, but just about fifteen years older.

"What have we got, Lamp?" I said, looking down at the corpse. My sneakers crunched over the uneven gravel as I took a step closer to the corpse.

"Female ennie, thirteen, maybe fourteen," he said, tugging at the fingers of the latex gloves on his hands. "Damn things always make me itch."

I retrieved a pair of latex gloves from my satchel. Ennie was local jargon for enhumans.

He continued. "Her teeth were removed, her fingertips singed, and—"

"We'll have to identify her through a face recognition program?"

"That might be a problem."

"Why's that?" I reached in my satchel for some evidence bags. "Hey, you're leaving when, next week?"

"Nope, this weekend. Jinni can't wait. It'll be just the two of us." He gestured at the body. "Take a look."

"Any CCTV footage?"

"No, this plant hasn't been in use for two decades. The surveillance cameras are all covered with filth. Everything's to shit."

I stooped down, and uncovered the top part of the body, and flinched. "Shit!"

"Yeah," he said. "Never seen anything like that. Her head's smashed in like it was run over."

I shut my eyes and fought with all my might not to vomit so that all the GAF could give me a hard time because the big bad coroner tossed her salad looking at a corpse. There was no mistake, however. She had been run over. It was the girl I'd hit.

This is not a cold case! How'd it get into the database so quickly?

Lamp had a smirk on his face. "You, uh, okay there, Examiner? Don't tell me after all these years of us working together it's starting to get to you?"

"Don't be silly," I said. "It's not that. I had some Waakye that been upsetting my stomach since I first ate it."

"Uh-huh, sure," Lamp said, and glanced up and around.

I leaned in. "Hmph. There's fluid leakage in her ears."

"What could've caused that?"

"A number of things, an ear infection...disease control already swept the area, right?"

"Yeah."

"It can't be a pathogen that killed her, or we'd already be in HAZMAT suits."

"Or dead."

"Yeah, you just keep the pessimism to yourself."

I took a bioswab out of my satchel, smeared a dab of the pinkish substance on the tip and swabbed it in a small glass vial before securing it and placing the sample into an evidence bag.

"Signs of compression and nail scratch abrasions on the front and side of her neck are consistent with asphyxiation via manual strangulation."

"She wasn't killed by a hit-and-run?"

"No, she was dead long before that."

Thank you, God! But who killed her if I didn't?

"Okay," Lamp said. "So she was lazy at catching fish, and they choked her to death?"

"Or killed her while having rough sex," I said, pulling the cover completely off.

"You say that with such an easy demeanor."

"It's not the first time we've had a case like this, is it? Here, take a look," I said, and pointed to her abdomen.

He flinched upon catching the first glimpse. "What in Shango's name happened to her stomach?"

I held in my rage, upset at the sloppiness of my brother.

This is how Kofi and Grunt took care of it? Do a pissant job of making it look like a dhole attacked the girl? No pathologist would ever agree with my findings if there was ever an alternative investigation on my autopsy.

Covering the body back up," I said, "I think the dholes got to her before we did. There are some scratches and jagged cuts that could be claw and bite marks."

"Every day I hear a new story about dhole attacks," Lamp said. "They say the radiation has made them highly intelligent, and now they can communicate with each other."

I stood up and chuckled. "What? You mean they're telepathic?"

"Well, no. But more like they're witch dogs. The villagers say that once you look into their eyes, you fall under a trance and can't run. That's how they catch you, even though some of them are deformed with three legs."

"Those are silly superstitious stories that have no basis of facts behind them."

"After decades of running through radiation zones, they'd become rabid four-legged beasts with insatiable appetites. I don't see how that's so far-fetched."

"I've got a bullet in Chucky, right now that says you're wrong."

"They say one bullet never put the stubborn bastards down, and I reckon a pack of them were damn near terrifying to stop."

"Did you have your guys secure the perimeter to make sure they don't return for leftovers?"

"Yes. There's a shooter at vantage points on all four corners of this facility. So far, no sightings of them."

"You guys are undermanned. You don't have the luxury of taking guys and putting them on dhole patrol."

"I put in a request for more bodies."

"Let me guess, as usual, the Inspector General said there aren't enough GAF officers in the region to go around."

"Look, I don't need you to criticize how we do things.

You're an investigative coroner, and we have to work together, but that doesn't mean you tell me how to do my job."

"What? You have something you want to say to me, Lamp?"

For a long moment, he just glared at me, his lips rising into a smirk, and then a snarl. "Our last case," he said, looking over his shoulder, "I would've gotten a promotion and double bit-credits if you didn't rip the throat out of that slave trafficker, but you wanted to drink his blood, didn't you?"

"This again? Look for the trillionth time, I'm an ennie, an enhanced human!"

"I know what you are," he said, raising his voice.

"You know that it's a civil criminal act to feed blood from a human, or any living species."

"Be honest. Blood lust got the best of you. That's why you tore his throat out—"

"Blood lust?"

"And you were abused in all those foster homes you grew up in. It was too personal, seeing what he did to those children—"

"And it didn't disgust you?"

"You lost control. Admit it!"

"Lamp, feeding blood from a human has been a crime punishable by death without a trial by the Enhuman Council."

"Just because there's a hefty price to pay doesn't mean it wouldn't happen. I mean, no disrespect but your species does get it's food from blood, mostly."

I got in his face. "Species?"

"Aw, Xo. Don't go trying to turn this into something racial. You know what I mean. Your people, your kind. You manufacture blood in processed foods, in beer, hell, even in energy drinks, it's not impossible that you ennies would be tempted to bite a human's neck or two. I get it. It's in your nature."

Blood rose to my head like liquid fire, but I maintained a soft tone. "I don't think you understand, Lamp. For centuries, that type of practice has not only been deemed sexually deviant but absolutely unacceptable. Like you humans, we are privy to flaws, mistakes, and downright fetishes. But I assure you, if I ripped out that slave trader's throat, it wasn't because I wanted to drink his blood, it was because I enjoyed thrashing his flesh, and making him pay with his death for all the mothers and fathers who have a black hole in their soul because he abducted their children and sold them to the highest bidder."

"So you just-just execute the suspect without a trial?" He asked, in a low voice.

"That's what your human bounty hunters did to us for hundreds of years! Now we're recognized and you still treat us like second-class citizens!"

He shrugged. "Yeah, I don't know. As with most new laws, that one needs a lot of revision."

"Lamp, one of the—I refuse to even say the scum's name— one of the slave trader's victim was only nine-years-old. You want to know why I always do so much investigative work? Your GAF cohorts are too frigging incompetent to do anything."

"Now, you're crossing the line!"

We were in a bonafide yelling match, which, believe it or not, had become a daily ritual. Lamp and I fought like family. We were family. I hadn't met him in real life, outside of the game, but we'd been streaming together for several years. It was our way of showing mutual respect like a crested porcupine standing ground against a lion.

I said, "You guys don't have the manpower nor balls to face anti-species traffickers without casualties but are too narrow-minded to recruit more ennies! Just last week, two of your guys were killed investigating the human trafficking ring in Tudu."

That seemed to tick him off. Now it was his turn to blow off steam. "You don't have to tell me what guys I lost in the field of duty! All right? I know who I lost, but the evidence is leaning to the fact that maybe they were attacks were by ennies."

"You sure it wasn't your witch dogs?"

He nearly blew a gasket. "Humans don't go around biting other humans in the neck and bleeding them dry!"

I walked away from him, seeing that we were grabbing eyes from all around. After a few seconds, I approached him, and in a calm voice, said, "Try explaining that to the people in Malawi."

He opened his mouth to say something, stopped, and then smiled, saying. "What happened to those victims in the Mulanje Mountains and Kadadzera is a result of superstitions and fear getting out of hand."

Laughing, I dismissed his claim with a wave. "Look who's talking about superstitions getting out of hand? The point is they weren't ennies, they were humans killing humans." I placed my hand on his shoulders. "We're not monsters, Lamp."

In return, he placed both of his hands on my shoulders. "But half the world still thinks you are. You've only come out of the closet, so to speak, within the last fifty years. You're going to have to play by the rules, Xo, for a few generations, if you really want to make a difference."

Turning away from him, I took a step and then shook my index finger at him. "I refuse to watch my people run back into the shadows of urban legend and Poe-esque fiction that have labeled us as savages for centuries. We are not asanbosam nor vampires—"

"Yeah, yeah, I know. You ennies may have heightened senses, and are stronger than we are, but you're susceptible to self-extinction just like we humans are, Examiner. Quantify your actions with excuses all you want. You had no right taking the law into your hands."

I got right up in Lamp's face, not caring who saw us. Lamp did, and he eyes darted back and forth at the officers who took notice of us, until I stabbed him in his chest with my finger and captured his full attention.

"That piece of scum was a convicted human and semi-human trafficker," I said. "He was indicted on eleven different counts!"

"There was never any solid proof, only a confession. One, I believe was coerced!"

"The jury didn't think so. Besides, eleven counts are proof enough! And because of an illegal search done by those idiot officers down at the Adansi North District, there was a mistrial and the sonofabitch was freed." I leaned in close to his ear and whispered. "He got what he deserved."

Lamp stepped back and cleared his throat. "Yeah, maybe. But do something like that again, and I'll put in for a request for a new partner."

"You do that," I said, and pulled out a pack of cigarettes and a lighter, annoyed by the entire conversation. "What are you looking at?" I asked a GAF officer staring at me. He had navy emblems on his uniform. "Go on, there's a crime scene here, that needs your attention. Go on! Nothing to see here!"

I offered Lamp a cigarette. "Do you want a jot?"

He shook his head. "Lung blasters? I don't think so."

"Suit yourself, then," I said, and turned away from him.

Lamp's hand clutched my bicep.

"Don't," I said, and took a gentle step away from his grasp. I suddenly had a flashback of Kofi's hand on my shoulder, trying to comfort me after the accident.

"There are some lines we're not supposed to cross, Xo," Lamp said, "and what you did, was one of them."

"There's no line I won't cross if, in my heart, I believe I'm doing what's right." I slipped the pack of cigarettes back into my sweat pants pocket.

"Even if it's to go against your family? Sounds like a contradiction waiting to happen."

"I don't give a care what it sounds like," I said, with a wan smile.

I let the silence between us rise in the air and lit my jot, took a few puffs.

"I'm on your side, Lamp. Come on," I said, walking off. "I'm going to the morgue and wait on the body. I'll do the autopsy and maybe my findings can tell us what happened."

"Don't you want to talk to the guy who saw them?"

I stopped and turned around. "There was a witness?"

"Yep. An old security guard at the plant."

"Well, where is he?"

"At the station. He's the one who called 1-9-1 and then swung by the station, right after. You drive? Your brother's car, here?"

"Uh, no. He junked it. I was actually on a jog."

"Way out here?"

"Yeah, it's only six miles from the dojo."

"Wow, between your running and martial arts, you're a straight badass, Examiner."

"Yeah," I said, feeling sick to my stomach.

Omigod, what exactly did the guard see?

"Well, you can ride with me," Lamp said.

"Sure. Sure. Um, one sec," I said.

I deactivated the House of Oware game and made it to the toilet in my bathroom just in time before I got sick.

3

01010100 01100001 01110100 01110101

I stood in the bathroom, staring at myself in the mirror, trying to get myself together. With shaky hands, I tossed two Zonegran pills in my mouth, feeling a panic attack growing inside of me.

There was a witness? Maybe that was just the game, tossing in a little fiction with the facts to make it exciting.

I rubbed my lips with the back of my hand. The taste in my mouth was unbearable. It didn't help that I had blut on my breath, either. Blut was blood beer. Humans didn't like it much but ennies like me, we couldn't get enough of it.

I drank way too much, way too fast, last night.

I rinsed my mouth out with mouthwash, and afterward, braced my hands on the bathroom counter. I held my head down, tried to calm myself, slow my breathing. Whenever I got too stressed out, I reminisced about that time when I scraped my leg on a piece of metal on Dad's boat. It was only a scratch, but I cried like it was the end of the world. My father took me in his arms and caressed my head. He kissed my boo-boo and sung the Ga lullaby:

> *Baby, don't cry.*
> *Where has your mother gone?*
> *She's gone to the farm.*
> *What did she leave for you?*
> *Yaa yaa wushi-o!*

It was one of my most favorite memories, ever. I missed him so much and would sing that song whenever I wanted the world around me to brighten. I inhaled a deep breath.

Okay. You got this, Feenie!

The only way to find out what was going on was to either walk into the real GAF headquarters and ask about the case, and then get humiliated while they laughed my butt right out of there for being a seventeen-year-old asking questions she had no business asking. Or...or go back in the game.

Damn, I have to know.

I went back into my room, crawled on the bed, and with a mere thought, activated the game.

~

I opened my eyes and was back in the game, standing in the ladies' bathroom of the GAF station. The lavatory was a single. There was one stall, one sink, a baby changing station, and a leather seating area, the width of the bathroom.

Yeah, I'm losing it. If the witness saw Grunt and Kofi dump the body at the water plant, somehow, I know it's going to lead to me. I have to find out what this guard knows.

I tossed cold water on my face and when I reached for a paper towel, swore I saw something move on the wall. My eyes shot up to the painting that sat above the changing station. The disturbing thing looked like the artist painted it right after having a serious nightmare.

Great. Not now.

One of the reasons why I loved the game was because it actually scanned the host's mind for their fears and input them in far more grotesque fashion to heighten the stakes of the game. I loved reading horror, therefore the program snatched elements of the stories that were stained in my memory banks and tossed them into the case.

The movie I watched last was called *Sisters* and was about conjoined twin witches. The painting was a chilling picture of two sisters with one head. They were dressed in identical blue dresses, except one had white ankle socks and shoes and the other one wore no socks and had canvas sneakers on her feet. They were holding each other as best as they could, and her eyes were closed as if trying to bear a painful experience.

I sniffled and bent down to wash my face with water. After a few slow calming breaths, I stared in the mirror while I washed my hands. My hair was a mess. I pulled it up in a ponytail. One of my nipples peeked over the neck of my tank top when I reached up and I pulled my shirt up a bit to cover it. I sighed.

What if the judge saw my brother in that water plant?

I placed my hand upon my head as if my father had reached down from the spirit world and raked his hand through my hair and I wanted to feel his large caring hands. Dad used to massage my scalp when he was alive to soothe me whenever I was troubled. My gaze drifted back to the surreal painting of the sisters on the wall. I took a step back. The eyes of the twin sisters seemed to follow me. It was unnerving, to say the least. I reached for the stack of brown paper towels by the baby station and stepped over to toss the garbage in the trash disposal sitting inside of the counter, all the while staring at the picture.

"Crap!" I said and flinched as if someone had just slipped ice down my back.

The twins in that painting just blinked their eyes!

Laughing at myself, I blinked a few times and shook my head.

It's just the game giving me a rise.

I had more pertinent problems that desired my attention. Lamp knocked on the bathroom door, giving me one helluva start.

"What are you doing in there?" Lamp asked.

I responded to my partner a little ruder than I intended. "I'm using the bathroom! What do you think I'm doing?"

The GAF headquarters looked like a museum of Gothic horror. It had influences of Mediterranean Revival and ancient Egyptian architecture. Stuccoed walls, doors, and windows in the shape of arches, wrought-iron balconies and large symmetrical façades, and of course as the dark images of my mind helped create, there were surrealist paintings and gothic Gargoyle statues hanging around like demonic creatures awaiting to possess the building and pull every visitor into an eternal nightmare

I left the bathroom and spotted Lamp speaking to the guard in the interrogation room. Butterflies scattered in my stomach, and I blew out a bubbled sigh.

Here we go.

The door squeaked when I entered and both Lamp and the guard's eyes landed on me.

Lamp gestured toward me. "This is the investigative medical examiner, Dr. Feeni Xo."

"I hate titles. Call me Xo," I said, and he nodded.

"I'm Kweku Bola," the man said.

He had a long white beard. His name, Kweku, told me he was named after the day of the week he was born. He wore an aquamarine dashiki decorated with white leopard print around the collar. By his dress, I gathered he was no longer in work attire.

Standing next to Lamp, I took the coffee cup from his grasp and took a sip. "I hear you had a pretty interesting night."

"Saw a pack of those witch dogs. I made sure that none of them looked in my eye, that's for sure."

"Let's just stick to the facts," I said.

He laughed. "Oh, I see we have a non-believer. They love those kinds of people. Most of the children that have disappeared, I hear was the science type. Did their neural studies with a stick up their behinds like they knew everything and the rest of us were illiterate-minded."

He was beginning to annoy me. "Look, Mr. Bola—"

"Kweku," he said, cutting me off.

"Kweku," I said, swallowing my irritation. "Just tell me—"

"Like you, I'm not big on formalities," he said, grinning.

I inhaled a deep breath. "Please tell me what you saw."

"I've already told the officers, even got it down in a neural report and sent it to your IGP."

"Yes," I said, nodding, "and I'm very grateful, but can you just go over it once more with us? Maybe those guys missed something."

"Well," he said, rubbing his beard. "I'd just gotten me a late-night snack of fufu when I heard them witch dogs yipping and yapping. I turned on one of the security floodlights and shined it out there. They couldn't see me from my vantage point. I was up on the second-floor office but still, I made sure I ducked, as to not give them heathens a chance to do their dog vodun."

"And then what happened?" I said, losing patience with the man.

"Then! Well, then they left, and that's when I saw him, or her. I couldn't tell from being so high up."

"You'd think you'd be doing rounds on the ground, huh?"

"I just told you, I was having a little bite to eat. Although I shouldn't have eaten fufu, it's always rough on my digestive—"

"Kweku!"

That made him flinch. "S-sorry. Like I was saying, that's when I saw the child."

"Wait. A child?" I asked.

"Yes, a teenager," he said, nodding. "But like I say, couldn't tell the gender, but I can tell you the fellow was wearing a hood, and when I yelled down and shouted that there was no trespassing, the little bugger turned around and looked up. It was an albino."

"You're sure about that?"

"Oh, yeah, about as sure as I'm sitting right here and feeling mighty gaseous. That much I know for sure. Had short hair, like a boy's but soft facial features. That's why I'm not sure if it was a boy or a girl. Also, the fellow had a really bright backpack on, orange, bright as a baboon's butt cheeks. The kid ran off when I said something, like fire was burning his, or like I said her, I don't know, but like fire was in their rump. That's when I saw what the witch dogs—"

I interrupted. "The dholes?"

"That's right! Those demon dogs, and what the child was looking at, and I got my shotgun and went down to investigate." His ashen face turned somber. "Nearly crapped my pants when I saw it was a dead girl. Called the authorities, right away. The rest is, as they say, His-toree!"

"Okay," I said, walking to the door. "Is that it?"

Lamp backed away from the chair.

The guard looked at us with a delightful surprise. "I'm through?"

"Yes sir," Lamp said. "But please contact us, if you remember anything else that might be of importance."

Kweku nodded. "Sure thing. Will do."

He got up and Lamp escorted him out of our office back into the main GAF room.

"Nice to meet you," Kweku said.

"Yeah," I said, my mind relieved but still a million miles away.

I leaned against the door frame and watched the man leave.

He didn't see Kofi nor Grunt.

Lamp came back up to me. "Hey, maybe your dhole theory works out. Do the autopsy, and we can close this case, and move on to the next one. We'll both get double bit-credits for solving this case."

I summoned up a weak smile. "Yeah. I'll, uh. I'll get to it, as soon as I get to the coroner's office."

"Well, I'm going to get me some brews, and maybe kick my feet up and stream a romcom and eat ice cream until my shirt buttons pop."

I laughed. "Didn't take a big guy like you for romantic comedies."

"Don't judge. We all have our vices."

"You're telling the truth there."

"Don't I always?"

I laughed. "Guess so. Hit me in the morning when you're up. Tomorrow, we'll follow up on the albino lead. See if we can find any in the area following Kweku's descriptions. Oh, yeah. I'll need a ride."

"Can't you just take your motorcycle?"

"I need a slave cylinder for my clutch," I said.

"You know you can just imagine it fixed, and it will be?"

"Yeah, but it's more fun this way to throw some obstacles in the way."

"Tomorrow," Lamp said, gesturing his coffee mug at me. "Wear something more appropriate than a jogging suit, will you?"

I took the mug out of his hand and gulped the rest of his coffee down. "Depends on what you deem appropriate," I said, gasping when the mug slipped from my grasp and the hot coffee spilled on his lap.

4

01010100 01100001 01110100 01110101

I deactivated the virtual sensory game in my neural implant with focused thought and opened my eyes just in time to see my favorite mug bounce off of my lap and break. An empty coffee mug with GAMER GIRLS DO IT BETTER printed on it, had shattered into a million pieces on the hardwood floor of my bedroom.

I was no longer Xo, investigating medical examiner, like I was in the neurogame, House of Oware. I was seventeen-year-old Feeni Xo, living a boring life in the city of Kumasi. My vision came into a hazy focus on my brother's faded tee shirt that said JOIN THE GHANA ALLIED FORCES.

"You idiot!" I said. "That was my favorite mug, Kofi! How did you even get into my room?"

Kofi's large dark brown eyes widened, and his mouth fell agape. His haircut was as fresh as the GAF demanded, but his face was shiny with perspiration. We were both the same age, but he had me by a few months. His eyes narrowed and a crooked grin twisted his lips.

"Well next time you won't pretend to ignore me when I'm calling you," he said. "You weren't really meditating. Your eyes were moving around in your eyelids too much. You can't fool me."

"Ugh!" I said, scoffing and leaped to my feet. "Aren't you supposed to be doing police work or something? How'd you get in at such an early age, anyway?"

"Grunt forged my paperwork." He pointed at my head.

"Is that horse hair or Indian hair?"

I was about to pop him good in his eye when Auntie Yajna poked her head into my bedroom.

"What in the world is going on, here?" she asked.

After dodging in and out of foster homes, and living on the streets for almost a year, Auntie Yajna took me in and treated me like her own daughter. She, Kofi, and the twins were the only real family I'd ever known since my parents died when I was young.

"Kofi broke my gamer mug!" I said, trying to get at him.

Auntie Yajna stood between us, and even if I tried, I couldn't get around her. She was a hefty woman and had the height to match her size. Kofi stood behind her and chuckled, making me more annoyed at him.

"I didn't mean to break it," he said. "It was an accident."

I reached my arm past Auntie Yajna and tried to grasp Kofi's shoulder. "Liar!"

Auntie Yajna stepped forward, her buxom bosom pushed me backward into a small stumble. "Now, now, Feeni. I've told you about that temper of yours! Give the boy a break. You know Kofi can get about as confused as flatulence in a fan factory. If the boy says he made a mistake, you better believe that he's well capable of doing just that."

That made me laugh, and I shook my head. "You got that right."

"Hey!" Kofi said. "What is this? Gang up on Kofi day?"

Auntie Yajna grabbed me, and stood by my side, hugging me. "More like *Women Unite Day*. You better recognize!"

"Feeni is not a woman," he said.

"Boy, just go on downstairs and make sure the twins are ready. I want to get in the rationing line before it grows longer than a politician's nose during election time. I can't afford to be late to work and now you can't take me to work, I'm going to be on crunch time from now on."

Kofi crossed his arms and leaned against the door frame. "I'm busting my butt on the force, so you don't have to work, Mom." He beat his fist against his chest. "I'm the man of the family!"

"Boy, if you don't do what I'll tell you to do, your station is going to have to put an APB of your B-u-t-t, because I'm going to bop you so hard, you'll be missing for days. Now go check on the twins, and make sure they ain't up to no good before you go to work."

"And while you're at it," I said. "Do some push-ups. Your chest sounded mighty flat when you beat on it, just now."

"At least my hair is real," he said.

"Boy!" Auntie Yajna said, failing to hold in a chuckle. "Get going before I have to tan your seventeen-year-old hide! You're not too big to still get a whupping."

Kofi sighed. "Okay, Mom! I'm going!" He left, mumbling, "I don't know why you don't make Feeni get them ready. I have to go to work."

"Because a man needs to learn how to take care of children the same way a woman does, and still work as hard as a mother does, to be a good father."

I laughed. "He doesn't even have a girlfriend, and you're teaching him how to be a father?"

"Look who's talking?" Kofi said. "Queen vibrator."

"Watch your mouth!" Auntie Yajna raised her hand at him, and he ran off.

When he left, Auntie Yajna helped me pick up the pieces of my mug.

"You were meditating, huh?" she asked.

"Uh, yeah."

"Well, I guess that means you're feeling better."

I didn't know why, but I hadn't told her about the game. Part of the reason was that I knew that no one else had a virtual construct in their neural implants. I've asked around, went online and even searched the archive streaming database. There was no such name as House of Oware, which is funny. As long as I could remember, I played the game that only Lamp and I seemed to own on our neural implants. It was my escape, but more than that it taught me all about pathology. One day, I knew I'd be one in real life.

"You're young. Why do you meditate?" Auntie Yajna asked and picked up my tin garbage can from beside my reading desk.

She stopped to look at some of my books: *Clone Forensics* by Kwesi Nzingha, *Transferring Consciousness onto Retcons* by Ama Selasi and *Soul Sleep* by Mahama Kwasi, among other books on pathology and science.

She nodded her head in a slow thoughtful motion. "You're too young to be so wise."

"I want to do big things, Auntie! I want to make a difference in this world."

"Child, you are doing big things!" she said, and tossed the broken pieces in my tin garbage can.

"You don't understand. That's not what I mean."

"Don't be silly. Helping me with the twins, keeping the place clean, it's a big help to me. A tremendous help. I don't know what I'd do without you. There's nothing more important than family and you help me keep this one together. Good families are what make a difference in the world. Many folks grow up in dysfunctional ones. Now, go on and get ready. It's almost time to go get food rations. You know I like to be one of the first in the line."

"Okay. I'll be ready in just a few minutes."

"Hurry up, child," she said, and left my room.

That made me feel good, hearing her say that I was a big help to her. None of my foster parents ever expressed love for me, but it also made me sad because Auntie Yajna truly didn't understand the black hole that was eating up my very soul. There had to be more to life. There had to be. I glanced in the mirror, and instead of my face, all I saw was that dead girl under my car. If I didn't kill her, who did?

5

The market square was packed. People were trading rugs, handmade blankets, clothes and a variety of other objects. Not depending on the government to supply our food, our neighborhood elders formed a secret hunting council and had gone hunting for tufted deer and Patagonian maras, leaving the village mothers and their offspring standing in the long line to receive our morning food rations. My brothers and sisters, Linga and Yoni were fraternal twins. They were running around, playing with other children without a care in the world. God, if they were ever abducted and trafficked, there wouldn't be a stone I wouldn't over-turn to find them. The thought gave me a chill. How could the GAF let it happen for so long? Many villagers said that they were more corrupt than the criminals they pursued.

Since there was a group of musicians singing and play-ing drums beside us, the twins were chastened by Auntie Yajna to be in her ear's reach. They did as told, but roused the hackles of everyone within ten meters of us, running between the people in line. There were at least twenty oth-ers in line ahead of us, but behind us, there had to be a hundred or more people. God, it was brutal. I just wanted to get back home and get back into the game.

About every fifty meters, the Kumasi Garrison from the Fourth Battalion of Infantry (4BN) were positioned to keep order and make sure no one skipped. They all wore cam-ouflage fatigues and carried rifles. Ever since a riot broke out when they ran out of food, two years ago, the Inspector

General enforced a stricter security detail to enforce crowd control and safety.

My mind bee-lined back to the House of Oware. The game was not only something to bide the time with, but it had also taught me forensics through intense tutorial drills, and tests through practicum. The repetition from doing the same things over-and-over again until I learned enough to move the plot along to advance to higher levels drilled into me investigative science.

I'd played the game near all of my life and I had a real knowledge of pathology. There was no doubt that I could be a real coroner in Ghana. But I was only seventeen, and even though I'd been down to the infirmary almost every month for the past year, they laughed at my offer to help in the coroner's department. No matter how I impressed them with my knowledge, I always got the same advice: Come back when you're older, and we'll see what we can do to get you a job in the records department.

Assholes. I'll show them.

I had much to offer the world and knew that I could make a difference if given a chance. Hopelessness seeped in deep and made my stomach turn.

A young albino girl stood by a dashiki seller, yelling, "Your judgment is coming! We have been treated like lepers long enough. You are nothing but lambs to stand by and allow someone to call a woman a slut because she is showing cleavage, or on the contrary, you say just because my whole body is covered that I'm oppressed, and I've been forced to dress this way. I am in a religion, dummies. It is my choice! My choice! And now, you have made a choice... to do nothing! To not vote; to be lambs! And you will be judged, accordingly because your religion is inactivity!"

There were many albinos in our village. Auntie Yajna said that the radiation caused them to be born that way. I didn't have the heart to correct her, that albinism was a debilitating disorder that existed long before the Final Event. I let it go. The albino girl reminded me of that person who hacked the radio broadcast and was spewing angst and disgust with the system.

Is there a resistance growing?

I shook my head, saddened by seeing the cruel state of our country robbing yet another young person of their mind. An old man with long dreads rode by on his bicycle, playing the news on the radio. The reporter caught my ear when he said: "The parents are asking for information if anyone has seen their daughter, Jinni, that they call the station or send them a neural message to the police hotline. Their thirteen-year-old daughter has been missing for three days, now, and as you can assume, their family are praying that she comes home soon."

Omigod! Lamp has a sister named, Jinni. What a terrible coincidence. The number of missing teenagers was growing. It was those damned slave traffickers.

The old bicyclist rode down the street, and with the musicians playing their drums with such bravado, was out of earshot halfway down the block. My attention shifted to a couple of men bickering. Alongside an old emerald green building, a couple of local elder men, one bald, and one with a white long beard.

That's the guard, Kweku!

The two men sat under a lean-to, smoking cigarettes, or jots, as I called them. The bald one, named Nana, wore a white tee shirt with the image of the superhero, Little Zeng, on it. The caption under the illustration said FIRST BLACK SUPERHERO 1963. They both sported over-sized earthtone shorts and were barefooted.

It was like they were putting on a two-man play for the people standing in line. The old men were loud and animated, and sought everyone in the line for reactions. Besides the musicians slapping their palms to the rhythms of Africa, those two men were our entertainment, and made it less painful, waiting in the long lines for food rations.

Kweku wiped the sweat off of his head, and said, "It's

not superstition, I tell you. Those pack of devil dogs, those dholes are killing our children, Nana. Something has to be done about them!"

"Man, you've been watching those tabloid news programs again on corneal stream TV. First of all, they're nothing but hungry Asiatic wolves. They're hungry, and the radiation has been in their blood for so long they're a little cuckoo in the brain."

"And that means what? They can come into the villages of Kumasi and eat up our children? If they look at you, you fall in a trance and walk right into their den of death—"

Nana interrupted him. "A bunch of old wives and superstitious scary husbands made that tale up! It's fiction! All fairy tale. Kick one of them dogs in their ass and they'll go whelping off back into the mountains with their tails in between their legs."

"You talk a big game," Kweku said. "But I don't see you going up into them hills."

"What is real, though was the *Final Event*. Now that squeezed the life out of our country and Ghana hasn't been the same since that idiotic nuclear war, ten years ago. It's 2025, and we're living like we're in one of them apocalyptic novels."

Kweku said, "Ghana isn't the same? You blind, man? The world, itself, hasn't been the same. Kumasi ain't no different from all the other cities that are struggling to supply food for its citizens."

"You don't have to tell me," Nana said. "Back in the day, I used to get a six pack of Pee Cola every Friday after a long back-breaking week working at the cocoa bean factory. Those days are gone. It's two cartons of lousy processed blood every day. Three, if one of my grandkids didn't drink theirs, and I give them a bit-credit for it."

"Hoo—wee! I sure miss gulping down a bottle of ice-cold bottle Pee Cola, and then burping out all that carbonation until the sun came up!"

Nana slapped his knee and laughed. "You ain't said

nothing, man! My wife, may she rest in peace, used to hate me burping like a gassy babirusa! Used to make her twist up her pretty little face every time. But now, there are no more supermarkets, retail stores, no merchandise shops, nothing that survived bombing and looting in Ghana, this market is all we've got for miles around."

"If I want to get batteries for my beard shaver, I have to wait two months before my order comes into the Accra Warehouse. Two months! Don't matter if I'm able to pay extra bit-credits to expedite delivery. And when I say delivery, I mean walking these two size twelves to the warehouse to pick it up! What happened to mailmen?"

Nana sucked his teeth. "Now you've got this girl hacking onto to all the streaming programs threatening to make the people of Ghana pay because we didn't exercise our right to stand up to the politicians."

Kweku blew out a puff of smoke. "What good does that do? Ain't nothing going to change anyway. The rich run the world and piss on the poor like a dhole marking his territory."

"Tell me something, Kweku," Nana said.

"Go on, man!"

"Did you vote?"

"You asking a trick question, Nana? You know I haven't voted since a Kenyan's son was President in America, almost two decades ago. What does one vote mean, anyway? Nothing. It won't change a thing!"

"The dumb get dumber," Nana said.

"Have you voted in the last decade?" Kweku asked.

"No, but-but-but that's not the point!"

Everyone started laughing at that.

Major Grunt walked toward us, and when he walked right by me, asked, "You okay, yeah?"

I nodded.

He whispered. "You owe me one."

"You do know the dead girl was found, this morning?"

"Already taken care of," he said. "Don't worry about it."

"You guys didn't come up with a smarter plan, like dumping her in Lake Volta, or something?"

"You guys don't have nothing to do with trafficking children to Lake Volta, do you Major Grunt?" Kweku asked, breaking up our conversation.

"How are you going to ask me an asinine question like that?" Grunt asked.

He shook his head in disgust and walked toward the back of the line.

Trying my best to act normal, I called out to him, "Hey, Grunt."

He stopped and turned toward me. His eyebrows buried in anger, but he knew what I was going to ask because I always asked him the same thing almost every time I saw him.

He shook his head. "Nope. Don't even ask, Feeni."

"What?" I said. "You know I'm a good shot, Grunt, by all the times you've taken me to target practice. When can I really go hunting with you guys? Kofi goes out with your battalion, sometimes, and I'm a helluva better shot than him."

"Like I told you three times, this past week," he said. "You're not ready, yet. For one, it's too dangerous. The dholes are very smart, and we have to make sure we keep them out of our village. We don't have time to babysit. It might get one of us killed."

"Dholes are nothing but wild dogs," I said. "Kill the alpha male and all the rest will go running."

He chuckled. "You may know a lot about pathology and that kind of stuff, but you know nothing about the nature of a wild animal. You have to almost be a wild animal to hunt and kill those radiation-mutated beasts."

"Hunting dholes?" Auntie Yajna said. "Girl, please! You better let the trained GAF do their jobs and worry about the house and children. That's where you belong."

I turned to her and sucked my teeth. "Home, doing meaningless house chores while Kofi gets to be a hero for our village?"

"Suck your teeth at me again and see if I don't knock some sense into them," Auntie Yajna said.

"When you're ready, Feeni," Grunt said. "Join the GAF academy."

I sighed. "That's really funny, coming from you! Where is my brother, anyway?"

Grunt clenched his teeth and I knew he was thinking of what we'd done the night before.

"He's doing paperwork on a case, and afterward he has to follow up on something," he said.

What did Kofi have on him to keep him from turning me into the police? Was it good enough to keep him silent? Was it that he forged Kofi's paperwork? Yeah, that's it.

Nana waited until Grunt was out of earshot and said, "Forget about hunting, Feeni. You look like such a sweet girl. Have you ever killed anything besides a mosquito?"

"She may act tough," Auntie Yajna said. "She's too much of a loving spirit to kill anything that breathes God's beautiful air. Besides, ain't nothing but rabid beasts out there in them damn jungles. Too many areas are still radioactive, and the poor animals won't ever be the same. Many of them run around in packs and will kill anything with a heartbeat."

"I know, Auntie," I said. "That's what everyone keeps saying."

Kweku said. "Your Auntie's right, Feeni. You don't want to be in any environment as volatile as that. Them witch dogs will have their way."

"There's no such things as dogs that can wield magic!" I said.

I didn't know how much more of that kind of talk I could take.

Nana continued. "But like I was getting ready to say, the government tattooed our wrists with numbers like we're prisoners. We're prisoners of technology, that's what we are! I quite remember when I was a boy we went to schools. Schools! When you took a technology class, you figured how to take apart a transistor radio. Nowadays, a person can read an entire book just by corneal streaming. Corneal streaming. What a joke. I remember how I used to get excited when the bookmobile visited my school!"

Kweku said, "Kids, today don't even have a clue what a school is, with their neural tutors telling them how to do everything, even wipe their balls, since neural implants became mandatory."

"Now you've lit the fire that's got my feet hopping!" Nana said. "It's been twenty years, now! Two whole decades since everyone had to get those damned neural implants."

Kweku said, "I remember telling my baba that would be the end of schools, libraries, universities, all of that, when neural tutors became the rave."

"Did he believe you?"

"Hell naw, he didn't believe me. My father is probably in his grave right now, shaking his head at how places like Ghana and Botswana were the first to endorse children learning from neural tutors."

"Put millions of teachers out of jobs, is what it did," Nana said. "And now, the children think they're smarter than their parents because they can learn calculus and name galaxies before they can properly get an erection or wear a bra. Well, I tell you what children. Ain't nothing like experience, and no virtual construct in the world is going to teach you the way a real live person can."

Kweku spread his arms wide and said, "Tell me all of you who are mothers. Was that fair? Putting schools out of business? Now, you have to watch your children round-the-clock. No more educational institutions to babysit your little monsters for six-to-eight hours a day."

A lot of the women in the line agreed and started clapping.

"All right, settle down," Grunt said. "You two are making my job harder," he said, looking at Nana and Kweku.

"It ain't a crime to speak our mind is it, Major Grunt?" Nana asked.

Grunt grinned. "I don't know, some of the jokes you make are so terrible they should be crimes."

They all laughed at that, even Kweku. I was too uptight to even think of a chuckle. Grunt turned and took a slow walk back down the line. Our eyes met. He nodded his head and I looked away.

Kweku continued. "All neuroschools do is make our children cynical and lazy. That's a bad place for anyone to thrive in."

"Thrive? Thrive? The only industries that thrive are the fishing industry and those that have tied themselves into IGP Sibaya's consciousness storing enterprise. They haven't even figured out how to transfer minds successfully, yet. But still, Sibaya holds all the power because he holds the keys to all the Consciousness Vaults, the world over."

"How in the hell does a man get that much power?" Kweku said and looked at us in the line. "The man used to be president of the NGS, the dag-blamed National Gun Society, way over in America."

Nana added, "Now, I understand that his parents were Ghanaian, but he was born an American. How does he come to Ghana, and not only become the Inspector General of Police but bamboozle the world to elect him to handle all affairs of the C-Vault?"

"He's a great salesman," Kweku said.

Nana spat on the ground next to him. "What he is, is a great con man."

"To hear you tell it. But see here? He didn't have much opposition after the war, that's how. After many nations fell from getting nuked, people were starving for a leader, and he stepped up to the plate. Yep, stepped up to the plate like he was Sir Don Bradman."

"It's like Sibaya Jedi Mind-tricked us all. We rolled over and barked whenever he told us to," Nana said, and started barking like a dog. "That's what that hacker on the radio keeps talking about. We're like lambs! Why don't we stand up to them? Show them a thing or two?"

"Shut up your noise, fool!" Kweku said, and coughed. "It's like that, everywhere! The nukes didn't just end the war, it killed the spirit of man and ennie, alike." He looked to see where Major Grunt was and when he saw that the officer was in a conversation with another GAF patrol man way down the line, he said, "No resistance, no change," and shook his fist in the air.

Kweku sneezed, and when I said, "Bless you," he sniffed and looked at me.

"And you know something, young lady?" he asked. "Even if the mainstream businesses were still open, our bit-credit means nothing anymore. Your bits mean nothing. How can you make a difference in the world if you don't have money? Money is power. How can anyone make a difference in the world without currency?"

I shrugged.

He stared at me for a moment, and then took another puff of his jot.

"Those damned hackers monopolized the bitcoin mar-ket," he continued. "Messed it up for everyone. I used to own a lot in bitcoins until I got bamboozled."

Nana's jot went out, so he lit it again, cupping his hands around the cigarette. "I know. I know." He shook the match out and flung it to the side. "It's now led by a bunch of gangster nerds—boy does that sound like a conundrum— gangster nerds of the internet, thug hackers, so bitcoins are losing value in a wasteland where the rich hide in their invisible kingdoms. What are we to do?"

"Find a way to properly download consciousness onto the retcons," Kweku said. "Those little data orbs that can be surgically implanted right in the back of the neck of those clones just like they are in us. That is the way man and ennies can live forever."

Nana inhaled a puff of the jot and blew out circle smokes. "What you're saying, brother, we should defy the Lord our Father's purpose? We should cheat death?"

"Damn, right!" he said and bellowed a deep laugh.

"Sentient beings will be able to live forever!" He gestured to us in line. "Wouldn't you people want to be immortal?"

Auntie Yajna said. "Honey, I'd be lying like a no-legged dog if I said I wanted to look in the mirror and see these big old sagging breasts frowning at me for the next umpteen eternities."

Nana cackled out a laugh and stood. His plaid shirt flapped open revealing his potbelly. He tossed his cigarette down and extinguished it with his large ashen foot. There were now only about ten people ahead of us, in line.

There was a woman behind us. She had her hair tied in two pigtail braids that cascaded down her back and almost touched the ground. On top of her head, the woman balanced a large basket. I supposed it was meant to hold the rations for her many children. It seemed like she had a herd of about six or seven children from the ages of four up to eight. They were the children that Linga and Yoni had befriended and drove all the other folks in the line mental.

"Maybe our scientists are playing God," the woman said, "and maybe that's a moral and theological issue. But food, on the other hand, is a different story. It doesn't matter if you have opinions on science or religion, we all need to eat to live. And I'm here to tell you that there's plenty of food, but the government is trying to control us, keep us sickly. Us begging for their help keeps us distracted on resisting their oppressive ways and keeps them in power."

They both looked over to her, and then at each other, and nodded. Nana was on his feet. Kweku remained seated but shielded his eyes because Nana stood in the line of sight of the sun.

"Damn, man," Kweku said. "Get out of the sun, will you? You want to blind me?"

"You're my wife, now?" Nana said, his face painted with anger. "Cause you're fussing at me like an old noisy generator that can't be fixed." He stepped to the side and placed his hands on his hips. "Better?" He turned, and scratched his chin, and spoke to the woman in front of us. "Now, what say you, Pigtails?"

"Food, man, food," the woman with the pigtails said. "Why do we have food rations? Huh? There should be no food rations because there's enough food to feed the world twenty times over every day."

Nana said. "You're talking foolish woman. The crops suffered from radioactive nuclides. Decontamination of the soil proved more difficult to overcome than anticipated."

Major Grunt joined in, saying, "I'd have to agree with the old man, there. Too many people are toxic from radiation and aren't allowed to handle, or manufacture food."

"Gloves don't stop radiation," Kweku said. "There is no way to manufacture food, properly without putting on a ridiculous HAZMAT suit?"

The woman said, "I don't mean no disrespect, Major Grunt, but..."

She waited for his response.

Major Grunt nodded, and said, "Go ahead. I won't take offense."

"Thank you," she said. "All I'm saying is that the government is lying to all of us when they say the machines are non-functional since the war. How is that even possible? A bomb that can destroy factories?"

"There is such a weapon," Major Grunt said.

The woman shook her head. "Yeah, but I don't know. Kill all of our computers and machines, though? All of them? I don't think so. I know there are viruses and EMP's but a thing that can destroy all of them? Some kind of computer virus? They're not telling us the truth."

Auntie Yajna joined in on the conversation. "What, sister? Kwame Gyekye the philosopher, you're not."

The woman faced Auntie Yajna and said, "What say? You don't know me to talk to me like that."

"Excuse me to say," Auntie said. "but these men got me riled up like a fat boy alone in a plantain chip factory. Now, forget about the machines being non-functional. That's not what we should be concerned with. Everyone knows that the vegetation, animals and plant life have been affected for the worst—that's why most of the wildlife is rabid, and have deformities, the poor creatures."

"And you know what?" the woman said. "The government has no solution, no solution at all to make things better!"

"Once all the proper operatives are in place," Major Grunt said. "I assure you the government will have solutions for the betterment of its citizens."

Auntie Yajna shook her head. "How? By harnessing our consciousness, like that's even possible, and put it in a dormant-clone of us?"

"Believe me," Major Grunt said. "It's possible."

I was surprised that he allowed himself to get sucked into the conversation. He was by far, the only GAF that tolerated talk against the government in his presence. I guess the topic was something that he was passionate about.

"That ain't no way to live!" Kweku said. "They don't even know how to make it work, yet. Look at President Mbutu. Three times they've tried over the past decade, and they've yet to successfully place his consciousness in one of the orbs and then put it a clone. They say there's too many complications, and already they had tragedies where a leader or two had their consciousness wiped clean, thrown into an abyss of nothingness."

"On the light," Nana said, which is a common Ghanaian phrase, "them hackers keep putting viruses in the system."

"We're being led by a bunch of bureaucratic idiots," Auntie said.

"Hey, hey, hey," Major Grunt said. "That kind of talk will get you into trouble."

Kweku said, "Now you know, people will complain about anything and everything they can, Major. Let the woman talk."

"Your funeral," Major Grunt said and put his hands in the air. He shook his head and took another stroll down the line away from our conversation.

"You think it's self-sabotage, woman?" Kweku asked my Auntie.

Auntie Yajna gave an adamant nod. "Yes, we voted for the IGP to be in charge of Ghana, but the truth is, he's there only because his predecessor, and other global leaders, are on life support due to radiation poisoning!"

Nana scratched his head, and said, "And because we have the most advancements in technology on the subject of consciousness transference, most of the countries of the world came running to us, making the Inspector General Bete Sibaya the most powerful man in the world."

"Do you really think he's still alive?" Kweku asked.

"Why? Because no one has seen him in public in several months?" Auntie Yajna said. "The man is a recluse. He can do his job from anywhere in the world."

"All we see of him are these tele-speeches on our corneal stream," Nana said. "Or street corner holograms of his National Address."

Kweku laughed. "It's not even him, it's an avatar of him. Some bigger than life recreation of him claiming how Ghana is the most powerful nation in the world."

Nana shook his head. "Yet, Ghana is a third world country, now?"

"The nuclear devastation made us a third-world planet," Kweku said.

Auntie Yajna said, "Since we've been manufacturing dormant-clones the last decade and developed consciousness vaults that truly keep the minds from corrupting, we are the country, and continent, I dare say, that holds the royal flush of humanity's future."

"Just because the body has been beaten, bruised and scarred," Nana said, "doesn't mean the heart, soul, and spirit can't still reign supreme."

Auntie nodded. "Yes! Believe me when I say, this land may look like it's dying, but our resources dictate that we're thriving! The government just doesn't want us to know that so they don't do anything to rebuild, for fear of losing their grip around our thirsty throats."

Kweku said, "Now listen to this sweet bosomy lady!"

"Boy shush," Auntie Yajna said, waving in a dismissive gesture.

Kweku tapped Nana on his shoulder. "She knows what she's talking about!"

The woman with pigtails said, "And I don't? So what? Just because Ghanaian scientists had a few snags transferring consciousness to the dormant-clones, it's a total fail?"

"Clones, scones! What in the world does that have to do with our food?" Nana asked.

"I'll tell you, Mr. Got something to say about everything," Auntie Yajna said. "What monies our country does have, is spent on a flawed technology. While the smartest scientists in the world, our people, are ignoring the fact that focusing on agriculture is going to save the world. Many of the plants that provided sustenance are dying out by the second? And advancements in fixing our broken system of feeding our people? Well, that's moving at a snail's pace?"

Kweku leaped to his feet and pointed at Auntie Yajna. "At best!"

"Boy, what's gotten into you?" Nana asked. "You done hopped up like you shat in your pants."

"I reckon you would know," Kweku said. "Ain't been a day, I've seen you that you don't smell like a walking sewer."

"You two are a mess!" Auntie Yajna said, laughing. "At the end of the day, it's not just our nation but many countries all over the world that are starving. Look around. We don't need television, iPhones, or computers to show us that the world is dying, we can feel it. We can feel it! Our souls can taste it, and you can breathe in hope all you want, you can't deny that the propaganda our government is giving us about a new life in a new body that can adapt to this toxic environment, smells rotten to the core."

"Preach on, priestess!" Nana said, and raised his fist in a gesture to honor Auntie.

She continued, "Forget about Ghana, never mind Mother Africa! If we don't rectify this global problem, or huh, find a magical doorway to a better world, we're all going to our graves and there won't be anyone after us to grieve!"

How could you follow that? There were no words spoken between the village philosophers for a few minutes. The sound of children laughing and screaming became welcomed fodder beneath the tribal drumming from the musicians. I kept my eyes on Kweku. The man was a caricature of intrigue. He seemed to be eating up everything that was said by Auntie Yajna and the others.

He finished his cigarette and flicked it away. "You say we're a third world country, but really we're not. Ghana will figure it out. It will. But did you know that it took the generous act of third world countries to show us how to survive during disastrous times?"

"It did. It did," Nana said, and walked over to the cigarette still lit, and twisted his barefoot over it. "Countries like India have become valuable resources to the world, even if the lady says we're really a first-world country. Come on, fool. Let's go! We were first in line to get our rations. I think I have some more tobacco back in my place."

"Well, why didn't you say so in the first place?" Kweku said, and nodded. "All right, fool. I'll just say one more thing to these intelligent women over here. Look here! That's why the leaders of this world founded the Global Consulate, to create a check and balances system for all heads of state. It was them that instituted the protocol of rationing our supplies. Say what you want, but we'd really be in trouble if there were no food rations."

Auntie Yajna and the women traded glances and nodded.

"Kwe," Nana said, "Your nose is bleeding." He reached in his shorts and produced a handkerchief.

"Boy, I don't know where that's been."

"Take the thing, before you bleed all over yourself. I haven't used it. Here, now!"

Kweku took it and wiped his nose. More blood came out of his nostrils.

"Just tilt your head back and leave it there for a bit, Nana said.

"I know what to do!" Kweku said. "Now stop pestering me," he said, and the two men disappeared in the crowd of people.

One of the musicians that was drumming stood up and started dancing while his friends continued beating a tribal tune.

"Fee-Fee," a voice said, behind me. "We're hungry!"

I turned around to see Linga, one of the twins, tugging on my shirt.

Pointing to the front of the line, I said, "Well, it won't be too much longer now."

"Stop pestering your sister," Auntie said, tickling her. "Run along. You'll be fed soon enough."

Linga's adorable dimples, her young wise eyes, and that infectious laugh brought me joy. The twins were six years old. Auntie Yajna adopted them when they were infants. Their parents died from radiation exposure. Most people died from that. If the ion radiation hadn't killed them, yet, they were affected with deformities and massive tumors.

When Auntie Yajna took them in, it was well after she had gotten a job with the Inspector General. After her time working as a nurse at the infirmary.

She got fired when they found out she was a blood addict and had been stealing bags and bags of blood from the infirmary's blood bank. They caught her red-handed when she was trapped after the building mysteriously caught fire. Auntie told me she was proud when the day came that she stood up at her addiction anonymous meetings and told everyone she went cold turkey and hadn't touched the evil stuff in almost a decade.

Since the GAF didn't charge or suspect her in the alleged larceny, when the entire wing of that building burned down, Inspector General Bete Sibaya gave her a second chance. Auntie Yajna was no longer an infirmary nurse. She had once treated his wife when she fell ill at a cricket event we were all attending. Soon after that, he'd hired Auntie Yajna to be the family's housekeeper, and she was just fine with that.

Although, she still talks about the IG like a dog for cheating on his wife. Auntie Yajna claims that his act of infidelity birthed a child that he does his damnedest to keep secret, but one day, she overheard him arguing with his former mistress about sending more money to take care of his child, and Auntie Yajna said, he stormed around his mansion the entire rest of the day, chewing out anyone who crossed his path.

I hadn't had proof, yet, but I knew he had something to do with the rise in human trafficking. It was the creepy way he looked at young children whenever I saw him speak at a public event. Soon as he was appointed Head of State when President Mbutu was put on ice, children started disappearing. If only scientists found a way to safely transfer the President's consciousness into a dormant clone, true order would be restored to Ghana. If that were true, maybe the girl I hit would still be alive. All we'd had needed was her consciousness to transfer to a dormant clone and she'd be as good as new, alive and breathing.

"Fee-Fee?" Yoni said. "Linga won't let me be the Tag Chief!"

I turned around toward Yoni. His big smile, and clumpy afro that seemed like a gopher had made a home there, made me want to kiss his cheeks until he squirmed out of my grasp. Linga's pale blue sundress crumpled against Yoni's already dirt-stained shorts, and they pushed into the lady in the line behind us, backward a little.

She just smiled at me.

"Where are your manners, Yoni?" I asked. "Say excuse me to the nice lady."

The lady wore a dress made of Kente cloth material, bright with the colors of green, black, yellow and orange. "Trust me, I have eight children in all. I don't get flustered easily," she said.

"Sorry, ma'am," he said, just as one of her children pushed him and ran off.

"Oh, no you don't!" he said, and ran after her.

Auntie Yajna laughed. "Oh, dear. I sure wish my old bones could still run around like that, but even if I could, honey, my bunions would have none of that."

"Girl, you're telling the truth," the woman said, laughing. "Well, seems like the line is moving faster today than usual. We'll be in front in a few minutes."

"I hope so," Auntie Yajna said. "I've got to get to work."

"Me, too, girl," the woman said.

"That so?" Auntie said. "Mind if I ask where?"

"Not at all," she said. "I work at the C-Tech."

"The consciousness vault?"

"Uh-huh. And you?"

Major Grunt walked by us, toward the front of the line, this time, ignoring me.

"I'm IGP Bete Sibaya's housekeeper," Auntie Yajna said.

The woman's face showed surprise. "You've actually seen him? In person?"

Auntie Yajna laughed. "Of course. He's not a ghost, just extremely private."

"I don't understand why you still have to get in line for rations? I would think he'd have your apartment full of whatever your heart desired."

"No, girl," Auntie said. "I wish that were true, but I've got to stand in this line twice a day to feed my family, same as you."

The woman shook her head. "Hmph. Who would've guessed?"

With that, nothing else was said between them. I got the feeling that Auntie working for the IGP made everyone else in the line pipe up. It was no secret that people were afraid of Bete Sibaya. He'd been known in the past to display a bad temper in public, even arresting some people on the spot for saying anything he found hostile and in opposition to his message.

Auntie had a good heart, and I don't think she realized that the people saw her more as an outsider rather than one of them. The moment they knew where she worked, they saw her as a spy. No, they wouldn't dare complain, bitch or moan in her presence for fear that it would get back to the IGP. Auntie Yajna was oblivious to that. Either that, or she chose not to acknowledge their ignorance.

After a couple of minutes, the children took turns, scrambling back and forth between us, until Auntie Yajna caught both of the twins in her grasp, their short arms doing their best to wrap around her for a big hug.

Auntie Yajna hugged them both. "Oh, I love those hugs, so much!"

She tickled them and they both laughed and slid down to the ground.

"Guess what day it is?" Linga said. "Hump day," she said, jumped up, and started thrusting her hips. "It's Wednesday! Wednesday, everyone!"

"Oh, child, stop being devilish," Auntie Yajna said. "Where did you learn how to move your hips like that?"

"From watching Feeni twerk while she worked!" Yoni said.

I didn't deny it, just shook my head while the others laughed. Auntie Yajna, and the woman with all those children, kept her eyes on their little brats, both shared faces of pride as the musicians allowed the twins and the other kids to play on their drums. As always, my mind drifted back to the House of Oware game. I couldn't wait to get back in and do an autopsy on the girl and find out exactly what did kill her.

A girl, maybe my age, maybe a bit younger, bumped into me, and I turned and met her eyes. They were green. She had albino skin and very short cropped hair. It was so short and the way she carried herself, made me think twice about whether she was female or not.

The green-eyed girl said, "Look where you're going."

I didn't respond but she was with two other girls and

they all laughed. They were all riding on skateboards and dressed in black hooded sweat suits, carrying bright orange backpacks over one shoulder. Up close, her features were soft, but other than that, the way she wore her clothes, and the tough raspy voice made me think she could pass for otherwise.

What did Kweku say in the interview? That the boy or girl was albino and wore a bright orange backpack. Could that be the witness?

I started off after, knowing that I had to ask her what she saw, but after one step, Auntie Yajna grabbed me.

"Where are you going, young lady?" she asked.

"I was just—"

She held her hand up. "Uhn-uhn! You see we are near the front of the line and I need you to carry the children's rations."

I bit my bottom lip and sighed. Auntie Yajna heard me and opened her mouth to say something but Yoni ran up to her and crashed into her hips.

"Breaker, breaker, 1-9," Yoni said. "Code blue, code blue. My sister just toot."

"Did not," Linga said, stumbling into my legs. "That was my stomach growling!"

He started giggling. "Sure it was."

Linga folded her arms and pouted. "Stop laughing. Fee-Fee make him stop laughing at me!"

"Stop teasing your sister, Yoni," I said. "Or someone may get a smack to their bottom."

Linga erupted in an obnoxious overdone laugh. That made everyone in earshot chuckle, and gaze at her.

"Not funny!" Yoni said.

"Is too!" Linga said. "Just like your dirty earlobes!"

"My ears aren't dirty!" he said. "I took a bath last night—but you didn't."

"Did, too!" Linga said, protesting. "I took a super-duper dry bath!"

That made the entire line of people laugh. We inched

forward, and the couple in front of us received their rations and moved on through the busy streets, putting us at the front of the line. There was a heavyset woman standing behind a table stacked with plastic packages. On her left were packages filled with apple slices, milk, rice porridge, and utensils. On her right were the same, except instead of a carton of milk, there was a carton of processed blood. That's the food rations that we'd get since we were ennies.

We saw that woman every day, and of course, had become quite friendly with her. She never went anywhere without her parrot, Snoopy, on her shoulder. The woman's skin was freckled with moles and she wore a hairnet. Her tee shirt was red and had an image of white wings on the front.

"Hey Yajna," she said, and held out the scanner gun.

"Kyoma," Auntie Yajna said, and extended her arm and turned her wrist up, displaying her identification number. The scanner issued a long beep and N/A flashed red in a small LED window on the gun.

"You still haven't taken care of that?" Kyoma asked. "You said you were going to fix it, yesterday, and the day before that."

"I'm sorry," Auntie Yajna said. "I was at the SSNIT, for three unbearable hours after work, yesterday. I swear it was working when I got here."

Kyoma said, "I don't have time for this. You want to start a riot with all these hungry people?" She glanced over to me. "I'll just scan Feeni's ID."

"Okay," I said, and held out my wrist.

Kyoma waved the gun over my wrist. My number, 01010100, blinked green in the LED reader.

"Hello Snoopy," Linga said.

Snoopy looked down at her, and then at Yoni, who was dancing in place.

"Hello!" he said, and squawked.

The children waved, and that made Snoopy flap his wings.

"Are we done, yet?" Snoopy asked.

"Not by a long shot, honey," Kyoma said, making the onlookers chuckle in amazement.

Kyoma passed me five packages of food rations, stacking them on top of each other.

"Why do we have to get one for Kofi," Linga asked.

"Because he likes a good snack when he comes home after work," I said.

Auntie Yajna was about to leave, and Kyoma grabbed her hand and whispered. "You work with the IGP. Get that fixed or next time we may just have a riot. We're almost out of food, and we just started."

"What happened?" Auntie Yajna whispered back.

Kyoma shrugged. "Problems with a shipment. Won't get the next one until tomorrow."

"Ay?" Auntie said. "Well, what about all these hungry people?"

The woman behind us, said, "There's someone behind you, you know?"

"All right, all right," Major Grunt said. "Move along."

Auntie Yajna said, "I'm going, Major Grunt, dear. Sorry."

"See you, tomorrow," Kyoma said, to Auntie.

We went about our way and the woman that waited behind us, placed her large basket down to fill it with food rations and called out to her children to join her. The twins skipped around Auntie Yajna and me, in their ritual hunger dance, begging to open up their ration package, and like every single day, Auntie told them they would eat as soon as we got home.

6

01010100 01100001 01110100 01110101

"Ooh, child, I have to use the bathroom like something awful," Auntie Yajna said.

"Good thing your ID number works, Fee-Fee," Linga said.

"I know it by hard," Yoni said. It's zero-ten-ten-one hundred!"

I giggled and poked him in the stomach. "Look at that!"

"I know it, too," Linga said. "Zero-ten-ten-one hundred!"

"You two are such brilliant children!"

"Feeni, baby," Auntie Yajna said. "Make sure the twins wash their hands before they eat."

"Sure thing," I said, and chuckled, watching Auntie Yajna rush to the bathroom, huffing and hissing like it was the end of the world.

I placed the food packages on the kitchen counter and hadn't been in the kitchen ten seconds before Linga ran into my bottom and collapsed at my feet, sobbing. "Fee-Fee, Fee-Fee, Yoni said earlier that he's going to feed my mind to the boogeyclone!"

"Did not," he said, ripped his shoes off, and ran into the living room.

"No coloring books until you wash your hands, first, and eat!" I yelled.

"Auntie Yajna's in the bathroom," he said, whining. "Aw, come on. I just want to color for a few minutes."

"Go upstairs!" I said.

He went stomping upstairs in as dramatic a fashion as he could.

Looking down at his twin sister, who was sobbing at my feet, I stooped down to her, and said, "Do you think it's even possible for him to get your mind? It's in your head, and it's invisible. You don't really think he can, do you?"

"Yes," Linga said. "If he downloads it into a wet-cum."

Wet-cum?

I almost lost it. Omigod, had she known what went across my mind when she said that, I'd have been embarrassed. "You mean retcon?" I asked, stifling a laugh.

"Yes," she said. "Wet-cum. That's what I said. Yoni said that it's judition for the boy twin to have the girl's twin's mind to do what he wanted."

"Oh, did he?" I grinned and picked her up in my arms. "Ooh, you're getting heavy. Are you trying to say the word tradition?"

The corners of Linga's mouth nearly touched the bottom of her ear lobes, her smile was so wide. "Yes, yes, Fee-Fee. That's it. I was close, though, huh?"

"Yes, you were, Linga! And that's such a big word to remember, too. Great vocabulary! You have a great mind!"

"Thank you," she said, grinning. "I'm a wordsmith!"

"That you are! Now go wash your hands."

On cue, we both smelled something, looked at each other and laughed.

"Auntie Yajna's stinking up the bathroom," she said, holding her nose, pinkie up.

"I think you better go upstairs like your brother and wash your hands," I said.

"Uh-huh," Linga said, making over-exaggerated nods. "Because downstairs is a danger zone to my nose. Auntie Yajna may be dead of self-fixiation."

Yoni ran down the stairs, falling to his knees when he hit the bottom and sliding across the floor.

"Hey, daredevil. Easy!" I said.

"You mean asphyxiation, Linga, and don't say that," I said, and placed her down. "It's not nice to speak about someone dying."

"Eew, what's that smell," Yoni yelled out.

"If I hear another word about it," Auntie Yajna yelled from the bathroom. "No blood snacks for either of you!"

The twins looked at each other, giggled, and covered their mouths. I went over to the kitchen counter to unwrap the food rations. One-by-one I placed them on our old wooden kitchen table.

"Don't think I haven't realized that you didn't wash your hands, yet, Linga."

"I washed my hands," she said.

"The same way you had a super-duper dry bath?"

"That's not funny," she said. "You're teasing me."

"Aw girl, don't be so sensitive," I said. "Now git!"

Yoni skipped around Linga, saying, "Duck, duck, goose!" and then pushed her in the head.

"Stop!" Linga cried out.

"Yoni, no!" I said. "It's not ever nice to hit girls."

"She's not a girl, she's my sister," he said.

Linga chased him around the table, them both laughing. "Guys, stop!"

Auntie Yajna yelled from the bathroom. "Go wash your hands now, Linga!"

And off she went upstairs, like a frightened rabbit.

Yoni skipped over to the kitchen table and climbed up into a chair. "Feeding our tummies is serious business!"

I chuckled, pure joy sweeping over me. I loved my family, and I loved the twins. By the time I placed Yoni's blood snack on the table and placed a spoon for his rice porridge on the table, Linga ran down the stairs.

"You did not wash your hands that quickly, young lady," I said.

"Did, too," she said, and ran over to me so that I could smell her hands.

They smelled fresh of soap. "I stand corrected."

"Yes, you do," she said, and climbed up into a chair at the table.

Outside the kitchen window, the drumming by the

market stopped, and I guess the musicians had finally taken a break. There was a house in back of ours. Their yard was mostly weeds. A rusted swing set sat in front of a two-car garage that never opened. Toward the side of the house was a colorful kid's cooking stove under by a large African mahogany timber tree. Scattered toys and dolls littered the ground. A little red plastic table stood in the middle of the yard with puzzle pieces on top of it. Dozens of puzzle boxes sat underneath the table. None of that stuff seemed like it had been played with, in years. I remembered seeing a cute little girl solving jigsaw puzzles on numerous occasions, many years ago. The parents were always going away on vacations and there was a girl around my age who used to live there, but I assumed she moved away right around the time I moved in with Auntie Yajna and the family.

Some laughter came from around the corner of the house. I waited to see what was happening. The husband chased his wife into the back yard, the two of them laughing. He grabbed her from behind and kissed her cheek. It made me smile, seeing how happy and in love they were. They suddenly stopped laughing and it looked like the husband had received a call.

Auntie Yajna came into the kitchen. "Is your rice water still warm, Yoni? Your porridge?"

"Uh, huh," he said, and put a spoonful in his mouth. "Delicious!"

I'm glad someone likes the food, I thought.

Linga asked, "Can we watch cartoons?"

"I guess so," Auntie said. "Feeni dear, I'll eat on the way to the IGP's mansion. I'm going upstairs to change."

I nodded, and then put my hands on my hips, and spoke to the twins. "Watch cartoons on your corneal streamers."

"We want to watch it on the TV," Linga said, whining.

Our flat screen TV sat on the wall behind the kitchen table. I kept the remote in the kitchen drawer filled with old crap, cereal toys, and papers. I found it buried in the pile of junk mail and turned on the TV.

"Okay," I said. "All right, guys. Which cartoon do you want to watch?"

"What time is it?" Yoni asked. His little eyebrows furrowed.

I glanced back at the digital clock above the stove. "Almost seven."

Yoni fidgeted in his seat and pointed at the television. "*Uncle Grandpa* is about to come on. It's on the Cartoon Network."

I pointed the remote at the screen. "Do you know what chan—"

"Thirty-six!" they both yelled out.

With the remote, I turned on the TV. A local cable news broadcast showed two scientists in heavy debate. The conversation between them was heated. The chyron at the bottom of the screen said that one man was from Ethiopia. He was slim with a large salt and pepper afro, about sixty. The other man was South African, lean like a cricket player, wore thick-rimmed glasses and seemed to be much older than his counterpart. They were sitting at a round table, separated by a very haggardly-faced brunette woman.

"That is preposterous," the Ethiopian said. "You are suggesting that all those natural disasters in the United States—right before the Final Event—Texas, Florida, Puerto Rico, and even in other countries like Mexico and Japan, was caused by CERN experimenting with the Higgs boson, and it becoming unstable, not an effect of some computer hackers over-riding satellites and monkeying around with the American government's weather modification weapon as in the High Frequency Active Auroral Research Program?"

The South African man's face wrinkled. "That—that—that's exactly what I'm saying if you let me finish!"

"That doesn't even make sense," the hard-faced brunette woman said. "CERN is in Switzerland. How could it affect that many different regions? The entire planet is dying because of the nuclear cataclysmic event, a decade ago."

The Ethiopian waved a dismissive hand and said, "Next, he'll be saying there's a fold in the universe and aliens will control all electronics over on Maple Street."

"I don't even know where Maple Street is!" the South African said. "Professor Stephen Hawking once told me that man will one day spread out into space, and to other stars, so a disaster on Earth would not mean the end of the human race."

The Ethiopian man said, "Yes, yes. I've heard you say it many times before on interviews, that Hawking, may he rest in peace, said that nuclear war, global warming, and genetically-engineered viruses are among the scenarios he believes are the ways that things have gone wrong for humanity, and that we will not establish self-sustaining colonies in space for at least the next hundred years. What's your point, since we have another eighty-something years to go?"

"That consciousness transferring," the South African man said, "in a way, is us going not outer space but into inner space. That's how we're going to self-sustain against punk kids with a high IQ and a fetish for developing the next killer virus that could wipe out humanity."

Linga pouted and started kicking her feet against the table.

"Linga, stop!" I said.

"Can I watch *Uncle Grandpa?* I'm missing it," she said, whining.

"Just a moment, darling," I said, and turned up the sound. "I want to hear this, real quick."

"There is no doubt in my mind that CERN's continual work on the God Particle," the brunette woman said, "has opened a portal, a black hole, that is going to wipe out humanity as sure as we all sit here arguing instead of trying to come up with a solution for closing it, not some genius hackers, sitting in the underwear watching porn on one screen and cartoons on their corneal streaming while trying to invent the next big virus."

On the bottom of the screen rolled a newsflash: POLICE HAVE FOUND THE BODY OF A YOUNG GIRL. NO DETAILS ABOUT HER DEATH YET, UNTIL HER PARENTS ARE CONTACTED.

There had been a lot of abductions in Accra and the surrounding area. My guess was that she was a victim of human trafficking. Linga mimicked one of my habits and blew out a bubbled sigh. She folded her arms and pouted. Her brother saw her and followed suit.

"Ehhhhn! Now I've got two spoiled brats sitting at the table like it was the last day in the world."

"I'm missing it!" Linga groaned.

"Okay, okay!" I said. "Channel thirty-six, eh?"

The twins lit up. "Yes!" they said, in unison.

I pressed the numbers, and poof, a green lizard-looking character rode on a tiger with a funny little character in suspenders. Keeping a joyful eye on how excited the twins were watching their cartoon, I blindly reached up and opened the cabinet hanging to the right side over the sink: the snack stash.

"Yay," Linga said. "This is my favorite episode!"

"Aww, we've seen this one a gazillion times, already," Yoni said.

Auntie Yajna came downstairs wearing a black dress, trimmed in white. "Cartoon reruns are about as uninvited as a knife fight in a phone booth. Ain't that right, twins?"

Yoni said, "Yup!"

"No, I like this one," Linga said. "I would watch this episode every day if it came on."

Auntie Yajna went over to them and kissed each one of them on their heads. "Now, Y'all be good for your big sister. You hear me?"

In unison, they said, "Yes, ma'am."

"The police found another body," I said. "I bet it was a victim of human trafficking."

"Don't go down that road, Feeni," Auntie Yajna said. "For the last time, Bete Sibaya does not run a trafficking ring. He's too busy running a country."

"A corrupt country, you mean. Ghana is worse than Nigeria, now, thanks to him."

"You sound like you're ready to join the resistance."

"Hah! Picture that. Me following someone else's rules."

"Isn't that the truth? You just make sure that when Kofi gets home from work, he helps you with your chores," Auntie said, kissing my cheek. "And clean up the children's bathroom. I was thinking where in the world is that wretched smell that's destroying the inside lining of my nostrils coming from? Hell, I was damned sure a bison moved into the spare room downstairs and died. It was their bathroom."

"Linga stunk it up," Yoni said.

"What's this and your obsession with stinky smells, Yoni?" I said.

"They're children, Feeni, darling," Auntie said. "What do you expect? Take care of the twins and your big brother."

"Hey, people are saying that Bete Sibaya is sick and that's why he doesn't come out in public anymore. You see him every day, is that true?"

"Child, you can't believe all those conspiracy theories. Of course, he's okay. I mean, yes he has become a lot more reclusive, and I see less and less of him, but he's not sick. I assure you of that."

Auntie Yajna waved one last goodbye and headed to the front door.

When the door closed shut, Yoni held up the empty carton his food came in. "All done. Now can I go color?"

"Yes," I said, and before I could get out my next sentence, he'd already jumped down. "but only for an hour and then it's nap time for you and your sister since both of you guys stayed up late last night, looking at the stars."

"We normally, don't have nap time until noon," Linga said.

"Well today," I said, "it will be earlier."

"Okay," Yoni said, and ran into the family room to color.

"May I be excused?" Linga asked.

"Yes," I said. "What do you want to do?"

"Will you read to me?"

"I would love to," I said, grinning

To be honest, I was surprised that I didn't have to fight tooth and nail to get the twins to agree to taking an early nap. I laid a Kente blanket out in the family room.

Yay!

The twins fell asleep within minutes. I guess they were tired after staying up late naming stars and talking about the galaxy. I just wanted to get back into the House of Oware game, and my plan worked. There was much more to investigate with my new case, and it was time to get back to some fun and forget about the crap in my life but first, there was something that I had to do.

~

My bedroom was the largest in the house, even more so than Auntie Yajna's. When she took me in, she insisted that I have it and that I had no choice but to take it. From the first time she saw me at the holograves, a place where both of my parents were memorialized, she treated me like someone special. She was there to visit her late husband. She had a special hologram made, showing one of their last conversations before he died to complications from radiation poisoning. The 3D image I had at my parent's holograve were made of stills.

On my olive-green walls were posters of cats. My floors were hardwood. I hadn't had time to wash my clothes, yet. There were a few piles of dirty clothes in front of my closet, separated between dark and whites. On the left side of the room was a twin bed, flanked by small oak wood side tables. The bottom of my closet was flooded with sandals and all my clothes were cramped into a closet that seemed far too small for a room that size.

I kicked off my sandals and went over to the area I had set up to honor my parents. There was a big scented candle on a table, along with photographs of my parents. There were three pictures: one of my baba, my mother and the three of us together capturing the time we went to a festival in Senegal. According to the data index, I was four-years-old in that picture, and didn't remember the occasion, but was happy to have the photograph, just the same. It had been nine years since I last saw them. It killed me that we didn't have more time together.

There was a drawer in the side table, and I pulled it out for a book of matches, struck one, and lit the candle. A little wax slithered down the wick onto the candle, and the aroma of cinnamon created an ambiance of sweet peace. The first time I discovered the House of Oware, in the game, a prayer appeared on two tombstones that sat side-by-side in a graveyard, outside of the church that was the starting place for the game. The names on the tombstones were Kulo Xo and Ruma Xo. They were my parents. When Auntie Yajna took me in, I created an altar to pray for my parents' peace in the afterlife. That prayer was the one I said, each and every time I bowed before their pictures.

I closed my eyes, and my palms kissed together in a reverence no less obedient than a gracious servant pressing her lips upon the Lord's feet, and said, "When the gods of my ancestors, my mother, and my father, come to the gateway that houses their souls, let this gateway be unfolded to KHUTI, and let the doors be opened to him that is in heaven."

I bowed my head to the ground, letting my forehead touch the cool wood of the floor, and continued,

"Come then, O thou travelers, who dost journey in Amentet. He who is over this door open it to Ra. SA saith unto AQEBI, open thy gate to Ra, unfold thy door to KHUTI. He shall illuminate the darkness, and he shall force a way for the light in the habitation which is hidden. Let their souls, their very consciousness, mend with mine and lead me to the path of righteousness. If I'm worthy to be approved by the Lord of Lords, the Kings of Kings and the ancestors who have opened once-closed doors, I may add to this community's legacy as a giver, and not take away from it as a taker, and shall prosper and give honor to my bloodline's name."

I blew out the candle. As always, the burned wick triggered an olfactory memory of a nightmare that always started with me standing in a broken-down motor boat among a sea of lit candles. Each one drifting on a square piece of wood in the middle of the South Atlantic Ocean. The black sky was illuminated by thousands of fireflies, holding their patterns like shimmering stars. It wasn't so much as the candles that disturbed me, but the water.

I despised the sea, no that wasn't the right word, I hated the sea. The late-night movie playing in my head when I went to sleep replayed over-and-over again of a yacht consumed with raging flames, the bone-tingling screams of a desperate couple drowning in their fate. Those screams were stained in the deep abyss of my consciousness.

My soul was torn into a hundred pieces each and every time I had that nightmare. I awakened, exhausted like I'd just ran a marathon to Somalia and back.

I smiled at the photograph of my parents and me. Those pictures that I downloaded from my neural implant onto an iFax and printed them out, were all that was left of my parents. Their deaths were tattooed to the depths of almost every object I encountered in my day. My wrist itched, and I looked down at my ID number tattooed to my skin: Zero-ten-ten-one hundred. Like the grave memory of Mama and Baba, it was a scar that ran as deep as my bones, but I could taste it like it was on the tip of my tongue."

"Stupid numbers," I said, under my breath.

I'd had my identification number memorized since I was able to feed on my own. It was a way that the government could track its people, no matter where they traveled. Auntie Yajna said it hadn't always been like that. But once trafficking got out of hand, and children were being abducted by the thousands, the Ghanaian government had to do something. Problem with that was, the human traffickers had found technology to overcome that, and were able to continue the big business of sex and slave trade.

It had gotten to be so bad that they added a new product to their agenda: ennies. Now, no sentient being was safe. Not that it made any difference. I wanted to stop it altogether.

If I did that, I could make a difference in this world, make a mark in history. Enough obsessing over things I have no power to change, time to get back to the game! But…

I stood and lifted the picture of my father in my hand, staring at it, trying hard not to see that I had his same eyes, even his smile. It wasn't but just a few hours ago that I thought I was a killer.

Now, because my brother and Grunt was so stupid, I may be found guilty of murder. If the right investigators find the clues that lead to me driving that damned car, I'm a goner. How could I have been so stupid, so mindless, so criminal as to drink and drive?

The hair on the back of my neck pricked, and a wave of nervousness swept over me. I trembled.

No, not again, I thought. It'd been months since the last one.

I rushed over to my dresser drawer, next to my bed and sifted through the junk of amulets, talismans and various ankh necklaces I'd collected over the years.

"There you are," I said, and clinched it in my hand.

I grabbed my bottle of panic pills. After twisting off the cap, I tried to pop a couple in my mouth. My hands shook too much and I freaking missed. The pills fell onto the floor, scattering like magic elusive beads. I concentrated so hard to pour a couple of more pills in my hands, but I couldn't hold my fingers still.

The pills bounced around my hands. I closed my fist tight and brought it up to my mouth. My body had started to convulse a little. I turned my head up to the bland milk-white ceiling and opened my fist a little. Two Zonegran tablets dropped into my mouth. I always gagged when trying to swallow pills, but I forced myself, grimacing. One would have thought I was trying to digest scorpions by my expression. Drool slithered down my face. I wiped it off and spat out sounds of disgust with every swipe of my hand.

Spasms of pain struck throughout my body. I let out a cry of agony. Curling over my parent's altar in a fetal position, I tried to will the seizure away, tried to relax my muscles, but shuddered without any signs of relief. After about a couple of minutes of gasping and moaning, the shaking subsided. The whole experience worked up my hunger. I needed blood and was glad that I had saved a stash of blood cartons for a rainy day in a small refrigerator Auntie Yajna let me keep in my room. I looked in my frig, took out a blood snack and a woman let out a horrific scream, just outside of my bedroom window.

7

01010100 01100001 01110100 01110101

Without looking out of my window, I unlocked my door and rushed down the hall to check on the twins. They were fine, sleeping like little pup wolves. It was amazing how they could sleep through just about anything. I glanced out of the kitchen window that gave me the best view of the side of the house behind ours. The woman who lived behind our house was hysterical.

What are they doing there?

Kofi and Grunt stood at her front door. The woman was flapping her arms and sobbing, leaning against her husband, who was also in tears. Her legs collapsed and her husband helped her to a lawn chair in her yard.

Something bad had happened to their family. Grunt and my brother were there to deliver the bad news. I didn't know the family. They never came out much, and when they did, kept to themselves. That wasn't normal. In my village, everyone spoke to everyone. We cooked together, danced together, and celebrated the several festivals each month together, but that couple stayed to themselves.

Auntie Yajna said that their youngest daughter had a little genius when she was younger and the reason why they were so protective was that other kids usually picked on her for being different.

Another female stepped out of the house. She was older, eighteen-nineteen, and dressed in a GAF uniform like my brother and Kofi. At first, I thought she was there as a grief counselor for that softer touch for the family of hearing such tragic news, but at a closer look, I realized that she, too, was in tears. She went over to the woman. I gasped when I saw that she had a gray strand of hair that went from the point of her widow's peak to the side of her hair. I knew that my brother was on official business, and I shouldn't have gone over, but something about that girl made me want to confirm a strange suspicion.

Checking on the kids again to make sure they were sound asleep, I slipped on a pair of sandals and eased over to the neighbor's house behind ours.

Kofi saw me coming and rushed over to me, saying, "Hey—hey. What are you doing? You can't be here. I'm working."

"They're making a lot of noise," I said.

"Where are the twins?"

"They're fine. Napping. I just wanted to make sure that our neighbors were all right."

"Bull," he said, grabbing my arm. "You don't even know them. You shouldn't be here. We're informing them of a death in her family. Their eldest daughter just got in town. She lives in Benin. This is tough as it is. If you have any respect at all for others, leave."

"That girl? The GAF officer?"

His eyes were jumpy, and he clenched his teeth. "You really have to leave."

"Okay, okay. I'm leaving. You'd think I was the one who killed their family member by the way you're acting."

Kofi stiffened, and I knew something was wrong.

"Wait," I said, and my hands started shaking. "No."

Kofi looked over his shoulder at Grunt. "Yeah," he said, in a matter-of-fact way.

"This—this isn't about the other night?"

Kofi didn't answer.

I looked over Kofi's shoulder and saw that Grunt had a look of distress on his face. The news report I'd just heard about the body of a girl being found but they hadn't notified the parent. It all started to make sense.

It was my neighbor?

I tried to breathe calmly but it was of no use, I had begun to hyperventilate.

"You...really should go," Kofi said. "I'll be over as soon as I can to check on you.

"I'll—I'll do that," I said, and turned around to leave, reaching in my pocket for my panic pills.

"Xo?" the female officer said. "Feeni Xo, is that you?"

8

01010100 01100001 01110100 01110101

Fear was something that could drive the most rational thoughts of a teenager into a recklessness that most adults couldn't begin to comprehend. Combine that with a set of visceral memories from thousands of recurring dreams over several years of seeing my parent's charred bodies swimming in rivers of screams, and you had one messed-up girl.

Many doctors (and there were many) diagnosed what I had as post-traumatic stress disorder. Believe me, it was more than just the nightmares or anxiety attacks that brought such disarray to my life. That's why I preferred living in the House of Oware game versus real life. I didn't want to face a world I did not control, a place where I had no significance as a sentient being at all. Even though I faced a myriad of problematic challenges in the game, I knew that it was I who ultimately controlled my destiny. I liked living in a world where the stakes were high, and impossible odds separated the average from the great.

I was a gamer, and I played to win, but not in the real world. But this time, I had to face life, knowing that the outcome was a lose-lose. The female GAF officer had a good reason for knowing who I was: she was Samora Lamp. Three hours later, she knocked on my front door. I welcomed her into the kitchen.

"I'm really sorry about your sister," I said.

"You look a lot younger than you do in the game," she said. "We're about the same age, right?"

"You're seventeen?"

"No, eighteen, or I wouldn't have been able to join the GAF."

"You, on the contrary, look a lot less male," I said. "Why did you pick a guy avatar in the game? You're going to be confusing me now after years of knowing you as a man."

"I don't know. I just did."

She looked at me with hopeless eyes. The kind that someone had who was drowning in quicksand with no one around to hear them begging for help.

"Sorry," I said. "I'm rambling about inconsequential things."

After I made a pot of coffee, we sat in my kitchen. Because of the House of Oware game, we had a history between us, an understanding, built on trust and a lot of time spent together solving cases in the VR construct. I looked at the door and thought about running. Running somewhere, anywhere, as long as I was far from those sorrowful eyes. She and her parents were facing the most heartbreaking times of their lives. The couple who took frequent vacations like they were always on their honeymoon saw their happiness ripped from under them, torn apart like a lion clawing out the heart of a rabbit.

How can I ever tell her what I did?

"Can I ask you a personal question?" she asked.

"Uh, yeah. Sure. Okay. Like what?"

"If Kofi and the twins are your siblings, how is Yajna your aunt?"

I chuckled. "Oh. Simple. When Auntie Yajna took me in, she told me to call her that, but she prohibits us from referring to each other anything but brothers and sisters, even though she adopted the twins and me. Only Kofi is her true offspring."

"There's no Mr. Yajna?"

"He died a long time ago, but girl, Auntie Yajna couldn't keep a man if she had him shackled to a wall in the basement. She's too set in her ways to be in something as compromising as a relationship."

"Ahh, now I understand. And where are Yoni and Linga, now?"

"When Kofi got off work, he took them to the market, along with some new friends they just made. There's a playground on the far end."

"I know it well, used to take Jinni there before she started getting picked on by the other children. You didn't tell your brother about the game, did you?"

"No, no. I just told him that we've known each other for years, and you needed some time with a friend."

"And he bought that?"

"I guess. Either that, or he wanted some quality time with the twins. He loves them so much."

Lamp's eyes fell into a tearful daze.

"Oh, I'm sorry. I didn't mean to—"

"No worries. I know you didn't mean any harm."

I got up and emptied my cold coffee in the sink, smiling at the writing on my mug that said I'M NOT A MISANDRIST, I JUST LIKE MY MEN DEAD written on it in fancy white lettering. "I guess I don't make the best coffee, huh?"

"The worst," she said, and a wan smile crept up the corners of her mouth.

I leaned my butt up against the kitchen sink, and she stood up and went to my sink.

"Jinni sent me a neural message before she died," she said, and poured her coffee in my sink.

"About what? Your trip to South Africa?"

"No. It was a peculiar letter that I didn't think was anything more than her paranoia, until now."

"What was in the letter?"

"I'll send it to your neural mailbox, now."

Just like that, my corneal stream flashed, alerting me of an incoming message, and I read it:

Dearest sister,

I think someone is trying to harm me. If you asked me how, I'd hate to admit that I have

*no proof but like a premonition, I know that
I'm being watched. I think someone doesn't
want me to help President Mbutu. Ever
since I agreed to go, I've had this feeling.
Please come home. I'm afraid something
is going to happen to me. I know I sound
schizophrenic. but I beg you, come home.*

Love Jinni

I asked, "When did she send that?"

"The night before last."

"And you're sure it's not a fake?"

"I did a GAF network intrusion scan on her neural
implant signature to establish if there was a TCP connection established."

"I don't know what any of that means."

"In other words, yes, the neural message came from her.
Did you do an autopsy, yet in the game?"

"No, I didn't get to it, yet. I was going to do it until I
heard your parents in the back yard receiving the news
about your sister."

"If someone was after her," Lamp said. "Why? To stop
her from breaking the code to allow First Lady Mbutu to
open the vault which holds the retcon with her husband's
consciousness on it?"

"There's only one man I know who does not benefit with
the President coming back in a clone."

We both said, "Bete Sibaya."

I sighed. "Which is strange because as far as I know, we
haven't yet developed the tech to safely transfer a retcon
into a clone without a full wipe of the consciousness."

"Why kill my sister? I'm sure there are other ways to
prevent her from moving forward. Why kill her?"

"Maybe why she died had nothing to do with your trip."

"What are you suggesting?"

"Her body was found at the old water plant, right?"

"Yeah, so what? You think since it was near Lake Volta,

it was a trafficking thing?"

"I don't know, maybe."

The more I think about it, why was she in that area to begin with? Was she left there to die? She doesn't seem like the kind of girl that would be in the streets in that part of town at that time of night.

"I have to find that witness," Lamp said.

"Hey! You know what?" I said. "I think I saw her today?"

"Where?"

I pointed in the direction of where we got our food rations, earlier at the market. "Right outside of my house, just around the corner!"

"She lives in this area?"

"I'd say the chances are pretty high. The CCTV probably has her walking around town. But how do we get access to it?"

"Leave that to me. Now that we've met," she said, looking out the window toward her parent's back yard. "You know what I think we should do?"

I grabbed a clean rag and poured a little dishwasher detergent on it. "Now what?" I asked and turned the water faucet on and started washing the coffee mugs in the sink.

"After we locate the witness. Let's talk to him, or her, together."

I stopped what I was doing and turned around. "You want me to help you solve the murder of your sister?"

"Why not, Examiner?"

"I'm not a real investigative medical examiner."

"You're more than qualified to assist me on this case than anyone I have ever worked with in real life."

"Thanks for the vote of confidence, but I don't know. Shouldn't you wait for your parents to come back from identifying the body? Maybe now is not a good time to dig into something so—"

"So what? Personal?"

"Look. You know as good as I do who killed my sister."

My heart stopped. "What?"

"One of those slave traffickers."

I exhaled a hard breath. "I don't think this is a good idea."

"Xo, come on! It wasn't a hit-and-run. You know that. I know that! Look where she was found! My sister's ten years old. She wouldn't be out in the bad part of town after midnight, wandering around. Not my sister! She was too smart for that. Jinni went to bed every night at nine."

"I—I don't know, Lamp. Maybe we should just let the GAF handle the case."

"I am GAF!"

It was obvious that she was too close to the case. I feared it may unravel her, but who was I to tell her no. If the shoe was on the other foot, no one in hell would stop me from finding out who killed my sibling.

"Come on," I said. "I know you're GAF. That's not what I meant."

"What are you trying to say, then? I'm not competent."

"No! No! I mean, you know? My brother. Grunt. Officers who aren't personally tied to the case. You're too close to this. It will tear you apart, and your judgment will be clouded."

She got right up in my face. "Let me tell you something, Examiner. There ain't a damn soul in all of Africa who couldn't do a better job at finding out who killed Jinni than me."

"Hey, I hear you," I said, and moved from under her. I walked to the kitchen door and glanced out of the screen. "Trust me. I know how incredible you are as an investigator. I'd never doubt that for a second."

"Then if you're my friend, you're in. Cut the bullshit."

I turned to her and nodded. "Yeah. I'm in. Let's go! Let's find your sister's killer."

9

01010100 01100001 01110100 01110101

"How are we going to get there?" I asked Lamp, as she slid on a shoulder holster. "It's way too hot to walk five miles in this sweltering weather."

She slid her revolver in the holster. "You do ride, don't you?" she asked, checking herself out in the mirror.

Lamp saw that I had changed into black jeans and a matching tank top and decided to get out of her uniform, slipping into blue jeans, and a midriff navy blue top. We both had on ankle-high boots.

"When you say ride, you mean what? A motorcycle?"

"Yeah," she said, and walked into the kitchen area. "I've got two bikes." She opened up a drawer under the kitchen counter and pilfered through junk until I heard keys jingling.

"In the game, you were always on a bike. Was that just fantasy?"

I was sitting on her parent's couch, looking at all the family pictures on the coffee and side tables in their cluttered living room. The walls were covered with art from Kenya, and dozens of warrior statuettes planted everywhere there was room for them.

"Oh, no, girl," I said, getting up. "I learned how to ride at my second foster home. My big foster brother taught me."

She tossed me a key ring with two small keys on them. "Then let's ride."

"You're sure you want to do this?" I asked.

"Xo, I just called in a favor to an ex-boyfriend and had him put his job on the line sending us a neural-video of all the pertinent footage with the witness in it. You damn straight I want to do this."

We walked outside of the house and Lamp unlocked the garage door. She manually pulled the door up. There were a ton of boxes everywhere, stacks of used paint cans and an array of furniture piled almost to the ceiling, but in the midst of all that junk were two spotless deep orange one-wheeled motorcycles.

"Holy crap!" What the heck are these?"

"It's called an Uno. Custom fiberglass body, self-balancing. Dad maintained them for me."

"Where in the hell did you even find one of these? Besides scooters, auto manufacturers don't even make vehicles anymore, except for the military."

"If I told you, I'd have to cut off your left tit."

"Yeah, right," I said.

She rustled through one of the piles of junk, producing a small leather satchel. "There are disposable gloves and a few other things you may need. It ain't much but it'll do the job."

I unzipped it and glanced in it. "It's perfect. Where are we going, exactly?" I asked, shouldering the satchel.

"We tracked the witness going to a house in Liati Wote. Stayed there overnight and left out in the morning. An older man and his wife, probably her parents, were in the yard doing various chores. I'm pretty sure that's where she lives."

"Got it."

"It would be the rough part of Kumasi she lives in, eh?" she asked, disappearing behind the pile of furniture. She came out holding two motorcycle helmets.

She handed me a helmet. "This helmet has iJet technology. You can pair your neural implant with it, I'll put in the address I have for the witness and the navigation will show on the bike's display."

I put it on. "That's pretty wild."

"It's all right. Look, I sent the CCTV footage of the girl to Major Grunt. He said he would put it through a face recognition program and see if anything came up."

"Sounds good."

My stomach growled and reminded me that I hadn't fed in a while.

"Damn, girl," Lamp said. "I heard that over here. You want to grab something to eat? I don't have any blood snacks, but I'll wait for you to get some from your house if you want?"

"Nah, I'm good."

"When's the last time you ate?"

"I haven't fed since yesterday."

"Why not? You're sick?"

"No, I just haven't had much of an appetite. I'm good. I'll feed tonight when we're done!"

"It's your body. So, yeah, um. In real life, have you ever fired a gun?"

"Yep. Plenty. Kofi's takes me target practicing all the time. I'm a better shot than he is, believe it or not."

"Cool beans," Lamp said, and started the bike.

I hopped on the other one-wheel bike and started it, feeling a bit awkward at first, but like she said, it was able to self-balance itself and I backed it out of the garage. I held Lamp's bike while she shut the garage door and locked it.

Lamp said, "I'm receiving a call. It's Mom. Hold on." She walked over toward the rusty swing set. "Where are you guys? ...Accra? What are you doing there?"

I gave her some space to talk, besides, I wanted to get a feel of the bike a bit and rode it down the dirt driveway to the road. A couple of older guys were walking by, and their eyes nearly popped out of their heads when they saw the bike. I sped past them before they could get a word out to me. They just whooped and hollered.

Before I turned around, Lamp was zipping by me, and off we rode. We were on Mampong Road toward Old Tafo in less than five minutes. I checked the time and saw that the news program I listened to every day was just about over, so I tapped into it with a mere thought and caught the last bit of the tough-voiced girl again making threats. I told Lamp that I believed this was the witness based on her voice, and to tune in to the broadcast.

It was not pretty. She said: People of Liati Wote, you will no longer be able to turn your head and say nothing. Nearly seven-to-ten thousand children are abducted and trafficked for labor and sex slavery! How? I don't care how many mouths you have to feed in your family, you don't barter a child so that the rest can get by! You lambs! You insufferable lambs. You sold away your children's spirit, but at what cost? I'll tell you the cost! The price of this madness is that now, you must pay with your soul. So tonight, you die!

Liati Wote. That's where we're headed. How does that skinny albino girl expect to follow through on her threats? Frankly, I believed it was all talk. What was she going to do, bomb the village? That is the same girl I heard speak last night on the radio after the accident. One thing for sure, I can relate to the pain she must've endured. There were many times I wanted to kill my foster parents for all the crap they put me through.

We rolled into the sleepless neighborhood and passed several streets that were filled with men hanging on the corner, drinking, talking and smoking jots. Some women hung out of their windows and talked back and forth to guys and girls passing by their house. The navigation led us down a narrow alley between two dilapidated old build-ings. We dodged through street debris, overstuffed garbage bins, and homeless people. Some were asleep while others glared at us ride past on the shiny one-wheeled bikes. I started thinking that it was a bad idea to have these expen-sive motorcycles in an area like that.

I was about one block away from the witness's home

when Lamp sped past me and made a right down an industrial area across from the boat docks. I figured she knew what she was doing so I followed her. We stopped in front of an old warehouse. The building's paint job looks like it was last done in the stone age. There was a metal garage with graffiti tagged all over it.

Lamp got off her bike and took off her helmet. "This area used to have the most amount of auto shops in all of Ghana. Now, there's only this one, and it's the best-kept secret."

Lamp tapped her helmet against the metal door, and in seconds it rolled up, making a metallic clanking sound. Inside the garage was so dark, I couldn't make anything out.

"We'll leave the bikes in here," she said, and rolled hers inside.

"Is someone going to turn on the lights?" I asked, rolling the bike in, and kicking the stand out so that it leaned next to her bike.

"Negative. But I trust this place."

"Whose shop is this?"

"A friend of mine. An older guy I met a few years back. He's sort of my uncle in a way, been looking out for me since I was a kid and went out on my own."

"What's his name?"

"I've been calling him Old Man, ever since I've known him. He gets a little sensitive whenever I bring up the past, so I don't"

Lamp stopped walking. "I'm getting a neurocall from Grunt."

"That was fast," I said.

"Yeah, Lamp, here...Frankie Lomas. Got it. You got a name for the folks?...Thomas and Meredith Benja. Good work, Major Grunt. You, too. Yeah. Right. Thanks."

She turned to me. "You get that?"

"Most of it. Different last names, Lomas and Benja."

"Yeah, I caught that, too."

"When I heard her speak on that radio broadcast the first time, she mentioned something about having nine or ten siblings, and how her parents died early, and her grandmother trafficked her to work as a labor slave at Lake Volta."

"Jeesh, no wonder she's all confused. And to top it off, she's probably been ostracized because she's an albino."

"She's had it rough, to say the least, but haven't we all? Doesn't mean you can go off killing people."

"No argument there," Lamp said.

"How'd Grunt get her name so quick? She has priors?"

"He didn't specify, but he said a group of boys were fishing and found Kofi's car in Lake Bosumtwi."

"What?"

How could they be so dumb?

Lamp laughed. "Easy, easy. Why are you acting like it's your car?"

"No, I'm not. I'm just surprised. I mean, I used to drive it a lot, so it does feel like it was my car."

"That makes sense. Grunt said not to worry, though. He and Kofi went to check it out. He said the funny thing about it was your brother just junked it, yesterday."

"Yeah, I know. That's what caught me so off guard."

"Uh-huh," she said, looking at me like she didn't believe me.

"These Unos are custom made, right? Is this where you got the bikes?"

"Nope."

"Liar."

"Well, you're not as dumb as you look."

"I was about to say the same thing to you."

We both walked out of the garage, giggling. Lamp whistled and the door clanked back down and closed. My heart was pounding, and I stuck my hand in my jeans, feeling for my panic pills. I didn't need them, but it felt good knowing they were near.

I hope those idiots cleaned the car outright. All I need

is for them to find some blood under the tire well or something and we're in deep trouble.

"You know where we're going?" Lamp asked.

"Um, yeah. I think. Just over a block on the other side of the street, right?"

"Affirmative."

When we got to the witness' house, an older white man, in his early fifties, was sitting on a bench in front of his house smoking a cigar. The tip of it, burned ash-orange. There were trees all around his house, and a lamp post standing at the edge of his property made his face look ghoulish.

An aye-aye sat on his shoulder asleep. It looked like it was somewhere in between a hybrid of a cat or a bat. Like a pug dog, it was as cute as it was ugly, if that makes any sense. One of its ears stood up when we approached but otherwise, it was either too old or too sleepy to pay us any mind.

"Are you Thomas Benja?" Lamp asked.

He raised his head, looked at us, and took a puff of his cigar. "Who wants to know?"

"I'm DCI Lamp, and this is Dr. Xo."

He squinted like the smoke burned his eyes when Lamp said the word doctor. "Doctor? Kids these days are passing all the tests in their neural schools without getting a day of real experience. Back in my day, they had to really work in a hospital in a residency to be called a doctor." He blew out a puff of smoke. "Hmph. What are you? Barely out of your training bra? Sixteen-Seventeen."

"I'm almost eighteen," I said.

He laughed, and coughed, the sound was filled with phlegm. "Same difference. Now, what do you want?"

"We understand you have a daughter named Frankie," Lamp said.

"What's this about?"

"Are you Frankie's father?"

"Yeah, I am. What of it?"

"We just want to follow up on a case," I said.

He threw down his cigar and crushed it with his foot. "Not that mess about the dead body police found at the run-down water plant, yesterday. Frankie reported it, as soon as she got out of there. They made her go over it, again and again. Do you people ever stop harassing innocent folk?"

"Is she here?" Lamp asked.

"No, she's out with her little skateboard dyke friends."

"Do you know who she spoke to?" I asked.

"I don't remember their names, but they were some cocky sonsofbitches. I think one of them was a major. The other one looked like he couldn't catch a thief if it stole the pants right off his legs."

I shook my head, in utter disbelief, and traded glances with Lamp.

A woman stuck her head out of the window. "Who in the devil are you talking to this time of night, dear? Thomas, everything okay?"

"Fine, Meredith. Go back to watching your American game shows on your corneal stream."

"Your food is getting cold," she said. "I know I didn't slave over this old-ass stove so you can let it go to waste!"

"I told you I'll eat when I'm ready! Now leave me alone, woman!"

"Well, hurry up! A news alert is saying that people should stay indoors, that the IGP has just called for a mandatory curfew, plus, I want you to rub my feet!"

"I'll be inside in a minute."

"Well, come on, then! My feet hurt!"

He turned to us. "Interview's over folks. Go harass someone else for a change."

"Can you tell us where we can find Frankie?" I asked. "It's really important."

Lamp said, "And it may help us to finally solve this case and give closure to the parents of the girl who died."

He sighed and took out another cigar. "Is that right?" Patting his pocket, he reached in and pulled out a cigar cutter. While he clipped off the end of his cigar, he said,

"To be honest, I don't think she's with those ruffian friends of hers. I think she went to meet her friend, Jinni."

That buckled Lamp and I caught her before she fell to the ground.

"Whoa, there, Missy," Thomas said. "What the hell's wrong with you?"

"Nothing," she said. "Sometimes the heat makes me lightheaded when I don't drink enough water."

She stood up straight and wiped her hand down over her lips. "Go on. You were saying."

"All's I was saying was that Frankie seemed mighty upset after seeing the dead girl, and I know that whenever my daughter got real uptight, her friend would always calm her down."

"You two adopted her?" I asked.

"What kind of fool question is that? Of course we did! Can't you tell?"

"How long ago was that? That you adopted her?" Lamp asked.

He started getting flustered. "I—I don't know. One day, about three years ago!"

"When Frankie was ten?" I asked.

"Yes, Meredith found her walking down the road late at night, nearly naked and bruised so bad we knew she's somehow found a way to escape from one of them filthy trafficking rings—wait-a-second, Frankie's calling me, now."

He started speaking to her, while Lamp and I backed off, and let our eyes roam around the place.

"Hey," I said. "Can you hack the computers in this house to see what's on their drives?"

"No, but I know who can."

"Who?"

"The Old Man. He is one of the best hackers in Ghana."

"Am I ever going to meet this mystery person?"

She shrugged. "I'm sending him a neuro-text and asking him now if he can gain access to—whoa, that was quick."

"What did he say?"

"He needed a physical address to find the IP address for the computer, and... There. I just sent it to him."

"Okay, he just neuro-messaged me, too. How'd he get my ID number?

"I gave it to him."

"You what?"

"Relax, sister. You can trust him."

"Yeah, well. He said that in order to compromise their computer, he'll need to find an exploit that has any vulnerabilities he can hack into."

"Yeah, he messaged me that, too," Lamp said.

"Maybe we can find an email or social networking account that can give us more background," I said.

"Well, I can tell you this," the Old Man neuro-texted us.

I asked messaged back, *"What?"*

The Old Man messaged, *"The owner of one of the computers has a Metasploit Framework, a Nmap, network mapper, a Nessus vulnerability scanner, and Maltego. Girls these are hardcore hacker software."*

"Hey, Old Man," Lamp messaged him. *"We gotta go!"*

Lamp and I went back over to Thomas.

"Everything okay?" I asked.

"Why wouldn't it be?" he said. After a breath, he offered, "Frankie never spoke about what happened. And we could never bring ourselves to ask her, but it didn't matter. Meredith brought her home, fed and bathed her, and the next morning went out and bought her some things from the market, clothes, toys and that stupid skateboard. That's all I can tell you. Now, if you're done wasting my time, I'd like to go inside my house, now."

I nodded and extended my arm to shake his hand. "Thank you, sir."

He fumbled in his shirt for his lighter and acted like he didn't see my hand. The aye-aye yawned when he stood and crawled down from his shoulder onto the bench. "Come on, Jubie," he said. "We're going inside."

Retracting my hand, I said, "Cute pet."

He spoke over my words. "Why don't you put an end to child slavery at Lake Volta?" he asked, walking toward his front door. "That's all them low life thugs in the underground city do is traffic kids from all over Africa, just so they can profit off of them kids. That's why we don't give 'em a dime of our hard-earned pension. I'd rather live in this dump than rub shoulders with people who turn their backs on their own."

"Sir," Lamp said, making him stop and turn around. "I sent my ID number to your registered neuro-mailbox, please give me a call if you can think of anything else that would help."

"Not gonna happen," he said, and slammed the door behind him.

The shades on his window rattled and we heard Meredith rip a hole in him for not fixing the stove, yet.

My corneal stream flashed alerting me of an incoming call.

I recognized the number and answered. "Kofi, what's up?" I said.

"Where are you?" he asked.

"Um, I'm out having drinks with Lamp. I mean Samora. You know? The whole being there for someone when they grieve."

"Get home, now!" he said.

"No! Dude, I just told you I'm out with Samora."

"For once, do as I say! Auntie Yajna's still at work. I have the twins and we're safe, but there's a—"

The temporal transmission ended.

"What the?" I said, and glanced over to Lamp.

Her eyes were welling up, her lips twitched, and she let out a weak smile. A tear rolled down her cheek.

"Oh, damn. I'm sorry," I said. "I didn't mean to—"

"It wasn't you; it was how he thinks Frankie is with my sister, now," she said, and sniffed. "What's going on?"

"I—I don't know. We got disconnected. Let me call him back."

10

01010100 01100001 01110100 01110101

With a mere thought, my neural implant dialed up Kofi's temporal transmitter, or rather his mind-phone, but he didn't answer.

"He's not answering?" Lamp asked.

"No, the jerk is ignoring me."

"Something's wrong. Did you hear Meredith say something about a mandatory curfew?"

"Yeah, let's get back to the bikes."

We walked off of Thomas' property onto the wide dirt road. A middle-aged woman, cradling a child bumped into me. The young boy in her arms seemed comatose. His eyes stared forward like he was in a zombie-like stupor. I tripped over her heel, but she didn't slow one bit, just kept going without a hitch.

"Hey," Lamp said, calling her. "What's happening?"

I tapped Lamp on her arm while looking down the street toward the village market area. "Hey," I said. "Check this out."

Humans and enhumans alike, poured through the streets in rivers of fear. Most of the roads outside of Accra were dirt tracks, so their feet clouded the air with dust and chaos. There were people running in every direction, pushing and knocking others down. A woman convulsed on the ground, gagging while being trampled.

"Hey," I said. "Don't trample that lady!"

A man ran by us, and Lamp grabbed his arm. His eyes were like blood moons under the shining street lamp.

"What is this?" she asked, but he tore out of her grasp, and dashed off.

People ran over the woman on the ground like a frightened herd of antelopes. Her hands were cranberry red like sobolo juice. Another woman stopped to help her but suddenly fell to her knees. The second woman hit the ground in jerky convulsions and rolled to the dirt road. In a wild smacking fit, she slapped her own head like she was trying to shoo wasps away.

"What's wrong with everyone?" I said, desperate for anyone to respond.

An old bearded man ran to the aid of both of the women, pushing people out of his way. But before he could get to her, released a guttural scream, and fell to the ground, holding his head. Stumbling through the streets, Lamp and I found ourselves gravitating toward the old bearded man. In split-seconds, his ears leaked red fluid and his arms stiffened like he had suffered a stroke.

I wanted to run over to them, to investigate what had happened to the man but thinking about the twins' safety struck fear in my heart. Again, I put out a mind-call to Kofi.

Nothing.

Maybe he wasn't ignoring me. Perhaps, someone had done something to jam our neural transmissions. I supposed something like that was possible but continued to hypothesize for any reason why the hysteria swirled around me in a whirlpool of madness.

I stopped a thirty-something-year-old woman wearing beehive braids.

"Hey!" I said. "What the hell is going on?"

She swiped my hand away, and ran off, looking over her shoulder at me like I was the one who caused all of the craziness. Lamp and I traded looks. I scanned the area, looking for someone watching the chaos in delight.

"Terrorist attack?" Lamp said.

"There's no one on the rooftops, nor peering through windows."

No one standing from afar to see his or her work in full display.

A motorbike crashed into someone's front door. The rider, a light-skinned boy with short braided hair, picked himself off of the ground just to get knocked to the ground again by a broad-shouldered man in a purple dashiki. The man kept going.

"They're holding their heads in a frantic rage like it's a migraine from hell," Lamp said.

"His hands are drenched in blood," I said, and bent down to see if the woman was still alive. She wasn't. "The leakage is coming from their ears."

The braided-hair boy cursed at the man who fled from him and ran into the house, shutting the door he'd damaged in his wake. A tall lanky teenage boy staggered past us. His eyes were also like dead moons.

"He's foaming at the mouth," Lamp said.

The disoriented teenager faltered like he'd lost a considerable amount of motor function, or perhaps he'd been born that way. He had a limp and held one of his arms bent like it had been fractured. Still, he managed to knock an elderly man's food rations out of his hands when he passed him. The frail toothless man wailed so loud it sent a shiver through my body.

"We have to do something," I said.

Lamp grabbed my arm and tugged me to follow her. "We need to get inside, away from this chaos."

I broke from her grasp and went over to the toothless man. I tried to collect his food among the shuffling feet, but it was like trying to grasp a ball being kicked around by footballers. I only recovered the toothless man's carton of milk.

I handed it to him and asked, "Do you know what's going on?"

The man seemed to have difficulty understanding me.

"What is wrong with everyone?" I asked him, shaking him.

He stared at me and his eyes widened. His head started to tremble, and his mouth pulled back into the grin of a man overcome with insanity. He fell on the ground and his body convulsed.

"Omigod," I said, and turned him on his side.

Vomit leaked out of his mouth and he started gagging.

I spread my arms out, trying to keep people from trampling us, and said, "Stay back! This man is having a seizure!"

No one cared or bothered to listen to me. They were dealing with similar crises, themselves. The toothless man's face twitched, but his eyes told me that he had traveled to a faraway place. Placing my hand on the man's shoulder, I watched his eyes roll to the back of his head. He started making a jarring sound. I planned to stay with him until the seizure was over and he had calmed down, but within seconds, he was dead. There was also leakage of fluid and blood trickling from his ears, and that confused me. The symptoms were all starting to show themselves: sudden neurological impairment, muscle weakness, seizures. But the blood leakage? That stumped me. It didn't add up with the other complications. It could have been a number of diagnoses, botulism, some deadly toxin, but the question I had was not what, but how? Nothing could be determined without a tox report. I needed to do an autopsy of this man to find out. But at the moment, that seemed ludicrous because it dawned on me that if they had contracted type of pathogen, there was a high probability that we had it, too.

A white van rolled a few meters beside us, and came to an abrupt stop, making dust rise in the air. On the side of the van was an image of green hands, palms facing upward. Just above that image was a moss-colored map of Africa. The words AFRICA CDC was printed next to the image of our continent.

I turned to say something to Lamp, but she was gone. Epidemic Intelligence Service officers exited the vehicle with a sense of urgency. They wore blue HAZMAT suits.

They each had yellow self-containing breathing apparatus equipment on their backs. Two more vans rolled up, and more EIS personnel got out. Those health workers wore white decontamination suits and SCBA's were also on their backs to ensure their air quality was self-contained.

"We need you to come with us," a voice said behind me.

I turned around. It was Major Grunt.

"Grunt, what the hell is going on?"

"Feeni, put this on," he said, and handed me a gas mask.

There were five other GAF soldiers behind him, one of them was Lamp. Her eyes were different. She looked at me like she didn't know who I was. They were all wearing gas masks and held rifles in their arms. They wore battle dress olive fatigues.

I pushed the gas mask back toward him, and said, "I can't."

"Sure you can," he said. "Just pull it over your that big head of yours and snap the chinstrap into place."

"What's the matter with Lamp? What did you do to her?"

"She's a Z3, which means during an emergency response, she only listens to the orders of the Head Dispatcher."

"Z3? I don't understand."

"There's no time to explain, Feeni. Now put the gas mask on! You, of all people, know you can trust me."

"Grunt, what is this? A terrorist attack?"

"We can't be sure, yet. We have orders to secure and quarantine the entire region until CDC gives us an all clear. That's why I want you to get your butt back home with your brother and the twins."

Lamp came up to Grunt and said, "Major?"

"Hold-a-sec," he said to her.

"Sir, you really need to see this," she said.

"Lamp!" I said. "Lamp, what is this?"

Grunt pointed to the military vehicle. "Get in there, Feeni." He turned around and spoke to his men. "Okay, the army boys of the GAF have been given orders to eradicate the entire village of the virus."

"Who would give such an order?" Lamp asked.

Grunt said, "Does it matter?" We have to clear out before they come."

Another one of his men shouted to him that they were already moving into the territory. I slipped the gas mask on and ran around the back of one of the CDC vans.

"Feeni!" Grunt called out.

I was not getting in that military jeep. There were too many questions, and no one seemed to have the authority to answer them. Peeking around the rear of the van, I saw Grunt scanning the area. His face showed obvious displeasure.

He'll get over it, I thought, and took off.

When he called out to me, again, I ran even faster, leaping over a victim who was squirming on the ground. Like all the others, the woman convulsed and held her head, yelling in agony. I stopped, knelt beside her and placed my hand over her forehead. Her head was burning up. She had a fever, and pus oozed out of her ears, telling me that her eardrums had ruptured.

Maybe someone had detonated some type of infrasound or ultrasonic acoustic weapon that blew out the eardrum.

I knew that the GAF had used infrasound for riot control once, but it didn't go well for them and they got a lot of backlash from the Inspector General. I doubt that they had used it that morning, but it was possible.

Perhaps the food did run out and things got out of hand.

"Just hold on, lady," I said. "Help is already here. Someone will be able to..."

Her head fell to the side and she stopped breathing.

"What the hell is this?" I asked, yelling in frustration.

I stood up and rubbed my forehead, one hand was on my hip. Two girls ran by me, one of them bumping into my arm. The girl didn't even know she'd bumped into me. I sighed and tried calling Kofi again. No answer.

"Dammit, Kofi!" I said, and looked back over my shoulder to make sure Grunt hadn't spotted me.

I ran up the street and came to a full halt.

"Oh, no!"

I saw a tattered coloring book under a toppled table and ran over to investigate. It was an Anansi the Spider coloring book. I'd hope not to see a child there. My head swiveled left, and then right, for any sign of a child in distress. A helicopter approached up above, and I looked up. There were two copters circling the area. On the sides of the copters, the GAF logo glimmered from the sunlight. One of the helicopters hovered above my head for a brief moment, before zipping away.

I glanced over my shoulder and scanned the area to see if I was still in the clear. I bolted toward a building and ran into the alleyway, placing my back against the wall. Fewer people were running around like chickens with their heads cut off. Most of them had fallen dead. Lamp was on the other side of the street, rounding people up like they were cattle. Her rifle did most of the talking and the people listened with god-fearing obedience.

Close by, maybe the next street over, one of Ghana's armed force officers spoke through a vehicle bullhorn: "Remain calm. Please walk. Do not run. I repeat. Stay calm. If you are in a safe environment, lock your doors until we clear the area and give you further instructions."

It was working. Even on the street I was on, things became less frantic. The area was cordoned off while GAF soldiers passed out gas masks to everyone, guiding them into specific areas.

The EIS officers in the blue protective suits walked around placing white sheets over the bodies that littered the roads with death. Someone moaned and stole my attention. About ten meters away me was a lean-to. A piece of metal from the structure was on the ground, a pale foot in a fluffy pink house slipper extended from it.

I lifted it and found, "Meredith?"

"Have you seen, Frankie? I can't...find her. Thomas told me not to go out, but she's my baby. My...baby."

Her shirt had been tattered and was soaking wet. She had lost a lot of blood and wasn't going to survive much longer without medical attention. Meredith's body trembled. Tears streamed down her face and she closed her eyes. One of her hands clenched over her head.

"Don't hurt Frankie." Meredith opened her eyes, slowly. "She's all I got," she said, and fell unconscious.

I absently dropped the coloring book and fell to my knees.

"Meredith!" Something caught my eye. "What in the world?"

There was a metallic liquid leaking from her ears.

Is she a clone? She can't be! I thought the technology hasn't been perfected yet to download consciousness onto a dormant-clone! Obviously, I'm wrong.

Meredith's hand slid off of her body and plopped on top of the image of Anansi the Spider on the coloring book. Her eyes were open.

"May the great Mawu grant you residency over the trees, streams, and mountains," I said, reached down and closed his eyelids.

Springing to my feet, I shot down an alleyway to a parallel street but had forgotten which street we hid the motorcycles. A child broke into a scream, and I turned toward the source. It was a yell so terrifying, my flesh crawled like maggots were moving under it. The GAF officer driving the personnel carrier with the bullhorn warnings had lost control and ran into a short obese woman. Two children, no more than six years old, stood a few meters away, bawling their eyes out. Feedback screeched through the GAF's vehicle bullhorn. One of the children, the boy, tried to pull his dead mother out from under the tires by her hands.

The armored car had smashed through the wall of a bright green building. Shards of glass from the windshields were everywhere. Half of the driver's motionless torso extended out of the front windshield. A thick cranberry fluid spilled from his ears. His eyes were open, locked in a timeless stare. He had a gas mask on but somehow had still contracted the virus.

Three teenage girls ran right toward the huge hole the GAF vehicle caused and one of them grabbed the children by the hands and tugged them farther into the building. Soon as they were out of sight, a tube from the fluorescent lights inside the building, swung from the ceiling and fell, making a popping sound when it shattered on the floor. I cringed and my jaws tightened.

At first, I thought I was having hunger pangs. Sickness swirled in my stomach. A lightheaded sensation made the ground seem to spin in a slow counter-clockwise movement. My shirt was drenched. The air was thin, and my breathing became labored. The sun scorched down on our community, but the fear of the twins being hurt was unbearable.

I called out in desperation. "Help!"

My fingertips were suddenly washed with a wintry chill. Voices crowded my head, but not voices of any particular language; a jumble of whispers. Better yet, not whispers, but more like a presence of a quiet rush of silent breezes brushing against my ear lobes.

What's happening? Is my mind being controlled? Is someone hacking my neural implant?

A young couple knocked into me. The man looked back and apologized just as his woman tugged him along. The pain grew inside of my head.

I have to keep trying to reach Kofi!

There were more and more voices chattering gibberish in my head, and that confused me. It was like a party line of monstrous voices. The sounds were like a chorus of demons dragging their voices at an inaudible slow speed. I couldn't focus, couldn't tap into my temporal transmitter.

Oh no! This is the second time, today!

My entire body jerked like an invisible giant slapped me in the back. I stumbled forward in slow motion like I'd been drugged, stumbling over bodies, and bumping into frenzied people as they ran through the alley by me. Something was about to erupt inside of me.

I need my meds quick.

Even though I hadn't had regular panic attacks in almost a year, I still carried a small Ziploc bag of anxiety pills in my pocket. I slipped the plastic bag out of my pocket, ready to dry-swallow a couple of them. I lifted the pills to my mouth, and someone bumped into me and knocked them out of my hands.

"No!"

The person kept running and disappeared around the corner.

God, I have to find my meds!

I stumbled over a broken clay jar, looking for the pills, and didn't see them. Colors started to melt around me. Everyone became a blur. I turned and the building behind me became a giant red blob.

My head rolled toward the heavens. The sky morphed into an endless abyss of tar. My head swam with dizziness, and my body felt heavy, useless. Things, perhaps cars, perhaps other people, knocked into my body. I couldn't tell. The world around me started growing darker and darker as I felt myself losing consciousness.

This mysterious sickness has now overtaken me too!

It was as if explosives erupted in my head, a mind bomb, creating fire and razor-sharp debris to shred into my brain tissue. Screaming, I tried to reach for my head but had no control of my arms, my legs, my breath. Everything spun, twirling, flailing. My head burned like molten lava had poured into it from my earlobes. All the sounds around me muffled into one confusing jumble of noise. My knees weakened and the ground rose up to me with unapologetic speed.

Smack!

Hands that didn't even seem like they belonged to me, slapped against the cool pavement, propelling me into a world filled with bright white stars. Blood trickled from my flaring nostrils, joining the saliva which oozed from my lips.

"What's happening?" I mouthed silently, closing my eyes.

My mouth opened again, spilling shaky breaths over trembling lips. The tears that ran down my cheeks like drips of red paint, tried to speak for me—tried to express that I was in too much pain to do anything but hurt. Thinking was like reaching into a cloud to grasp a breeze. Impossible.

I saw the pills, hiding under an empty carton that once contained a blood snack.

There! There they are!

I reached for them just as a pair of faded gray Converses stomped over the pills and crushed them.

"Shit!"

Exasperated, I rolled over to my bag and retrieved the plastic bag from my pocket to see if there were any more. Usually, I carried four tablets with me. Nothing was in the bag. I berated myself for not putting enough in the Ziploc bag. A thought hit me, and I patted my front pocket.

"Yes!"

The other two pills had somehow slipped out of the Ziploc bag and were in my front pocket. I struggled with everything I had to gain control of my motor functions and with great effort, reached into my jeans pocket and found them. I popped those sonsofbitches into my mouth the second I tugged them out, grimacing at the thought of dry-swallowing them and retched twice before they went down my throat.

It took a few minutes to take effect. Legs ran around me in blurred colors, and it was my luck that only one person stepped on me. With each second, the excruciating pain in my head subsided, and my muscles became less tense.

After another minute or so, I wriggled my fingers with ease and sat up, relieved. With the back of my hand, I wiped tears off my cheek.

That was intense. What I just went through wasn't a panic attack. That was something else.

The streets started to thin out a little, but now there were more bodies on the ground, some wriggling, others still. It was a literal war zone. We had been attacked, but by what or whom, I didn't know. What kind of pathogen could do what it just did to me, and why wasn't I still affected?

Or maybe I still am. At any rate, I was a helluva lot better like a fireball had been extinguished in my brain.

I managed to pick myself up when I received an incoming neural alert and recognized my auntie's ID number flashing in my corneal streamer.

Trying to control my breathing, I answered my temporal transmitter, "Auntie Yajna."

I wandered absently toward the side of the building next to a food rationing station. Our neural implants made it easy to hear m-phone conversations, even though our environment was noisy.

"Child," she said. "Are you all right?"

"Auntie Yajna, I don't know how to say this. I—I messed up bad! I left the twins with Kofi."

"You didn't mess up, baby. The twins are here with me."

"Do you know what's going on?" I asked.

"Not really. A terrorist attack on our town, perhaps. The Inspector General is getting briefed on the situation and will update everyone on the details soon. I got that from the horse's mouth."

"How did the children get there? You're two tro-tros stops away."

"Kofi used a military vehicle and dropped them off. Honey, you need to get out of there, and I mean, now!"

"All right. All right, Auntie. I'll come out there to you."

"Well, how are you going to do that?"

"I'll find a way."

"Feeni?"

"I'll find a way, Auntie. Trust me. I gotta go."

"You just better—"

"Bye," I said, jumping on top of her words.

"Okay, baby. bye bye, sweetie. I love you," she said, and ended the transmission.

Had it not been so much going on around me, I might have noticed that she said goodbye to me, for like the first time, ever.

A sound, like someone had popped bubbled plastic wrap, exploded through the air. I took cover beside a building. Five military jeeps rolled toward us, screeching over the curb flanked on each side of the point car like birds in a V-flight. A grenade launcher sat on the top bar of each vehicle unmanned. GAF officers, all donning purple gas masks and wearing black fatigues, started firing their assault rifles at people in the streets.

"Hey!" I said. "Hey, Assholes! Hold your fire!"

The spray of gunfire drowned my voice out. Pandemonium broke out. Even the EIS officers ran for cover but it was of no use. Most of them were dead in seconds, the HAZMAT suits riddled with bullet holes. Major Grunt's battalion retaliated. It was a standoff until one of Grunt's men was hit and spun to the ground. Another few shots ended the man's life. Grunt blasted the driver of the soldiers in black. The guy had positioned himself behind the vehicle but as soon as his ammo was out, Grunt fired through the front windshield and managed to hit his target right between the eyes.

Another one of their soldiers shot at Grunt and braised his shoulder. Grunt let out a guttural yell and ran toward their vehicle. Lamp covered him, shooting a rain of bullets at those soldiers.

"Shit," I said, realizing what was going on.

The government sent those soldiers to eradicate everyone in the area!

I watched in shocking horror how one-by-one the EIS officers and other CDC health workers were taken out. It was obvious that I didn't have much choice. I had to run for cover in the midst of the rain of gunfire or get torn to shreds like so many others who were in the streets. I was vulnerable where I was out in the wide open. I took a deep breath and sprinted for the building that had a huge hole from that armored car ramming into the wall.

Shwip—shwip!

Bullets barely missed my head. I ducked, covering my head with my arms, with the thought that one more inch and my brains would've been splattered all over the dirt road.

I kept moving but glanced over my shoulder quick enough to spot Lamp chasing after me. Her eyebrows were fueled with a ton of aggression, but her body language showed the type of awkwardness that reminded me of a marionette being manipulated by a puppet master. She pointed her gun at me and fired. I leaped over the lip from the hole in the wall and slid in front of the olive-green vehicle. The front end of it had limited damage, but after bullets painted the metal with multiple indentations and cracked the passenger side window.

"Lamp! Snap out of it," I said. "It's me, Xo!"

She was about fifteen meters away, bolting toward the vehicle. I climbed inside the military personnel carrier from the driver's side. I only had a few seconds.

One. Two. Three!

I threw the passenger-side door open. Gunshots tattered into it.

Shit.

She anticipated my moves and positioned herself to kill me, waiting like a panther about to pounce her prey. Using my momentum, I rolled onto the ground. Bullets riveted into the asphalt around me, spraying bits of cement into my face. I sprung to my feet. Lamp's gun met the center of my forehead.

"Nothing personal," she said, her eyes wide. "But all infected have to die."

Her fingernail began to flush red.

She's pressing the trigger!

Grabbing Lamp's arm, I grappled her wrist, spun away from the muzzle of the gun and twisted backward into her body. I threw an elbow into her jaw before she even knew what happened. She dropped the gun, probably surprised I could take her like that. It really wasn't a fair fight. She was human. I was an enhuman. The advantage was mine on strength, alone.

I back-kicked her in the shin with the heel of my shoe. She doubled over, released a low grunt, and just when I bent down to grab the gun she dropped, she knifed my arm.

Where the fuck did that come from?

I stumbled to the ground, grunting in pain, and clambered to the opposite side of the crashed car. Trying to get as far away from the scene as I could, I continued to move until the pain was unbearable, and I collapsed on my stomach. There were more gunshots fired, and Lamp was hit. She spun and fell to the ground.

"Gotta keep going," I said, under my breath. Reaching for the pain, I took in the damage.

There was a deep gash in my upper arm, and I was bleeding out pretty bad.

That's going to feel like crap unless I feed on blood soon."

Rising to my feet, I held my shoulder and winced. It burned like crazy, but I knew I could get it to heal if I fed to speed up the process. Just the idea of what crossed my mind was an abomination, but if I wanted to survive, it was something I was prepared to live with, as long as no one knew what I'd done. Lamp lifted her arm and started reloading her sidearm. That little distraction was all I needed. I ran toward her, leaped in the air and slid on my knees across the hood of the military vehicle. She stood and shot at me. The bullet whizzed past my ear like an angry wasp.

"Dammit, Lamp," I said. "I'm going to kick your ass when all this is over with!"

I grabbed the corner of the windshield, lifted myself up, and straddled her neck with my legs.

We fell to the ground. I stood up in a low crouch and jabbed her semi-hard in the throat with the heel of my hand, not enough to kill her. She gawked, and I leaned down close enough to whisper something in her ear, planting my teeth into her neck.

She shrieked. "Eeeyah!" and fought with hopeless desperation to get me off, pushing and shoving her knees into my back.

But there was no way. I was not feeding off of Lamp. Maybe had I eaten over the past twenty-four hours, I wouldn't have done it. I drank a few sips of her blood, and an overwhelming endorphin rush came over me. I almost blacked out. It was like I'd had a double dose of epinephrine injected right into my heart. Lamp almost threw me off of her, but I regained my composure, and slammed her wrists to the ground, staring into her eyes.

Her body softened, and the fight in her died.

While still mounted atop of her, I wiped the sweet remnants of her blood from my mouth with the back of my hand while shame moved me to spit the taste on the ground. Someone strong, stronger than me, grabbed my shoulders, and stabbed me in the neck with a needle.

Grunt ran over to Lamp and injected a needle in her neck. Lamp looked up at me, and her eyes widened.

"Old Man?" she said, smirking. "You've betrayed me?"

I knew it was an anesthesia that we were injected with, and I had less than fifteen seconds before it took me down. I fought like hell to escape, but darkness took my fight away. Before I fell unconscious, the man who grabbed me said,

"Otsoo, meet me in the House of Oware by the tombstones. I think Frankie has found us and has compromised the game."

In Ghana, if you were clumsy as a kid, Otsoo was a nickname your parents gave you. I was the epitome of clumsiness, growing up. My eyes became blurry with a film of tears, as I glanced into his tender gaze and said, "Dad?"

11

01010100 01100001 01110100 01110101

When the House of Oware game construct materialized a virtual world around me, I sniffed, catching a waft of familiarity. Formaldehyde stirred in the air like vultures. My neural implant tapped into my temporal lobes and added sensory texture. No matter how many times I dry-cleaned my favorite lab coat, that odor persisted. The game had decided to put me in that lab coat, along with a conservative pantsuit underneath.

The cemetery was the starting point for the game. The night air was clouded with fog. Trees towered over many of the tombs and created elongated shadows that swayed in slow ominous movements at the insistence of the strong wind. For as far as the eyes could see in every direction were stone homages paid to the dead. Mom and Dad's tombstones stood before me. A patch of South African sugarbushes grew along the side of each grave and illuminated the gravesite with hope.

"They are quite lovely, aren't they?" Dad asked.

I turned around. He was standing behind me.

Like the many times, as a toddler when Dad came home from the lab, I ran to hug him. A flood of emotions poured through me, dripping through my eyes like joyful morning dew. Not wanting to let go, just yet, I said nothing but squeezed him harder. I was too overwhelmed by the shock of seeing my father again after so many years of hopeless goodbyes. His body was rugged, strong, and his scent colored the room with a bright splash of manly cologne.

"In real life, you're alive," I said. "I thought you died."

"For all intents and purposes," Dad said. "I did die."

Pushing away from his tender grasp, I wiped my eye with the back of my hand and asked, "How is this possible?"

"I'll explain everything later," he said, and walked over to his tombstone and sat on it. "As for now, we have a difficult situation at hand."

"Frankie," I said, and walked up to him. Reaching for his hands, he took mine, and as we talked, he swung my arms like he used to do when I was a child.

"Yes, this girl has found a way into the game."

"But how?"

"That horrific act of genocide in Liati Wote was of her doing. I'm sure of it."

"But how? Those people died of some type of new pathogen. I'd never seen anything like it."

"Tell me something," Dad said. "Were you affected?"

"At first, I thought it was a panic attack coming on—"

"By the way, I will show you how to overcome that."

"You will? How?"

"Later, Otsoo. We have much to talk about but later. Tell me the symptoms you had during that attack."

"Well, it all seemed like a hallucination. The pain was real, of course. I'd gotten a migraine but one like I'd never experienced before."

"How so?"

A random but necessary thought crossed my mind. "You met and befriended Lamp in real life?"

"Yes, her part in my plans are monumental, but Otsoo please, tell me about your experience."

"Nothing to tell except it felt like my neural implant was going haywire, like someone had hacked my brain, and I had no control over it anymore."

"That's what I thought," he said and stood. "Come, it's time for you to meet the others."

"You have other children?"

"No, no, Otsoo. These are ennies who have played the House of Oware game all of their lives, like you."

"But Dad, how? What is all of this about?

"Be patient with me, Otsoo. When the time is right, I will explain everything, but I have to leave the game and transport the two of you to a safe house. Stay in the game, meet the others."

"Where?"

"In a simulation of a bar called the Kings' Shelter. I've finally found the real one, and will take you there to meet everyone face-to-face, in real life."

"How will I even know who they are or how they look?"

"Samora will be there."

"She tried to kill me!"

"It wasn't her doing. You must forgive her. The same way she will have to forgive you when you tell her what you did."

"You—you know? Dad, how do you know all of this?" I turned around, and paced, trying to make sense of it all, and said, "It's like you've been spying on me all of this time. I'm not going anywhere until you tell me what's going on."

I turned around, thinking my stubbornness was enough to make him come clean. But he was gone, and a door appeared in front of his tombstone. I scoffed and walked through the door.

~

The Kings' Shelter reeked of beer and roasted peanuts. Aside from the rock 'n roll, the bar was like every other dive in Ghana: plasma screens showing cricket games, buxom waitresses with short skirts, watered-down drinks, funky bathrooms, and sticky floors. Hovering high above the bartender's head, a hologram of Little Ghana Boy screamed from an old jukebox projector singing *Ready Teddy*.

When I went through the bar's door, the game changed me into riding gear, leather jacket and pants, boots, and a helmet. I spotted Lamp, a female version, just beyond a tiny dance floor and gripped my motorcycle helmet while I maneuver past the bar tables seated by buzzed chatterboxes and shouldered through the dancing patrons.

Lamp was sitting on a stool toward the back of the bar by the pool tables, holding a beer on her thigh and a lollipop in her cheek. There were a few more people back there watching one table in particular. The closer I got, the more I realized a white woman was putting on a master class in kicking someone's ass in pool.

She was tall, towering over the others. As if a character in a Bradbury novel, her ginger hair was a lamp burning, cascading down her back. The woman wore the kind of clothes that told everyone she had a lust for expensive things. She had thick, well-drawn reddish eyebrows that furrowed over drooped eyelids, and her mouth never seemed to stop jabbering.

Ginger-head's accent told me she was from South Africa. "A decade ago, global warming has made it possible for scientists to find an ancient virus—one ball off of the six," she said, and aimed for the corner pocket. "And now after finding a fourth giant virus..." She struck the ball with the force of a pro, and the one ball slammed into the pocket. "French scientists revealed recently that they plan to resurrect the harmless virus that had been locked in the Siberian permafrost for more than thirty-thousand years."

"Of course, you're speaking of Mollivirus Sibericum," a large man in a charcoal gray pinstripe suit said. He sat next to Lamp holding a pool stick. His black-framed glasses were thick, like his mustache. "But I'm not sure if disturbing a prehistoric virus is wise."

"What are some concerns that you think scientists are deliberating?" the ginger lady asked, standing and chalking her pool stick.

"Where should I start?" he answered. "There are many."

"I agree with Lt. Tanaka," a woman said, interrupting. She wore an earth tone scarf around her long neck. A black snood covered her hair and her face was Geisha-white. "Even though these scientists may have said the virus is harmless, they don't truly know the potential dangers that it could pose."

Lamp stood when she saw me. Her face was all

wide-eyed and loopy. She handed me a beer. It was cold and the label said flavored with fossa blood. The name of the beer was called *Kings' Shelter* and had an image of a white moon shining over a gold pyramid. I took note of the pyramid on the label and popped that bitch open the second the cool jar hit my hand.

Lamp interrupted the conversation. "Hey everyone, this here is my pathologist friend, Xo. Feeni Xo." Lamp said. "That there is the one and only, Felicia Shaw," he said, referring to the pool shark. "She heads the Africa CDC. And the Indian woman over here who wishes she was black—"

"Watch it, Lampers," Durga said.

Lamp giggled and stumbled forward a step. "I mean the one with the pretty braids—"

She nodded. "That's more like it."

Lamp continued. "That's Shaw's assistant, Durga. Every Tuesday, Shaw comes here and robs us law folks out of our money."

"What's up, Xo?" she said, nodding at me with a genuine smile.

Tanaka said, "These phonies wouldn't know if they were being robbed if a thief took the glasses off their very noses."

Tanaka held up a credit card and tube of lipstick.

Shaw gasped, and said, "That's mine!"

Everyone in the small group laughed at that. Tanaka tossed the items to Shaw. She caught them and shook a fist at her. I took a sip of the beer and thought I'd gone to heaven.

"Good beer, huh?" Lamp asked, grinning, and taking a sip of hers.

I nodded. "Damn sure is," I said, and looked at the label, again. "Kings' Shelter. You sure know how to pick 'em."

I pulled Lamp over to the side. "You tried to kill me."

"But I didn't pull the fatal trigger," Lamp said, and took another swig of her beer.

"No, but you tried."

"That's where you're wrong. I tried my damnedest not to, but someone was in my head."

"Here's to making whomever hacked into our brains, pay with their life."

"My hunch is it's Frankie."

I nodded, and clinked the bottom of my bottle against hers, before taking a refreshing swallow.

"My Dad is the Old Man?" I asked.

"I guess."

"At first, I thought he'd betray me, but he said he was only protecting you."

"You spoke to him at the cemetery?"

"Yes, right before you did."

"You know what's going on?"

"No, like I said, he's a man of mystery, but believe me, before all of this is over, we'll know exactly what hand he plays in all of this."

"I second that. Does Dad think these guys can help us tie your sister's message and Frankie's part in all of this?"

"Although I just met them, I'm convinced that they can."

"Why?"

"These folks have also been playing the House of Oware game. They're not just characters in the game, they're real-life people, all our ages."

"And each one of them has been trained for all of their lives in a particular profession?"

"Yep, just like us."

"How'd you find them?"

"I didn't. They found me. Durga is a whiz in computers. She found a back door into the program and found the info that revealed who was playing the game."

"So who did this to us?" I asked.

"The real question," Lamp said, taking a sip of beer and then continuing, "is why?"

Shaw pointed her stick at the man with the thick-rimmed glasses. "Now back to the topic at hand. I agree, Tanaka, that we don't truly know the dangers, but if every scientist was afraid to take risks we'd running around in our cars like the Flintstones. Look, Pithovirus Sibericum, one of the other viruses they found, has five hundred genes—"

Durga asked, "Whereas the influenza virus has only eight!"

Lamp jumped in, saying, "And now these arrogant French researchers want to awaken the Mollivirus Sibericum? Maybe *Molly* doesn't want to be disturbed!"

"Molly?" Shaw. said, one eyebrow raised.

"Look guys," I said. "I know science is beautiful to us, but some of the most beautiful things in the world are the most dangerous, space, the ocean, animals, hell even us women, but these viruses we're playing with, they're pathogens of Jurassic nature! Jurassic! So, I don't care if the virus seems to only attack single-cell amoebas—"

"I follow you, Xo," Shaw said. "The binomial nomenclature known as the *Homo Sapiens* may not have the biological structure in their immune system to fight off a virus that carries sixty-two point five times the punch of influenza."

"Exactly," Lamp said, pointing at Shaw.

Tanaka shook her head. "Hey, you think the Spanish Flu kicked the world's ass? Wait until Molly throws on her stilettos and prances across this globe. All humanity will be able to do is climb its way up the mountain and claim itself queen of the most endangered species."

"Not on my watch," Shaw said. "That's why my team and I work tirelessly at the CDC, to make sure we do all we can to thwart not just that virus, but all viruses."

I turned to her. "You work at the CDC?"

She nodded.

"So explain to me," I said. "Why did an entire village come down with a virus like I'd never seen before and the government came in and killed everyone off, even the CDC health workers?"

12

01010100 01100001 01110100 01110101

"I had nothing to do with that," Shaw said. "But based on what you just told me, silver fluid coming out of the ears, people holding their heads, and screaming, I have an idea of what's happening."

Shaw, Durga, Tanaka, Lamp and I were standing outside of the bar passing around a lipstick-smudged cigarette like we were participating in some kind of female bonding ritual, and perhaps we were. The streets were empty, except for the wet residue that covered the dirt roads with rain puddles. Outside, the village was quiet, yielding to the yips of a pack of dholes high in the mountains, and a chirping cricket hiding in the crevices of darkness. Light flickered from a street lamp. Moths flew around the dampened bulb and wisps of cigarette smoke careened upward into the cool night air.

"I know what you're going to say," Durga said.

"Someone please fill me in," I said.

"It was a computer virus," Shaw said.

"But it's not possible to get past the security systems of neural implants. They're impenetrable."

"Durga, humor me," Shaw said. "Tell us exactly how a computer virus works."

"Malware, logic bombs, those sort of things are software that piggyback on computer programs," she said. "The malicious virus replicates itself to spreads to other machines, wreaking all kind of havoc for the host."

Shaw extended her hand to me for the cigarette. "This

is what the retcon virus has done with clones, destroying the consciousness, and literally erasing it from existence."

"Since the very first neural implant was surgically inserted in man, the capability of a virus getting past security walls were a non-factor," Durga said.

Tanaka said, "But somehow in clones, scientists didn't get something right in their biological gene coding, and that's why the clones were susceptible to viruses."

Durga tapped her index finger to her chin, and she fixed a gaze on me. "But this mysterious malware acts like a double-edged sword, attacking the neural implant and attaching itself to a virus already present in the body."

"I'm not following you," Lamp said, leaning against the side of the building, her heel on the brick wall.

Tanaka went over to Shaw and extended her hand. "Pass and puff, sister. Pass and puff," She inhaled deeply, blew out smoke circles and said. "Okay, so you know that the viruses that cause the common cold are always present in our bodies, yes?"

Lamp nodded. "Yeah, yeah, I know."

With the jot dangling in her mouth, Tanaka clapped her hands and pointed at Lamp. "Good! Not to be stating the obvious but so many people think they get sick because they were out in the cold, yes?"

Shaw nodded. "Unfortunately, that's true. But we know it's more about the behavior of the host that allows the virus to attack the immune system," Shaw said.

"Yeah, I follow," I said, "if a person is extremely exhausted, it's that behavior that weakened the immune system, allowing a variety of some one hundred different strains of rhinoviruses to mutate and replicate at such rapid rates, it's impossible for a vaccine."

"Okay," Lamp said. "I'm starting to understand.

"Like cold germs," Durga said, "which we all know are present in our cells, this retcon virus is a replication of software that is present in all of our neural implants. I don't know when or how it gets in the host but it's there, waiting for our immune systems to be weak enough for it to become active."

"And what better time to attack is when the body is nearly expired, and the consciousness is being transferred?" Lamp asked.

"Those people weren't asleep," I said. "They were out and about the town, trying to make the best of an oppressed life."

"That's it!" Shaw said. "The virus feeds on the oppressed. When we're stressed, the limbic system and the cortex are activated."

I tapped the top of my lip and thought out loud. "Elevated cortisol levels lower immune systems, triggers elements of mental illness—"

"And decreases bodily resilience," Shaw said.

"Hence," I said, "the more someone fears something, the higher the level of stress hormones are released in the brain."

"Frankie has found a way to infect our neural implants with a malicious virus," Lamp said.

Tanaka flipped the cigarette into the streets, allowing the wet ground to extinguish it. "You think it's this Frankie person?"

"I know it's her," Lamp said. "But what I don't know is how this ties into my sister's death?"

I flinched and turned to her. "Do you feel that?"

"Yes," Lamp said. "Water. Something is wrong." She stumbled forward and placed a hand on her head. "I'm losing consciousness."

13

01010100 01100001 01110100 01110101

I disengaged the game and opened my eyes, but there was nothing but darkness. My body was dripping wet. There was a sound that was as familiar as the crashing of beads draping over my shoulders during the initiation ceremony of Dipo. It was a something burning, and flooding around that sound was waterfall crashing into a watering hole.

Where am I?

Raging waters splashed into a watering hole less than a meter away from me. Something raged like the wind ripping through bed sheets hanging on Auntie Yajna's clothesline in our backyard. The odor of oil amidst the thick smoke in the air led me to believe it was a vehicle on fire.

How did I get here?

Sniffing, I caught the faint scent of a human, female. There was a hint of feminine deodorant. For a few intolerable seconds, I couldn't remember my name. My pulse thumped hard in my neck. Blinking, I sat up. My head was also on fire, pure agony. I blinked again, in desperation, reaching around my surroundings blindly.

Am I blind?

I grasped the earth, and let the dirt slip through my fingers. Anxiety seemed to be the only thing that was tangible. Taking slow, calming breaths, I stood, tasting human blood on my tongue. I retched, my stomach protesting in violent convulsion. The nearby flames bathed my skin in warmth. I lifted my hands and did not see them.

Why can't I see?

I climbed to my feet and tripped over something. After regaining my balance, I reached down and felt for what tripped me up and realized it was a body. The person was still breathing.

Who is this?

Taking a cautious, still perplexed step forward, a faint noise swelled from the distance, growing louder with each passing moment. At first, it was an eerie clicking sound, similar to a door creaking or...*a strange bird call, perhaps. This is my neural implant. The game construct is malfunctioning.*

The more the sound grew, the more it pierced my ears until it became unbearable. The only way to describe the sound was to say that whatever it was, it was screaming, as if in deep agony, bringing with it a sound like magazine pages flapping in the wind.

Birds! I can see them! Birds! But...this is not real. I'm experiencing a literal virtual illusion, a conundrum to the tenth power. A waterfall? Are those birds singing? Insects buzzed over my head, and small critters crept and crackled softly over leaves. Am I in the woods?

I wasn't in the game anymore, I knew that. I was in real life mode. Somehow, in my mind, a world materialized. Even though I was blind. I knew it wasn't the House of Oware game, but something else. Something quite different.

I believed that my neural implant executed an override of my optical nerves once signals went to my brain, communicating my blindness.

I had no idea something like that was programmed in my mind. Was it a form of neurological appeasement? A way for me to cope until my sight came back? Would it come back?

I stood in a rainforest. The sun was bright, the sky fiery as the skin of red bananas and the trees towered like giant Maasai warriors protecting their tribe. A roaring waterfall spilled into a watering hole, and birds flew above in a v-formation. My neural receptors recognized my environment and built a virtual world based on my perceived environment. Sprinkles of light illuminated the air and filled the sky with tiny balls of fire.

A Cape Glossy starling landing on a branch stretching over the river bed. Her shimmering feathers looked like she'd been bathing in an oil spill. She eyed me, jerking her head in curious twitching movements. Three other starlings landed, and they ranked on the tree branch like soldiers during morning inspection. One of them belted out a throaty musical call.

What's that?

A swarm of bright yellow butterflies surfaced from out of the watering hole and swirled around me, sprinkling droplets of water. Suddenly, something shook my body.

I wanted it to stop.

My body was wet, cold. Something sent a riveting jolt throughout my body.

I'm hungry.

My senses were dull but the hunger inside of me ate up all forms of rational thinking. Someone spoke to me, but it was incoherent, like a muffled voice from behind a hundred walls of cotton. There was only one voice that came to me in full clarity. My own. Inside my head.

Feed me...

Someone shook me, and shook me, and shook me.

Then I will feed from you...

I reached my hand out and grabbed whatever thing it was that attacked me. It tried to resist me but was no match for my power, even in my weakened state. It was obvious what I needed, what I wanted, how my thirst drove me to an autonomous yet maniacal desire to survive. A hunger brought on by innate instincts.

I'm hungry...so very hungry...

There seemed to not be any scent to the thing, but as I said, my senses were dulled. Yet, I knew.

I must feed...

With every part of my being, I knew what I had to do; the way a chick knows when to break out of the eggshell, or a flower knows how to grow through concrete, or a salmon has no doubts that it can swim upstream. I knew that this creature would be my source of sustenance, and without thought, doubts or hesitation, my teeth found her neck.

Its blood was warm. Delicious. Fulfilling. Satisfying. Yet, not satisfying.

I want more...

No, I needed more. I was high as the sky, euphoric like a thrill addict's first ride on a rollercoaster ride that seemed to not have an end in sight. (Well, here's another fine mess you've gotten me into, Stan.)

Where did that come from? Who is Stan?

My lips and my tongue caught every drip, each drop that tried to flee from the wound. I meditated on the deliciousness, and dropped my head in a wonderful ine-briation, until...a moaning purred from a woman.

A woman? A human? I just fed on another human, again!

My eyes snapped open, this time for real. It wasn't day but rather night. At last, moonlight welcomed me back to the world of the seeing. I stiffened.

Lamp!

I backed away, scraping my palms on stones that pro-truded from the earth.

Omigod!

I'd fed on Lamp like I was some kind of savage beast.

What am I? An adze? An asanbosam.

I was an enhuman, not some kind of vampire told in folklore on the porches of an old shaman priest. I scur-ried backward on my bottom in pure horror, stopped only because of a tree.

What have I done?

Gasping, trying to absorb the enormity of my sins, I stared up at the waterfall, and at the mountain behind it.

I know where we are.

Mt. Afadjato, or Afadja as the locals called it, stood nearby. Tagbo Falls splashed into the watering hole. The village of Liati Wote was no more than a forty-minute hike from there. I'd done it several times, myself.

Near the base of the waterfall, on level ground was a small wooden house. I scratched my head and found it odd that a cabin was there. It hadn't been there the last time I hiked to the waterfall. The wood, even in darkness looked as if it had been new.

Nearby, a jeep was turned on its side, and was engulfed in fire. There was a massive dent on the driver's side of the door. A meter or so away, a man's body lay on the ground. His arm lay limp in the river like seaweed.

"Dad!"

He was hurt. I scrambled to my feet and stumbled over to the jeep. The fire was intense. Scorching. There were dents in the door of the passenger's side. I checked over his body. His head was bruised. He probably had a concussion. There didn't seem to be any life-threatening injuries, but his ankle had blown up like a water balloon. I grabbed his hands and dragged his body by the arms, away from the jeep.

When I backed up into a tree, I slid down it to my butt, satisfied we were far enough from the vehicle in case there was a gas explosion. Wiping the sweat from my brow, I looked down at Dad.

He opened his eyes and said, in a weak voice, "Otsoo, we have to get to the cabin."

I used the tree to help me climb to my feet and ran over to Lamp. I dragged her halfway toward Dad and an explosion from the vehicle erupted. The force of it threw my body so far, the impact of hitting the ground stunned me. After, I'm not sure how long, Lamp moaned and stirred me from a deep daze. I lifted my head, thinking that the endorphins secreted from my saliva and the anesthesia Dad gave us must have given her a stronger analgesic effect that what occurred to me. Crawling to my feet, my body protested with body aches and burning pains on my arms and elbows.

How could I have fed on a human? I can't believe I stopped to such low—

I stumbled over to the water and vomited. The current from the waterfall flushed the remnants of my agony toward the opposite bank. When I heaved until the point of deep cramping, I washed my mouth out with the cool water in gasps of labored breath.

The watering hole was vast and stretched wide. Beyond that, the breathtaking tones that had been colored from the amalgam of tropical weather and the beasts who nurtured their habitat with unapologetic nightlife. There was a vast amount of vines, and fungi growing about and along the trees.

Seeing an entire village shot down like animals, made me temporarily fall to acts of insanity.

There is no way for anyone to prepare to experience seeing such heinous acts of death.

Lamp seemed to be awakening and I went over to her. I crouched down for a closer look. She was perspiring. I placed my hand on her head, checking to see if she had a fever. Her hand caught mine, her other hand punched me in the throat. To be honest, I don't know what caught me more off guard, the fact that she sucker punched me, or that she was responsive so soon after all the blood I drank from her. She was human, and I thought something like being nearly drained of blood had weakened her. I was wrong.

The pain of being struck in the throat is by far, one of the most grueling attacks. It's why I do it. Not only was my neck on fire. Imagine what enduring asphyxiation for a full week but not dying was like, or having a knuckleball thrust in your neck. That's what it felt like. While I gagged and rolled on the ground spitting out breathless expletives, Lamp placed a knife at my throat.

"If I hadn't played hundreds of hours with you in the House of Oware game," she said, "I'd have no problem slicing your ass up and letting your rotten corpse fertilize the grounds of this of good old Mother Africa."

"Shh," I said.

"You can't tell me to be quiet!"

"Something's here with us."

Lamp stiffened, and we both listened and scanned the woods for movement.

I heard a twig snap from above and glanced up. High along the steep hills were about a dozen pairs of amber eyes, gleaming under the moonlight.

"Dholes," she said.

Their stench was more putrid than usual. Lamp reached in her shoulder holster for her gun, but of course, found nothing. Grunt, or whomever threw her in the jeep, confiscated it.

A large pack of dholes began running down the slopes of the mountain toward us, some of them bumping into each other and tumbling down. The radiation-mutant canines ripped hungrily into each other, others fought, nipping and howling for position.

We backed up to where Dad was on the ground. He picked himself up and started limping.

"We've got to get to the cabin," he said.

I went to him and helped him move faster.

"Samora," Dad said. "Your weapons are in the jeep!"

"Got it!" she said, and made a dash for the torched wreckage.

I hurried on, with Dad's arm around my shoulder.

"Hurry, Lamp!" I said. "Hurry!"

I turned around and saw her trying to reach inside the jeep, but she snatched her hand back. The metal must have been lava hot. My foot hit something hard, and I tumbled forward, bringing Dad down to the ground with me. The dholes yapped and were gaining ground on us.

"Come on," I said, and helped him back up.

The dholes were getting closer. It was dark and there was nowhere to go in this vast forest but that cabin. Those wild dogs would be upon us within a minute, tearing our flesh apart. Lamp found her guns and started firing at the dholes. I didn't dare look back this time. Dad and I were only a few steps away from the front door of the cabin. He was going in and out of consciousness, and that made each step a laborious effort, but we made it. I reached for the doorknob and turned it.

"Locked!"

"My keys," he said, coming to. "They're in my pocket."

I reached in his pocket. Nothing. Looking back at the dholes fast approaching, I reached into his other pocket.

"Dad!"

I shook him.

"Dad!"

He lifted his head.

"They're not there!" I said, and glanced back at the dholes.

"Must've fallen out," he said, and dropped his head.

One of them was standing there watching us. His paw was right where I'd tripped and beneath him, sparkled the keys under the bright moonlight.

The other dholes slowed their approached, snarling and growling while they flanked us like soldiers coming up on their enemy.

"It's like they know we can't get in," Dad said.

"The sneaky bastards are surrounding us," I said, trying to kick the door in.

"These doors are fortified," Dad said. "No way you're going to just kick it down."

There are too many of them," Lamp said, reaching us. "No way I can shoot them all, but I did find this."

She pulled a long, curved machete from a shoulder scabbard, I hadn't even noticed she had on.

"That's mine," Dad said.

"Well now, it's mine," I said.

Lamp kept firing at the ones closest to us, each time making the pack bark and back up. But after a few seconds, they inched closer, their backs hunched, ears erect. Gripping the kukri knife tight in my hand, I spun around. The pack of dogs was closer. Much closer. A few of the dholes had bits of pink meaty flesh in their jowls. That dog food was prize meat from when they caught Grunt trying to divert them away from us.

Lamp fired two more shots, and that held them at bay. There were now only five dholes left.

"Cover me!" I said.

"What?" Lamp said.

"The back door! Cover me!" I said, and sprinted to the back of the cabin.

The dholes didn't chase after me.

Where are they?

I remembered Grunt saying that they were intelligent and learned fast. They knew that Lamp would kill them if they followed too close.

Smart devils.

I reached the back door and twisted the knob. The back door opened.

I closed the door, ran through the dark cabin, hopped over the couch and unlocked the front door. "Go!" I said to Lamp.

She ran in, carrying Dad.

"So dizzy," Dad said, and stumbled inside. He disappeared. Seconds later, I heard a door in the house close.

I slammed the front door shut, but it didn't close all the way because Dad's boot had fallen off and was blocking it. Kicking the boot out the way, I had almost closed the door when two of dholes crashed into the door and whelped. That knocked me on my butt. I scrambled backward and climbed to my feet. The lights were off in the cabin and it was too dark to see much of anything, but I did see a wooden chair just to the side of the entrance by the window. With the knife still in each hand, I shoved the chair in their path with my free one, and jumped over the couch, stumbling into a table.

The lamp on the table fell to the floor and shattered into pieces. The dogs yipped and growled. Two went after me, the other three chose to have Lamp as their late-night snack.

One of them sprung at me. I stabbed him in his side. It yelped and fell to the floor with a loud thud. Another came at me and was about to bite down onto my arm, but I kneed it in her torso hard enough to knock it away. She landed on her paws and scrambled right back toward me.

There was a wooden dining table in the middle of the floor. I ran for it, but a dhole bit into my boot, tripping me. I crashed into the table and fell to the ground. The mountain dog continued after me, its jowls snapping at my leg. I rammed my heel into its neck and shoved the machete into his head.

When I rolled back to my feet. The other dhole that pursued me, growled. Her teeth were wet with thirst. The bottom of her torso was translucent, revealing muscles that were pinkish and sinewy.

Three dholes had Lamp cornered. One of them was between her and a bedroom door. She pointed the gun at the closest one and pulled the trigger.

Click!...Click!

She was all out of bullets.

"You want some of this?" I said, and banged the hilt of the kukri knife on the table. "Come and get it, bitches!"

They all scattered backward a few meters and turned to me. Behind me was the kitchen. A marble countertop counter separated the living room from the small kitchen. I leaped over the counter, my butt sliding over the smooth marble, and landed on the other side of the counter, knocking an eighteen-piece knife set on the floor. Their paws clattered against the floor as they pursued me.

Lamp had run into a bedroom opposite the kitchen.

"Stop with the heroics, dipshit, and get in here," she said.

I scrambled to my feet, bouncing against the oven, took two steps, leaped and somersaulting into the bedroom. Lamp slammed the door behind me, just as the wild dogs reached it. With her back to the door, she slid down it. Gasping for breath, her body shook against the door while it vibrated from the dholes trying to get in.

14

01010100 01100001 01110100 01110101

"Where's the Old Man?" Lamp asked.

"He's in the other room. I heard him close the door behind him."

"What is this place?"

"And I would know that, why?"

I caught a glare from Lamp, but ignored her, busy scouting the room like a student moving into her boarding school dormitory room for the first time. The floors were hardwood and carried the scent that told me they had just been stained.

"Dad!" I said, calling out to him. "Dad, are you okay?"

"He hit his head pretty bad," Lamp said. "He's probably out cold. This must be his cabin."

"Actually, I remember him saying that this was a safe house."

"A safe house?"

"Yeah."

"For who?"

The most frightening thought came across my mind.

What if Dad was the one responsible for the virus? What is this was what he used to traffic girls?

Two twin-sized beds had white sheets neatly folded back from the top and tucked with meticulous precision like they were made by a disciplined overzealous cadet in the military academy. A white pillow and rust blanket sat opposite of each other, on each bed.

"You don't think he's involved in—"

Lamp didn't let me get the question out. "Of course not!"

I didn't know if it was the fact that I'd been fighting off a pack of dholes or if it because I'd just fed off of Lamp's blood and it had an ergogenic effect on me, but I seemed more hypersensitive than normal. My olfactory senses were in overdrive. Even her heartbeat seemed louder, and her movements, slower like my corneal streaming turned down my sight sensory down to a half-speed slower. I came to the conclusion that all of my senses were more acute.

"I'm calling my aunt to make sure she and the twins are okay."

"What about Kofi?"

"He hasn't been answering my calls. Have you tried your parents?"

"They're not answering either. I just tried them."

"You think the reception is bad because we're up here in the mountains?"

Lamp didn't answer that, instead, her face turned sour and she snapped at me.

"So what are you, some kind of cannibal? Your family are cannibals?"

"What the hell are you talking about?"

"Is that what your people really are?"

"What?"

"Obviously, you're not a vampire, I've seen you out in the sun, before, and it doesn't feel like it, but you sure as hell don't have any fangs—"

"There's no such thing as vampires, idiot," I said, jumping over her words.

"Then your people are cannibals, and you eat each other? You consume flesh to live?"

"What the hell are you talking about? This is not the cerebral Lamp I've played—I mean known, for so many years. You could've killed me with that thrust to my neck, you know?"

"Karma is a bitch, huh? I didn't do anything that you didn't do to me."

135

"Heifer, you were trying to kill me! Wait-a-minute, I thought you couldn't remember what happened at Liati Wote."

"Most of it is still hazy, but I remember fighting you. So I finally meet you in person, after all these years. So, where'd you get the upgrade in your neural implant to give you access to the game?"

I didn't have time for such frivolous small talk. "Who sent you to kill all those people in the village? Grunt?"

"I don't remember."

"Was Kofi also ordered to kill innocent people."

"I don't know."

"Bullshit!"

"I don't care what you think. All I know is that one minute we were on our way to the bikes, and the next your teeth were planted into my neck!"

I pointed at her. "You're lying. Who do you work for? Some kind of uprising resistance? A terrorist group? You seem to know a lot about hacking. Maybe you had something to do with Frankie and her tirade against the week. Why suddenly show up, today?"

I regretted those words, as soon as they left my mouth.

Her face twisted in such a way, I thought she was having a stroke. "Did you kill my sister?"

"What?"

"You heard me! There's something fishy going on between you and your brother and Grunt. Now Grunt's dead!"

"What—what are you saying?" I asked and took a step back.

"I'm saying that I saw the glances you all traded whenever I mentioned my sister. You think I'm stupid? I know that you're hiding something."

"No, no. I'm not."

She pushed me against the wall. "You're lying!"

There's something about guilt and shame that can turn the strongest denial into a weak confession.

Lamp slammed her fist against the wall. "Tell me! Did you kill my sister, dammit?"

She started shaking me. "Did you? Huh? Did you?"

"All right!" I said, tearing up. "At first, I thought I did."

She recoiled from me. "What did you say?"

"I—I thought I did."

"You thought you did what?"

"It was raining, and I'd been drinking. I knew that I shouldn't drink and drive, but I always had control of it before."

"You were driving drunk."

"No, I mean, yes. I was driving Kofi's car, and I don't know, I got distracted. The next thing I know, I hit something. When I got out of the car, I saw that it was a girl—"

Lamp gasped and fell back onto the bed. She sat there in shock, looking at me with disbelief.

I had to make her understand. "But I didn't know it was Jinni. I think Kofi knew."

"He was in the car with you?"

"No, I called him and told him what happened. He was in the area and came to me pretty, quickly. He called Grunt and the two of them figured it best not to say anything."

She stood up. "They what?"

"Grunt said it would ruin my family, and my future would be destroyed."

She walked up to me. "What about my family?"

"I know—I know. I was wrong. I'm sorry—I really am, Lamp. But someone else had killed her! It wasn't me!"

She scoffed and turned away from me, holding her hand up over her mouth.

"I wasn't in the right mind, Lamp. And-and I didn't know what to do. It was Kofi and Grunt's idea to move her body and take it to the water plant."

Lamp turned and rushed toward me. She stabbed her index finger into my chest. "I pulled you from the lake, gave you mouth-to-mouth resuscitation, and come to find out, you've been lying to me the whole time? You're the monster, not Frankie! You are! You're the monster!"

"Stop!" I said, and pushed her off of me.

Lamp swung her fist at me. I knocked it away.

"I don't want to fight," I said.

Damned, if she didn't throw another punch. I swatted it away and had my hands around her throat before I knew what happened.

"In case you haven't noticed," I said, "I'm an enhuman, faster than you ever dreamed of being. Lucky for you, I didn't choke you out for hitting me in the throat."

Lamp took another swing at me.

I batted her hand away. "I don't want to hurt you."

Before I got all of the words out, she tackled me. I shoved her off of me, but she recovered faster than I anticipated and bounced to her feet. I rolled over just as her boot slammed against where my head was supposed to be had I not moved. Rolling over on my side, I sprung up and caught a kick to the head. That sent me to the ground and a million stars floated in my head. She kicked me in the side, and I let out a guttural yell.

I shook my head and said, "I didn't kill your sister!"

Lamp said nothing. She pulled her leg back to shove her size eights back into my side, but I caught her foot and twisted it. That gave me enough time to recover and get to my feet. She was on her feet almost as quickly. We circled each other, both of us using Nigerian fighting stances.

I threw a combo, left-right but she blocked it. I countered with an elbow to her face, but she blocked it with her forearm. She threw a jab and caught me in the mouth. Just as quickly, she followed with an elbow slicing up toward my chin. I dodged it, countered with a kick to her side, and almost connected but she slapped my leg down. I snapped my leg back to my body just as she swept my heel and caught me good.

I fell but rose quickly. She came at me fast and hard, swinging. I moved and she passed me. I turned and forced her backward all the way over to the beds. She swung fast and hard, but I dodged, ducked and swerved out of every strike. Auntie Yajna would've said I was Azumah Nelson in his prime. She couldn't land any more punches. Lamp was good, though. Real good. However, I grew tired of fighting her, plus I had so many questions that took precedence over everything else.

"Time to end this," I said.

"Shut up, Liar—"

I ran toward her, gathering up about four steps of momentum. She swung a fist at me and corrected her swing when she realized I leaped in the air, but I was too fast. I leaped over her reach, and she missed me by mere millimeters. With one leg, I bounced my foot off of the bed to her left, spun and landed behind her, clothes-hanging her to the floor with a powerful swipe around her neck. Her back hit the hardwood with a thud, and the impact knocked the air out of her.

I said, "It's over."

She dropped both of her arms to her side, gasping for air. I placed the heel of my boot at her neck.

"We done, here?" I asked.

She didn't answer but started sobbing. I felt like crap for fighting her.

"I said, are we done, here?"

"Yeah," she said, gasping for air.

"Just let me explain."

"There is nothing that you can say that will ever make me forgive you."

I lifted my boot, and she knocked my leg away from her. Extending a hand to help her, I said, "Can we now figure out what's going on?"

Lamp swatted my hand away and picked herself up. She went over to the door and placed her hand on the doorknob.

I grabbed her hand, and said, "Lamp, please. I'm sorry for everything. I really am, but I need you. We need each other.

"I don't need you."

"But if you open up that door, what's going to be out there, doesn't care about your sister's death, or anything that's happened to our people...Please? I can still hear them flesh-hungry canines out there."

She relaxed her shoulders and dropped her hand.

"I just want to find my sister's killer."

In a sudden jerked action, she doubled over, throwing her hand out to brace herself from falling into the door frame. "Dammit! My period's early."

Her eyes were dilated, and her head was hot with fever.

"I don't think you're having cramps."

She swatted my hand away, "What are you talking about. I know my own body!"

"That may be, but I think..."

"You think what?"

"I think—"

~

She collapsed on the floor, and not knowing what to do, I did what I thought was best: I searched the news feeds via a corneal stream to see if there was anything on the pandemic and came up with nothing.

How could there not be any news about it?... Government cover-up!

I dared not call emergency. I would've been jailed on the spot for breaking ennie law. I tried a search in the Ghana National Library Archives for any incidents regarding an ennie biting a human, and to my surprise found over a thousand entries. They weren't dated centuries ago like I thought they would be, either, they were dated within the last couple of years.

How is this possible?

I wasn't the only one to have done such a horrific thing. There were others. Many others. I researched a few informative entries and knew what I had to do for Lamp. I opened the window, carefully, popped open the screen and crawled outside. I made sure to close the window and crept around the front. The dholes were lounging inside the living room part of the house like house guests that had no intentions of leaving any time soon.

With my back to the house, I stood right outside the door and whistled.

"Here, Cujo mutts! Come to mama!"

The dholes came scurrying out of the house, and they were going so fast, even though they saw me plastered up against the wall, weren't quick enough to turn around by the time I ran inside and rammed the door shut.

I tried turning on the lights, but none of them worked. There seemed to have been no electricity in the house. There was another door, on the east side of the house. The one Dad went into. I peeked my head in there, seeing half of the king-sized bed.

"Dad?"

I took one step inside and tripped over something. It was my father unconscious on the floor. I lifted him, and with some awkward effort got him on top of the bed. This must have been the room he slept in. All of his stuff was thrown across the bed, over by an office desk and in the closet. Over the desk, framed in mahogany wood was a degree decorating the wall. I saw a name on the degree that was way too coincidental.

Written in Old English Regular font was UNIVERSITY OF CAPE TOWN, DEGREE OF DOCTORATE OF Medical Sciences AND Virology and it was awarded to my father, Kulo Xo. There was a small bathroom inside the bedroom, and I checked the wall cabinet. There was nothing of use there, toothpaste, a crappy toothbrush, and some dental floss. I checked under the sink and found what I was looking for: a first aid kit. Within a couple of minutes, I cleaned up the bruises on his forehead and patched him up using the gauze and band-aids I found.

He let out a moan. I kissed Dad's cheek and went out into the main part of the cabin. I didn't hear it before with all the fuss of trying not to get eaten, but there was a generator humming right outside the cabin. An extension cord came through a custom-made hole in the wall of the kitchen and connected to an electric refrigerator. It was quite impressive for being in such a non-descriptive cabin. The frig had double thermal glass doors and stood against the wall, storing blood packs. A digital temperature logger indicated that the temp was +2 °C. There were three rows of cabinets topped with a steel surface that literally stretched from one end of the room to the other, barring a few feet on either side.

I opened the left side of the fridge and found ice. According to my research, we needed a lot. Before I made use of that, however, was the task of telling Lamp the news. I went into the room, and she turned away from me, in a strong fit of contempt.

"Lamp," I said. "There's something else I have to tell you."

15

01010100 01100001 01110100 01110101

I placed more ice in the tub, while Lamp called me the kind of names that would make a Vodun priestess turn to ashes. She wasn't happy at all with the news that she was turning into an enhuman.

"It's too cold, Xo," she said. "Stop it. Don't—don't put any more in!"

"Just a little while longer," I said.

I placed the tip of my finger on her forehead. She knocked it away, but not before I got a reading. Her temperature flashed across my corneal stream. After hundreds of thousands of people died from radiation poison, every person born after the Final Event had an upgrade put in their neural input to continuously scan their vitals and hers were off the charts.

"Lamp, you have a temperature of 105 degrees!" I said.

"You don't think I know that," she said, shoving ice off of her. "My thermochromic sensor readout is blinking like crazy on my corneal stream. All I see is red!"

"Then you need—"

"Just stop—I don't need any more ice, you ingrate! You're making me feel worse!"

"I know what I'm doing, and STOP throwing the ice out of the tub! You're making a mess."

"Get away—Don't—Just leave! I don't need your help. You've helped enough. Now, I'm becoming a freak, and it's all your fault! It's your fault."

16

01010100 01100001 01110100 01110101

Lamp was hot, and she was cold, and then hot again. Her screams were ear-splitting. She reached out and squeezed my leg so hard, I grunted, but I didn't complain.

"There you go, Lamp," I said, caressing her. "Let it all out. It'll be over soon enough."

"I'm dying," she said, her nose running. "I'm dying!"

"No, you're not, Lamp. Quite the opposite."

"How do you know?"

"I looked it up in the archives of the Ghana Library."

She blinked her eyes, and I knew that she did a quick search on her corneal stream. "You're right," she said. "In the news feed, two other people have anonymously reported the incident within the last few hours but wiped the data from their neural implant clean before authorities could triangulate where the mind-call came from."

"Yeah, I saw that."

Suddenly, Lamp had a sneezing fit. Her arms flopped over the porcelain tub and drooped to the floor. She closed her eyes, gasping for air, begging God for just one second of relief.

Over and over, she repeated, "Please...please...please God...make it stop...please stop...you...sonofabitch...hurts so much!"

I didn't mean to, but I chuckled softly because it reminded me of the first time I heard Pastor Limerick curse when he accidentally slammed his car door on his finger. When he saw the horror on my face, he angrily said he's only human, and no one's perfect, while shaking the hell out of his swelling finger.

Upon recent observation from all the times we played House of Oware, I was sure that Lamp didn't believe in God. Auntie Yajna once told me that when people have nowhere else to go for mercy, they come crawling to God with fair-weather sincerity.

Her eyes grew dark like embers of wood swallowed up by a gluttonous high tide. I knew she was thinking of Jinni, and how her parents and she can no longer enjoy life the way they did as a family. I never said a word but continued to soothe Lamp by rubbing her back and placing a cool rag on the nape of her neck. After a few long minutes, and her breathing quieted, she opened her eyes and stared at the ceiling. Her eyes blinked like a child fighting their best to stay up after bedtime but losing the battle with every passing second.

Lamp groaned and sweat streamed down her forehead when she slowly turned her head toward me.

"I'm...dying..."

"Stop saying that. You're not going anywhere, but once you recover, you'll be stronger than ever. Maybe as strong as me."

She coughed, and said, "You ain't shit."

I chuckled and raked my hand through her head. "I know, Lamp. I know," I said, and placed the back of my hand on her forehead. "Come on. Let's get you in the bed."

There was a linen closet beside the bathroom, stocked with big white fluffy towels and wash clothes. I wrapped a towel around her and helped her to the twin bed. I pulled the covers back and eased her down onto the mattress. She didn't want to lie down. Instead, she sat up and rocked back in forth in bed.

"My stomach..." she said, grasping it with her hands.

I sat on the edge of the bed, holding her hand. "Do you think you can eat something?"

"There's food?"

I nodded. "Plenty."

She shook her head and curled up on the bed in a fetus position. "Not unless you want me to hurl again."

"Okay. You can eat later when your appetite comes back."

"The pillows hurt," she said, and shoved them onto the floor.

Tossing and turning, she couldn't get comfortable.

"Every muscle in my body aches," she complained. "Feels like a knife's crammed into my rib cage."

I crawled up on the bed next to her, leaning my back on the headboard. She eased onto my lap, placing her hand beneath her head. She brought her knees up toward her stomach and started sobbing.

"It hurts so bad," she said.

I started singing the song my father used to sing to me, first in English, and then in the Ga language.

> *"Baby, don't cry,*
> *Where has your mother gone?*
> *She's gone to the farm.*
> *What did she leave for you?*
> *Yaa yaa wushi-o!*

At first, Lamp's tearful eyes found mine, her neck twisted in an uncomfortable position, and then she smiled, nestling her head into my lap. That made me smile. I continued to rake my hand through her hair.

When I finished the song, she asked, "Did you lose your parents when you were young?"

"Yeah," I said, and my whole body shuddered.

"How did they die?"

I inhaled and blew out a hard sigh. "Fire. They both burned in a fire."

Lamp sat up. "Omigod."

I pushed her head back into my lap with a gentle touch.

"I barely remember it all. I was so small, like seven years old. Sometimes, parts of it come in my dreams like pieces of a puzzle."

"So you were with them? In the fire?"

"Yep. We were on my father's yacht when the fire started. To this day, the police aren't sure what started the fire. All I remember was that I woke up in my bed on the yacht, coughing, and someone, I think it was my father, covered my face with a blanket to protect me from the fire. He ran through the flames and got me to safety. I passed out as soon as he got me on the pier. When I woke up in the hospital, a nurse reluctantly told me that they didn't survive the fire."

"Oh, I'm so sorry," Lamp said, shaking her head.

I didn't want to talk about my parents anymore, so I shifted the conversation to her. "So what about your parents? What do they do?"

She chuckled. "Nothing. They're both recently retired and have renewed their vows every year since. They were so surprised when mom got pregnant with..."

We sat in silence for a long while. I'd brought so much tragedy to Lamp.

"I'm sorry, Examiner," she said.

"Wha—what?"

"Here I am crying over my sister's death like I'm the only one in the world whose faced a horrific experience when you had both of your parents taken away from you. I don't know what I would have done if Mom and Dad left me."

I was speechless.

"And from what it sounds like over the years," she said, "You had a terrible time with all of your foster homes."

"The worst. Hey, look. Let me get you a blood snack," I said, changing the subject. I got up and went out to the refrigerator. "I'll just set it by your bed. It will make you stronger. Trust me, you'll feel one hundred percent better."

The entire top row was stocked with blood bags, the kind blood banks used to store for patient emergencies and transfusions. Lamp let out an abrupt yell. I shut the refrigerator door and went over to her. Tears flowed down her cheeks, and she moaned loudly, curling back into a fetus position.

"I just want to stop crying," she said. "I want the pain to stop."

She covered her head with her arms, and I slipped the pillow she tossed on the floor back under her head. After a few minutes, she started dozing off, but something she said was eating at me.

Lamp received a temporal transmission.

"I'm getting a call," she said, and sat up.

Transmissions were being jammed. Maybe they're just poor because we're out in the mountainous area.

"Lamp here," she said, her eyes full of curiosity. "Thomas! Yes, thank you for getting back to me. Hold on one sec, will you, sir."

She put him on mute, and said to me, "I'm going to do a three-way so you can hear. Don't say anything."

The call came in before I finished nodding.

"Sorry, Thomas. I just had to turn off the stove. Go ahead."

"Meredith told me not to call, but she went over to her sister's and this has been gnawing at me for years, and I have to tell somebody."

"What's that, sir?" Lamp said.

"Frankie wasn't alone in that water plant when the GAF found that poor girl's body."

"I'm listening," Lamp said.

"Yeah, well you better, because I think she's the reason Frankie's got in so much trouble over the years. She was there at the plant, too."

"Are you saying that she murdered that girl?"

"Hell naw. Why would I say a thing like that? That would implicate my child. You think I'm stupid?"

"No, sir. Sorry."

"Don't be sorry. Just shut your pie hole for a minute and listen."

"You got it," Lamp said.

"That girl, Cadence was her name. She and a couple of other girls, I think. They were trying to get Frankie to set up a meeting with one of his bosses at the fishing dock to meet with them."

"For what purpose?"

"Not really sure, but I know Frankie was always talking about joining the resistance, and shit like that. I said, 'Frankie, stay out of it! 'cause all that kind of talk no matter which side you were on, ending up turning the cause into terrorism' but no one ever listens to me."

"You may be right."

"Damn skippy, I'm right. I think they were trying to get back at the sonsofbitches who were responsible for trafficking all those children. And now, after I hear what happened tonight. I think Frankie had something to do with it—not answering my calls, nor returning my messages—I'm afraid something happened to her. Promise me you'll find her. I just want her to be safe. I don't know how I'll live if she's not around."

"Sir, we'll do our best."

"You've got to do better than that. Your best hasn't done crap but allow corruption to be as common as the cold."

"Do you have any idea of where Frankie hangs out?"

"Yeah, after work there's this bar, Cadence works at, Kings' Shelter. Yeah, that's it. I do believe that's the one."

"Where is it?"

"Beats me, but I don't know if this helps but Frankie says that Cadence loves dragons, and always has them around her. I figure she's talking about one of those punk street gangs."

"We'll find that place and bring your daughter home," Lamp said.

"Oh, Jesus. Will you?"

"Yes, sir. You have my word."

I looked at Lamp like she was crazy. You never make promises like that. More times than none, it set up the family for a huge disappointment.

"If Frankie's there when we find her," Lamp continued. "We'll bring her back."

"God bless you, child...Bye, now."

"Goodbye, sir."

"And thanks," he said.

"Sure thing," Lamp said, ending the transmission.

"Well there you have it," I said. "Dad knows where the bar is."

"We still don't have any concrete proof that Frankie is the one who released the retcon virus. My sister thought someone was trying to kill her, but I still don't see how this connects."

I scratched my head. "Was Jinni on any social networking sites?"

"I don't know. Why?"

"We need to know who her friends were. If we're lucky, we may also find threatening posts or something that could give us a better lead."

A little time passed before we spoke. A pack of dholes yipped and howled in the distance. I racked my brain, trying to put all the pieces together. I knew that she was still suffering, and I placed my hand on her arm, but she shrugged it off. Her breathing seemed like such a laboring task.

She muttered. "You changed my life, forever, Xo."

Having had no more energy to say anything else, her tears spoke for her. Lamp brought her knees up to her face, arms covering her head, and rocked. I said nothing, but she let me hold her. In my arms, she bawled and shivered until the chills and fever died. While she trembled in my arms, I wondered if I would ever make it up to her.

Even though I'd just met her face-to-face, I'd known her most of my life playing beside her as a partner in the

House of Oware game. She would hold a grudge against me, forever. That much I knew. In just a matter of hours, my life had gone from bad to worse.

All I wanted to do was be significant in someone's life; to matter. I wanted to prove to the world that I had something to offer, but all I did was prove why I didn't belong.

17

I hadn't realized that I was asleep until Lamp's snoring awakened me. I wanted to check on my father. The cabin was hot and unbearable. Before I went into his bedroom, I went around the house and opened all of the windows. There wasn't much light in the room but enough moonlight for me to see.

Dad was fast asleep. His head wasn't warm, and his breathing was normal. I pulled the quilt from under him and covered his body. I just sat there watching him sleep. It was great having him back. For years, all I ever wanted was to have another chance with him, to be a family again. I had many questions to ask him and couldn't wait for him to be fully rested.

After a while, I got in the bed and lay beside him, putting my head on his chest like I used to do when I was a child. His chest moved up and down and I listened to his heartbeat. We had many wonderful times as a family. I started nodding off to sleep and sat up when I heard claws scratching at the front door.

"Oh, no you don't," I said, and hurried to the front door. "I know you dholes are highly intelligent, but today is not the day you figure out how to turn a doorknob."

I double-checked the front door to make sure I locked it. It was.

"Damn, it's hot," I said, wiping the sweat from my face. My clothes were drenched, and I felt sticky.

It seemed the cabin was getting hotter by the moment, even though it had to be close to midnight. I decided the only way I was going to cool off was to take a cold shower.

Dad's bedroom had a bathroom, but since it was best to let him get some get some much-deserved rest, I thought it best to take a shower in the other bedroom. Besides, Lamp was snoring so loud, I doubt the running of the shower would disturb her.

I headed back to that room, and paranoia from having the *witch dogs* right outside, made me check the doors again to make sure they were locked. Slipping off my boots, I wiggled and squirmed until I slipped my jeans down my hips, stepped out of my panties and unlatched my bra, letting everything fall to the floor.

I went into the bathroom and turned on the water in the shower, and wouldn't you know had to pee all of a sudden, so I plopped down onto the toilet. The bathroom was as plain as it could be: chalk-colored walls, white tiled ceramic floors, and the only thing that had a little pizazz to it was the pink floral shower curtain.

Shoot!

I'd forgotten to get a washcloth and towel from the linen closet. Glancing up and behind me, I found that there was a set of spotless white towels and washcloths. As I remember, Dad always was meticulous. I appreciated a man like that.

There were only a few sheets of toilet paper left, but it did the job, and I got up, flushing the toilet. Glancing in the mirror at my nakedness, it exposed a body full of nicks, cuts, and bruises,

I checked the water and stepped in, sliding the shower curtain closed. It seemed wrong to be taking a shower. The world was in full chaos, and all I could think of was personal hygiene. Grabbing the washcloth from the shower rack, I picked up the bar of soap that sat in the dish awaiting its first use and made the rag sudsy. There was a travel size shampoo fighting for space in that soap dish too. It slid over a little when I picked up the soap.

Letting the water run in my face, I washed my chest, and stomach, thinking, *I can't be too hard on myself. Frankie did this! She gave us all the warnings. But who is she, really? And how does she connect with Jinni? They are the same age. Maybe they knew each other.*

What was a thirteen-year-old-girl doing in that part of the town? She was too young to drive. How did she get there? It was strange Kofi was over there, too. He said he was working on a case, but I didn't believe him. Aw, I'm not making any sense. I'm tired. Things will make more sense after I get some rest. When I wake up, I'll check on Dad, and try to reach Kofi and Auntie Yajna.

The water felt good. Real good. So wonderful that I wanted to lose myself in it and forget all my problems. Wouldn't it be great to just wash them away like dirt swirling down into the drain that led to an abyss, never to be seen or thought of, again? I wanted to stay in that shower forever. A loud noise clapped and gave me a start. I hadn't realized that it was the bottle of shampoo. The sound was so jarring it triggered my memory of watching all those people in Liati Wote die.

People were screaming for help all around me, and I did nothing. I was in the eye of a genocidal storm like a helpless lamb, watching my brothers and sisters fall to the ground and convulse. My thoughts ran wild like a rabid beast in a field full of injured prey.

Guns don't kill! People do! Don't spit on the rich and powerful. Spit on the weak and lazy. Deploy a virus that not only kills the mind, but it kills the spirit. It not only destroys the body, it destroys everybody. Humanity. Yes! Fire upon them. Fire! Fire!

The water suddenly got hot, becoming liquid flames, oozing lava on my skin.

Fire! Fire! I couldn't stop the flow of liquid flames

because I was a part of the ocean (we are the lamb) and the yacht was on fire.

"Daddy!" I screamed. "Daddy, Daddy, help! The fire!"

I heard my mother call him, too. We were both calling him, until she heard me and told him to, "Go save our baby! Kulo! Go save our baby!"

Why won't the smoke stop burning my eyes? I can't see! I don't want to see, but I still looked out of the cubby hole of my room. The water outside was so red. Why was it red? Was that blood? An ocean of blood? There's so much red! So much red! We are lambs but our wool is not white. Our wool is red. Blood red. The death of the children is on our hands.

Mom and Dad's face emerged from the water. Their faces were badly burned, and their lips were blackened strips of skin, hanging off of their faces like used fly strips. I wanted to stop looking, to turn away—but they kept calling me.

"Feeni! Feeni!" they said, calling out to me.

I wanted to answer, but in my mind, I held Lamp's sister in my arms. Her face was deformed, crushed in from the weight of the car rolling over her head. Mom and Dad called me, to be with them, to be one happy family again, but I didn't deserve happiness. I deserved eternal torment. What could I say? There was nothing to say. I killed her. I killed Lamp's sister.

I don't even know her name. I don't want to know her name. Knowing her name makes it even more personal. I was reckless and got distracted. All it took was a millisecond of distraction and the insides of his brain were spilling onto the road.

I didn't answer. I couldn't.

Jinni was in my arms. That was her name. Damn, why did I remember? Now, it's personal. (Well, that's another nice mess you've gotten me into).

Flames.

So hot, yet so cold. Cold like an emotionless lover. Cold

like the last breath of someone trapped under an ava-lanche. Breathing. Breathing. Breathing slow. No slower. Slower! Not breathing. Hold me, Dad. Cover my face. No, don't smother me. I can't breathe. Stop. Stop. Barely breathing. Dying. So young. So smart.

"Xo! Xo," Lamp called.

"Jinni!" I screamed. "Yes. That's her name. I told you. She could've been anything she wanted to—what, what's that—what's happening?"

Something draped over my shoulders, and I shuddered, opening my eyes. It was Lamp!

"You're shivering," she said. "Here, let me help you up."

I looked up at her, and I swear, for a moment. I didn't know who she was, or why she was touching me. Her hair was now wet, and part of her clothes. There was sadness in her eyes like a priest who had lost his faith, like a dog who had learned being mistreated was a daily part of life.

I recoiled and wanted to cover my nakedness, looking down, expecting to see blood. I was covered with a large white towel, not Jini's blood.

It seemed so real.

Lamp gently guided me out of the shower. The water from the shower continued to run. I don't even know how, but somehow, I ended up leaning against the bathroom sink, shivering. Lamp held me, her arms comforting me like a warm blanket. I was cold. So cold.

Why was it so cold?

"It's going to be all right," she said.

"I don't know what got into me," I said, my lips quivering with fear.

I don't know why I was afraid, I just was, and I didn't know how to make the feeling subside.

"Shh," Lamp said. "That...was guilt leaving your body."

"I was the one who did it. I killed—"

"Shh," she said, and placed her fingers against my lips. "You hurt me, and I may never forgive you, but that doesn't mean you can't forgive yourself."

I wanted to thank her.

Can she forgive me?

She was there when I needed her most. Knowing that brought to surface something so confused, but so sure, at the same time. I kissed her finger. And I kissed it again, this time opening my mouth, and letting a sliver of her skin into my mouth.

"Whoa," she said, and stepped back. "What are you doing?"

There was such horror in her eyes, I froze, scared, embarrassed, humiliated. My towel fell, and there I was, standing in front of her, nude. Part of my body was still wet from the shower. The anger in her face softened. Her mouth opened slightly. I saw her eyes fight not to look, but they lost the battle. Lamp rushed me, slamming me against the side wall of the bathroom. I gasped and before I could close my mouth, she bit my bottom lip.

"This is...wrong," I said.

The words had barely escaped my mouth before her lips were on my neck, sucking. I inhaled abruptly, and she bit hard, breaking my skin.

Lamp drank my blood. And it was good.

I cradled my face on her shoulder, and let the darkness swallow me.

18

01010100 01100001 01110100 01110101

The lock on the door clicked, and the door opened. I opened my eyes. I'd fallen asleep. Lamp was in the other twin bed, snoring.

Someone just came into the cabin!

I jumped up and grabbed the first piece of clothing I found on the floor. My shirt, and then I slipped into my jeans, switching my hips until the damn things snuggled over my curves. I went out into the living room. Kofi was standing there, his face, emotionless.

"I knew you'd make it," he said.

"What are you doing here?"

He turned around toward the door. His face softened, and his lips curled into a slight smile. Lamp walked out, unapologetic in her jeans and a bra, yawning and traded glances with me.

"How'd you find us, Kofi?" she asked.

"Wait," he said. "Grunt didn't explain everything to you?"

We didn't answer.

Kofi's smile faded. "I saw the wrecked jeep outside. What happened?"

Dad came out of the room. "Major Grunt saved my life, son," he said.

"Who are you?" Kofi said, and drew his gun.

"Kof, wait," I said.

"Grunt didn't tell me we'd be having company, Feeni. Who is this man?"

I stepped in front of his gun with my hands up. "He's my father."

"I don't understand. How could that be? And where is Grunt?"

I placed my hand on his arm and lowered the gun. "He—"

"He what, Feeni? Where-Where is he?" Kofi asked.

"Son, he's no longer with us," Dad said.

"What?"

"He's dead," Lamp said.

"Damn, can you tone it down, just a little," I said to her.

"Oh no," Kofi said. "That can't be! I—I looked! I didn't see a body by that jeep."

"That's because when we crashed, he jumped out of the car and ran up the hills, making the dholes follow him up there, and diverting their attention away from us," Lamp said.

Distressed, Kofi sat down a chair by the front door. "Now what? I was supposed to meet him here. He gave me a key and told me he'd explain what to do when I got here. This is all a big mess."

"What exactly does that mean?" Lamp said.

Kofi shot a confused look at her. "You smell different."

Dad's eyes sparkled with pleasant surprise. "Your deductions are very good, young man," he said, and stepped toward Lamp. He sniffed in the air. "You're—you're no longer, human."

"How's that possible?" Kofi asked.

Dad ignored his question, placing his hands on Lamp's shoulders. "How are you?"

"I feel like shit," she said. "I was trying to get some sleep, but Xo was snoring like the Battle of Adwa was going on in her throat."

"You think I'm the one who snores?" I asked.

"Like a Pekingese with sleep apnea," she said, making my father erupt into laughter.

"Seriously though," she said. "Everything looks clearer,

sounds are excruciatingly intensified, and basically all of my senses are on overload. So yeah, I have a migraine that would make Shango call in sick."

"Only temporary," Dad said. "You'll soon not only get used to it, but you and Feeni will learn how to use your senses like specialized weapons."

Lamp cocked her head to the side. "Damn, really?"

"Yes. First, you will go through a sort of gestation period during which you will consume a tremendous amount of blood."

"Won't I get sick from doing that?" Lamp asked.

"No you won't get sick from over drinking," Dad said. "When my daughter turned you, your red blood cells went from circular to oval in shape. Therefore the molar concentration of the blood will allow your stomach to have the osmotic pressure to absorb more fluid without rupture?"

"I have no idea what you are talking about," Lamp said. "I'm the detective remember. Not the scientist."

"I get what he's saying," I said. "In a nutshell, we're like camels. We can drink a helluva lot of blood if we want to, and the oval blood cells make it so that we don't bloat like a whale."

Dad nodded. "As I was saying, yes, you can go long periods of time between feedings if you stock up every once in a while."

"How do you even know about any of this?" I said. "As far as I know, Lamp is the first person to ever turn. We're born enhanced humans like queens in a beehive, we're not made."

"Wait," Kofi said. "You don't believe that load of hyena crap that we were born like this, do you?"

I stuttered. "Well—well, we were...were we?"

Kofi and my father traded glances.

"We've both had an emotional day, so far," Dad said. "Let's not spoil it with things that no longer matter. Just know that on occasion, there may be times when you have to feed off of a human. When you do feed, make sure you don't literally drain a human. That would be murder."

Kofi said, "We don't kill in hunger. Only psychopaths murder humans for blood. That's why certain enhanced human laws were put into effect to prevent our kind from developing Blood Lust Syndrome, or BLS, and becoming blood addicts. Once that happens, kidnapping humans always come next because donors never volunteer for long no matter how much they're paid."

"Except for endorphin junkies," Dad said.

"Well, yes, of course," Kofi said.

"It's a bit much to swallow," Lamp said.

Kofi said, "School time's over. Now, will someone please clue me in as to what is going on, here?"

Lamp moved past my father and asked Kofi, "Did you and Grunt kill my sister?"

"That's a pretty hefty accusation," Dad said. "What grounds do you have to ask such a question?"

Kofi stood. "Because, sir. Grunt and I messed up."

"What are you saying?" I asked. "You killed Jinni?"

"No, God no! But when you—" He looked at me and stopped mid-sentence. "When Grunt accidentally hit her while he was driving. We didn't know that she was already dead."

"That doesn't make any sense," Dad said. "What? She was a zombie and limped across the street and you hit her?"

"No, she was already in the street," Kofi said. "I mean, on the ground, and we didn't—"

"Stop!" I said. "Just stop, Kofi. You're making it worse. No more lying, okay. That stops now." I turned to my father. "I know this isn't something you want to hear from your daughter on the day you finally reunite back with her, but I was drinking, and driving."

Dad threw his hands up. "Oh dear ancestors! Don't tell me you killed the girl!"

I went to Dad. "No, no. Kofi's right. We found evidence to suggest that she had already died when I found her—"

"When you ran over her," Lamp said.

I threw my hand up as a gesture of defeat. "Yes—yes, when I…did that. She had already been killed."

"And how do you know this?" Dad asked. "Had you done an autopsy?"

"No, Dad. I didn't. I'm not allowed to do that, yet. But "There were signs of compression and nail scratch abrasions on the front and side of her neck that are consistent with asphyxiation."

Dad lifted his chin and cocked his head. "She was strangled."

"Wait," Kofi said. "How would you have access to that knowledge? We haven't released those findings, yet." He turned to Lamp. "You told her! You just met her today, and you're compromising our case by jabbering off at the mouth to a civilian?"

"That's cold, Kofi," I said.

"No, it's not, sis. It's the facts. I'm a GAF officer. Lamp is a GAF officer. We have rules, regulations, and one of them is to not jeopardize catching a psychopathic killer because your new girlfriend is cute!"

"Actually, I told her, jerk off!" I said. "Not the other way around."

He laughed, but it wasn't because he was amused. "I thought you just said that the lying has to stop!"

"It does, Kofi!"

"Then tell me how you could know in-house information like that?"

Lamp and I looked at each other, and then I turned to Dad.

"Just what I thought," Kofi said. "You don't have an answer."

"We do," Dad said. "It's just complicated."

"I can't do this," I said, and walked toward the bedroom.

"Where are you going?" Lamp asked. "We're in the middle of a murder investigation."

I stopped and came back to her. "Right! Right," I said, and gestured to Kofi and her. "You all are in the middle of a murder investigation! Not me. I'm out of it. I'm done caring about any of this!"

I went into the bedroom, closed the door, and broke down crying on the floor. As crazy as it sounds, the whole thing felt like my fault.

If I hadn't gone out drinking, that night. None of that night would have gone the way it did. Lamp would have no reason to hate me. I would not have pulled Grunt and my brother into a snowball of career-ending choices, and Grunt would still be alive. I broke enhuman law! I'm a sexual deviant, a criminal that deserves to be punished!

Kofi and Lamp started arguing, and then the door slammed. After that, there was silence. Auntie Yajna got it wrong. We were more dysfunctional than any African family I'd known. The funny thing about it all was that normally, I'd want to just escape, to jump right into the game, and pretend nothing happened.

That doesn't feel right, anymore.

I took that moment to review the digital feed showing Kofi and Grunt interviewing Charlie, earlier that day. Getting back to the case got my focus off of me and back on to gathering evidence on the case. I was glad that there was audio to go along with the video clip.

From one angle of the GAF security camera, Grunt, the parents and their child sat in the waiting area, right outside the interrogation room at the police station. The mother was hugging her tomboyish daughter, and the father sat lazily in the chair, holding a cup of coffee in his hand. They were both white, but their daughter was black. Her skin was as pale as theirs, though, because of her condition.

Thomas was wearing an over-sized pale brown suit and his wife was dressed in a soft blue dress with floral patterns, both leaning to a rather conservative style of dress. On the other hand, Frankie wore a lime green Morocco football club jersey and baggy green shorts. Her hair was cut short, and from that vantage point looked like a cute teenage boy.

Kofi went over to the vending machine that sat just beyond the men's room, bought a chocolate bar, and slipped it into his pocket.

Lamp hopped up when he saw my brother and rushed toward him and whispered something. After a small exchange of words, Kofi put on a smile for the parents and the boy.

"Thank you for coming in," Grunt said, and extended his hand to the Thomas.

"Frankie has had a hard day," Thomas said. "I hope this doesn't take much longer. We're missing the match on the telly. Tonight, we're going to finally beat Mazembe, right, Frankie?"

Meredith grunted.

Frankie kept her eyes to the floor. "Yeah. I guess."

"I don't think so, Francis," the mother said, making him look at her. "If you think after all the trouble you've been in today, skipping school and hanging around those trouble makers you never let me meet—"

"I already told you," Frankie said., interrupting. "I was there by myself!"

Meredith spoke over her daughter. "Hanging with those female street thugs against my adamant wishes. No, you're not going to go home and watch soccer with your father! Think again."

She extended her pale wrinkled hands to Grunt. "I'm Meredith, and this is my husband, Thomas."

My brother shook her hand. "I'm Officer Kofi."

"Let's get this over with, shall we?" Meredith said. "We're exhausted, and I just want to go home and tend to this throbbing migraine."

Lamp gestured to the interrogation room. "Sure, this way please."

"You have some really cool artwork in this place," Thomas said. "Isn't it, Frankie?"

His daughter didn't answer.

Thomas continued. "I'm a collector of Surrealist art, myself."

"You're a junk collector and a hoarder," his wife said.

Thomas scoffed. "Junk that paid for the house you live in, and all your excessive indulgences, too, huh?"

"So, Frankie, what games are you good at?" My brother asked, trying to get her to open up more.

She looked up at him but kept walking. Her behavior was shy, a far cry different from the loud indignant voice I'd experienced from her on her hacked broadcasts.

Kofi chuckled and said. "Shoot, I used to stream games on Twitch Prime, I'd play RPG's like Diablo VII and Monster Hunter."

Frankie mumbled. "Monster Hunter has glitches with research points."

"What's that?" Kofi asked.

"That game sucks balls," she said.

"Francis!" Meredith said.

"Yet, you still play it," Kofi said.

Frankie looked up at my brother and smirked. "Only because the graphics are good."

They entered the interrogation room. A sign above the door read *INTERVIEWS*.

"Just the graphics are good or do you like the storyline, too?" Kofi asked.

Frankie smiled for an instant but then it faded. "Don't try to butter me up. You don't care about me! You just want to dig info out of me."

Kofi shook his head. "That's not true, Frankie. I'm a people person, it's in my nature to care. Especially for someone who has seen such horrible things like you have, today. That's got to be hard on you."

My brother shoved his hand in his pocket and pulled out the chocolate bar.

"See?" I got this for you.

Frankie didn't hesitate to take it. The wrapper was half-way open, the second it was in her hands.

"God, you're giving her sugar," Meredith said. "You know Francis has ADD and will be all over the place in a matter of minutes."

"In case you haven't noticed, Frankie's in eighth grade, now, hon," Thomas said. "And every kid loves chocolate."

There was a rectangular table in the center of the room. It was big enough to seat three adults on either of the long sides. Three beat-up chairs sat on one side and one opposite it. The girl and her parents grabbed a seat with their daughter, sitting in the middle. Kofi chose not to sit.

Grunt cleared his throat and sat, saying, "So, Frankie. Why don't we start from the beginning? Tell us about everything you saw at the water plant."

Someone knocked on the door, but I didn't say anything, wanting to review the rest of the video. After a few seconds, the door opened, and I stopped the neural video.

"Otsoo," Dad said. "Can I come in?"

I was still sitting on the floor. I threw my hand up, and said, "Just leave me alone."

He went over to the bed. "Now you know I can't do that."

Dad groaned when he sat down, and it concerned me. He was just in a car accident. There could be some internal injuries.

"Aw, don't look at me like that," he said. "I was the captain of the Accra Rugby Club in my heyday. I can take a little tumble."

"Yeah, but how old were you when you played? Eighteen, nineteen? That was a long time, ago."

He patted his hand on the bed. "Come here. Sit next to your baba."

I hesitated.

"Come on, Otsoo! Come on."

Instead of sitting beside him, I sat at his feet and leaned back against the bed.

"Ah," he said. "Looks like my daughter is yearning for a famous baba head knocker."

I turned around, and said, "A what?"

I started to get up, but he laughed and pulled me back. "I'm just kidding."

His hand raked through my hair, and I closed my eyes,

remembering all the times he did that, and I fell asleep while he massaged my scalp. I could be having the worst day of my life, but as soon as his magical fingers walked on my head, all was forgotten.

"How do you do it?" I asked.

"Do what, Otsoo?"

"Turn bad days into good, rubbish into gold?"

"If I blow the dust off of my eyes, two antelopes can walk together."

"What does that mean, baba?"

"It means that the benefit of having a supporter is to help you see through things. You see, Otsoo. It is better to be in a group or have a partner than to be alone."

"I'm independent. I like doing things on my own."

"The idea is more of collaboration, rather than isolation. When we walk together, we do not do it in competition but in love."

I thought about that for a minute. His strong hands were so soothing that I didn't speak for a long while.

"Who left the cabin?" I asked.

Dad did not answer right away. "Today is Samora's day of learning how to cope with the advantages and disadvantages of betrayal."

"What advantages could there be from being betrayed?"

"The advantages, only if one chooses to see it, is that you understand that no one is free from making mistakes, sometimes the dumbest of mistakes, the worst of the worst of the worst of mistakes,"

I giggled. "Okay, I get it, already, but what good does that do?"

"Ah, Daughter. If you begin to understand that, you begin down the road to empathy, and that journey is one of great honor."

"Do you consider Lamp your daughter?"

"No, you are my daughter. She is my student."

"Why can't I be your daughter and your student?"

"Otsoo, that is a question that only you have the answer to."

"I don't understand, Dad," I said, and got up to sit on the bed with him. "If you were alive, why didn't you find me?"

"First, let me say that I've dreamed of this day, Otsoo. I regret, and will so until my last breath, not being brave enough to see you for all these years."

"Brave enough?" I asked.

"Yes. You see, I've always been afraid that the instant I told you I was alive, you'd be taken away from me again."

"Why?"

"Do you remember the day of the frightening fire on my yacht?"

"Yes, there's not a day that I don't think of that fire."

"After that fire, I woke up in the hospital with third-degree burns. My face was literally unrecognizable, I went through months of self-loathing and pitying myself."

"All this time I thought you died in the fire."

Dad continued, "It was your mother who had been declared dead but Dr. Shaw, who you will meet as soon—"

"I met her in the game!"

"Yes, you did. Dr. Shaw had been the receiving doctor at the hospital, and she had been working on developing the retcon so that it could not be affected by that nasty virus."

"Wow," I said.

"She came to see me every day for two months in the hospital and hounded me until I gave her permission to save my sweetheart's consciousness onto a retcon."

"Mom?"

"Mm-hm. After she did that and proved to me that it was successful by tapping into my neural implant, I eventually asked her to do the same for me when my body conked out."

"I don't understand. You died?"

"Yes. I had a heart attack just a few hours after I made the request to Dr. Shaw, and expired. I'd already signed the paperwork—"

"You're a clone?"

"Yes...I am."

I was still in shock, thinking my father was alive and sitting beside me. In the blink of an eye, I discovered he's not beside me but rather a clone. It was overwhelming.

"Can we just take a step back for a moment. This is a lot to absorb."

"Sure Otsoo," Dad said. "I came in here with a plan but knew, as always with children, one has to be able to adapt on the fly."

"I'm not a child like you once knew, Dad. I'm seventeen, now."

"And more beautiful than I could have ever dreamed of," Dad said.

He was so much more charming than I remembered, and handsome. "So you and Mom's neural implants survived the fire, and scientists were able to transfer your consciousness into a dormant-clone? But if your body is terminated, you're not really alive, are you? Not technically."

He smiled. "My clone, all clones, are living organisms, not much different from our original bodies. We are alive, Otsoo, very alive."

Another knock came on the door. This time, I answered.

"Come in!" I said.

"I looked all around for Lamp," Kofi said. "I can't find her."

"She's been trained remarkably well," Dad said. "Don't you worry about her. She can handle herself. I assume she's getting used to the enhanced senses, right about now."

"But the dholes," Kofi said.

"If I were you, son, I'd be more concerned about the dholes than her, especially now that she's an enhuman."

Kofi folded his arms and looked at me. "Yeah, how did that happen?"

"Not to be a bitchy sister, but you kind of walked in during a father-daughter moment."

"Oh," Kofi said. "My bad." He pointed to the door. "I'll—I'll just be leaving, now."

"Sit down, dork," I said. "We're family. You're always invited to sit with us."

That took him by surprise. "Really?"

"She knows what she's talking about," Dad said, chuckling. "I'd listen to her."

Kofi smiled and plopped on the other bed, placing his hands beneath his head and stretching out his legs on the bed.

Shaking my head, I said. "I don't understand. How—how did you even? I thought that Ghana had not yet had the technology to successfully grow clones."

Kofi sat up on his elbows. "He's a—"

"Shh," I said. "Just try to keep up. "What were you saying, Dad?"

"That's exactly what Bete Sibaya would have the world to believe, that we don't have the tech to successfully transfer retcons to dormant-clones. IGP Sibaya has been doing everything he can to suppress the news of our advancements."

"Why?"

"I can answer that one," Kofi said. "Greed and power."

Dad nodded. "I'm with you on that one."

"Still," I said. "None of this has anything to do with the albino girl that's going around committing genocide with her retcon virus."

"You'll soon understand everything I've done in the past couple of decades has been for this moment now. Everything is connected. I've just been waiting for the four of you to be mature enough to be ready."

"The four of us?" I asked.

"Yes, you, Samora, Durga and Tanaka."

"So, we're all in this, whatever this is, together?"

"The four of you are going to change the world."

"You really think highly of these girls," Kofi said.

"And with good reason." Dad stood, and his knees popped. "I must admit, there's still some getting used to this new body."

My father nodded at Kofi, and he returned the gesture.

"What's that all about?" I asked. "You two buds, all of a sudden?"

"I think, Otsoo, the best way to answer your question, is to show you. Get dressed and get your energy up by feeding on the snacks I put in the refrigerator. Afterward, I'll show you just how I think we can catch that killer."

~

"Follow me, children," Dad said, heading for his bedroom.

Kofi and I followed.

"Wait, why are you going in there?"

Dad chuckled, and said, "Watch."

He went over to the bookshelf and pulled out a book next to the photo albums.

An electrical mechanism came to life, whirring like a drill struggling to drive a bit into a piece of metal. The sound emerged from beneath the king-sized bed. The bed flipped over on its side, and revealed a dark stairwell leading into the ground.

"Now that's what I call a hidden passageway," Kofi said.

"Where does this go?" I asked.

"Mount Afadja," Dad said. "This was the President Mbutu's secret entrance into his underground city."

"But there's a house over it," I said.

"Sibaya's people were getting close to discovering this entrance, I had to camouflage it."

"Impressive," I said.

"Come on, children," Dad said.

We went down the wide stairs into the dimly lit area. Once we were a few steps down, the bed frame eased down over the entrance and tunnel lights illuminated the entire corridor. At the end of the hallway stood an elevator.

The doors opened the moment Dad stood in front of them.

He said, "We are about to travel close to two kilometers deep beneath the mountain."

As we descended, Dad shared with us stories of what he did when he first discovered the doctors had successfully transferred his retcon into a clone. I would have enjoyed the stories more if the strangest feeling of never seeing Auntie Yajna and the twins again hadn't swept over me.

19

01010100 01100001 01110100 01110101

We went from the topsoil of the earth to the top of an underground penthouse. I stepped out of the elevator into a furniture-less living room.

"Welcome to our glass-walled home," Dad said. "I'm still in the middle of fixing it up."

"This is a rather modernist home," I said.

"Hardwood floors, two-story vaulted ceiling, highly-sophisticated security drones, chic bedroom suites, and over there," he pointed is a beautiful kitchen with granite counters."

"What a grand night-life view," I said.

"It's like New Year's Eve in Times Square except we're sunk beneath the earth," Kofi said.

"There's a whole world down here," I said. "How is this possible?"

"It's a bit of an illusion," Dad said, taking a remote-control unit off of an instrument panel on the wall, and depressing a button. "Ocean view..."

We now seemed to have been in an aquarium with sea life swimming outside of the walls.

He pressed another button. "Jungle life."

The penthouse sat in a tropical rainforest. A mother fossa tended to her litter of six pups under a tree. On the glass wall, opposite us, there was a wide door, lined in gold.

Dad pressed another button and the view returned to a magnificent vantage point of the lively underground city.

Our shoes knocked against the pristine floors on our

way across the room toward a steel-trimmed door. He placed his index finger on a biometric fingerprint scanner pad located on a silver lock. The mechanism beeped and he turned the handle, opening the door.

"Can I do that?" I asked.

Kofi said, "Once he programs it to your fingerprint."

"This way," Dad gestured and held the door open allowing us to walk into a pitch-black tunnel.

It was too dark to go on, so Kofi and I stood in the dank tunnel awaiting instructions.

"Lesson number one," he said. "As an enhuman, you have acute vision and hearing, but only if you focus, can those senses become an ability that few have the skill to master."

"I can't see a thing in here," I said.

"Look into the darkness, but don't focus on what you can't see, focus on what you can."

"That, uh, would still be a negative," I said.

"Kofi, would you do the honors?"

"Um, yeah. Amplifying image enhancement in our neural implants."

"Whoa," I said. "Night vision. How'd you do that, Kofi?"

"I allowed you to collect the available light, including infra-red."

"Now look at me," Dad said, and waved his hand.

"I see your hand," I said. "It's red. As a matter of fact," looking at my own, and then turning my attention to Kofi, "all three of us are showing red."

Dad said, "That's the infra-red light giving us thermal readings. Come on," he said. "Let us continue into the tunnel."

The three of us resumed walking into the dank tunnel, our footsteps echoing down the corridor.

"We all have this capability?" I asked.

"Yes," Dad said. "But just like we all have the capacity to learn an insurmountable amount of data, it all depends on the individual and how they process knowledge."

"Wait until I teach the twins this," I said. "Yoni will never be able to cheat again in hide-and-go-seek."

Dad chuckled. "I guess not."

"Lamp knew how to do this already?" I asked.

"A little. However, now will she be able to fully appreciate her skill sets. What we're passing through is actually a twenty-five-ton blast door, made by the most brilliant architects and engineers the world has ever known."

"The others you mentioned, Tanaka, Shaw and Durga have these capabilities?" I asked.

"Tanaka and Durga do," Dad said. "As well as Samora, now."

"This doesn't make any sense," I said. "There is no way, you could've had access to all of us when we were infants."

"I know it sounds, impossible," Dad said. "You see, many years ago. A group of science-geek friends got together on a drunken night and decided we didn't like the way the government treated its people. It was Samora's father who actually decided that we should do something about it."

"That's why you've taken her in?" I asked. "Out of personal obligation?"

"Yes," Dad said, nodding. "Her father had an amazing mind. Jimmy could see numbers like we could see a flower growing in a garden."

"Her father was one of the engineers of this place?" I asked.

"One of?" Dad said. "He was the chief architect."

"This is incredible," I said.

We were approaching the end of the tunnel. "The ten of us, the five couples, decided that we would create a safe haven for our children," Dad said. "One they could play in, and flourish, and be as brilliant as they wanted to be without any immoral or political pushback, or people telling them what they couldn't do."

"So you guys built this underground world," I said.

"No," Kofi said. "They built the House of Oware."

"Holy ancient elders of Accra!" I said, stopping in my

place. "You—you made the House of Oware game?"

"Your mother and I created the game, right before the boat fire." Dad stopped. "Had I known it wasn't safe for you to be in contact with us, Otsoo, I would've put you in foster care myself. Believe me, I fought with your mother on many occasions, but I was too naive to believe anyone would go to the lengths they did to stop our progress on gene coding and recombinant DNA technology. There are many people who disapproved of the work we were doing. It's why I contacted Kofi, years ago, to be my eyes and ears."

"You knew about this all this time, Kofi?" I asked.

"Cat's out of the bag, now," Kofi said.

"Why torture me like that?"

"I had to keep up the appearances," he said.

I punched him. "Dork!"

He laughed and tried to dodge me. "At your service."

We approached the end of the passageway and walked out into a dark alley that had locked iron gates on each end. The air was cool, and the odor of granite was irrefutable. We followed Dad, as he picked up his step and hurried down to his right. He held his hand up, gesturing for us to stop where we were, and he opened the gate. Dad's head turned left and then right. He walked out.

"Clear, he said, gesturing for us to come. "Let's go."

I was the last to walk through the gate. A CCTV drone whizzed by, overhead. The air held wafts of nastiness like an abandoned unfinished basement that had been flooded ages ago and never fully recovered. Still, the streets weren't deserted but were full of life and electric like a Las Vegas lounge casino.

In the narcissistic temperament that irony worked, the liveliness was just a facade of the pain endured by every city dweller. My flesh crawled, observing sidewalks filled with people whose private woes seemed displayed for all the public to see due to the radiation-exposed deformities they carried on their faces and bodies. Many of their gazes carried deep hopelessness but their attire said otherwise.

They wore robes, dashikis, and dresses colored with pride and branded for expensive tastes.

I'd seen disfigured people before, I mean, who hadn't, but never had I seen so many all at one time. For the first time, I wondered why I hadn't seen more. There had always been rumors that through generations of genetic stubbornness, some families developed bloodlines that became immune to the effects of radiation. I, for one, didn't think that was possible.

Maybe our community hadn't been hit hard by the consequences of nuclear war, or maybe those people had gone into hiding. I had a pretty good guess to where they'd gone. These people turned their backs on the poor who couldn't afford to live in such a place and escaped underground, to a city where radiation didn't affect them as much. I hated to admit it, but some of the things Frankie criticized made a lot of sense. That still didn't give her the right to kill innocent people.

An old lady in a Kente cloth dress whizzed by me on a ten-speed bicycle. There were no cars nor trucks driving on the streets but instead, young and old alike rode by on pedal-bikes, scooters, and skateboards. The underground city pieced together a jigsaw puzzle of errant sounds: murmur and laughter from an array of conversations, the shuffling of wandering feet, and the stereophonic sounds of voice-overs delivering sales pitches for their commercial products on larger-than-life billboards and holograms.

Neon signs flashed and popped with vibrant color. One sign boasted *BEHIND ON YOUR LIFE TAX? DON'T BE EXILED BACK TO THE UPPERLAND, CALL ZABARI AND SONS AND LIVE DEBT FREE!* Another sign proclaimed *DONATE TO THE SIBAYA FUND TO CONTINUE A RADIOACTIVE-FREE LIFE.*

"How is this possible?" I asked. "The sights, the sounds. Why doesn't everyone live down here? At least we'd be safe from the dholes. People wouldn't be exposed to nuclear fallout that's still strong in many regions."

Dad sighed. "I believe that it was something President Mbutu wanted, but after the Final Event happened and he, like so many global leaders, transferred their consciousness onto a retcon because their health was failing due to radiation poisoning, it got lost in the planning."

"And that allowed Sibaya to run Ghana any way he wanted," I said.

"Don't you find it strange that every global leader downloaded their consciousness onto retcons and stored them in C-Vaults—those who didn't die of radiation poison—that is?" Dad asked.

"I don't think it was a coincidence, at all," Kofi said. "Politicians and billionaires are the most dangerous people in the world. Killing for power is a way of life for them."

"I'm not so sure about that," I said.

Kofi chuckled. "Yeah? Well, did you know that billionaire families hand down a thousand-year trust fund from offspring-to-offspring?"

"A thousand years?" I said.

"Yeah, imagine that?" Kofi said. "They make sure that the wealth stays in their families, forever. Also, they make sure that the family's ideologies stay intact. You disobey your great-great grandfather's rules, whether they be racist, or conservative, or whatever, and you forfeit living a posh life."

"So what if you have your ideas, your own mind, and disagree with a way of thinking that may be prejudiced against others?" I asked.

"Oh, that's no problem," Kofi said. "You just live in poverty. Because even if you become successful on your own, the patriarchs will find a way for making you pay for going against family tradition."

"That sounds a bit far-fetched to me," Dad said.

"You were down here, at a club partying with your fellow officers, and didn't bring me?" I asked Kofi.

He turned to me, confused. "What? What are you talking about, Feenie?"

"That mark on your hand. It's a club stamp, right?"

"My what?" He looked at his hand. "Oh," he said, chuckling. "This?"

"Yeah. why haven't you ever brought me down here? It looks like a lot of fun."

"It's not a hand stamp, stupid. I used to have a tattoo, there. When I first started hacking and joined this dumb hacker's group online."

"Oh," I said. "A tattoo of what?"

"It was a pyramid. That was the group's logo. When I quit the group, I had the tat removed."

"When was that?" I asked.

"When I got the tat or had it removed?"

"When you inked it."

"About four years, ago," hc said, and sucked his teeth. "Eh? What's with all the questions?"

Dad said, "If you haven't noticed, you'll soon discover that your brother, Kofi, is one of the best hackers in Ghana."

"Excuse me?" Kofi said. "You mean in Africa."

"The world," Dad said.

Kofi nodded. "I do like the sound of that."

A woman walked by holding the hand of a young girl; a girl who looked so similar to Lamp's sister, I'd thought I saw a ghost. It wasn't, of course. My face must have shone a deep sadness because my father placed his large hand on the back of my neck, squeezing it gently.

"What's wrong, Otsoo?"

The question caught me off guard, and I shook my head like a mosquito pestered me.

"Nothing," I said, and summoned up a fake smile. It was a genuine effort.

"Wait," I said to Kofi. "You can hack our brains?"

"Yup," he said.

"You created the virus?" I said.

"No," Kofi said, "But I expect to find out who did, and put an end to them once and for all."

"Fascinating," I said.

"You sound like Mr. Spock," my father said.

I shrugged. "Who?"

My father blew out a long sigh and shook his head. "Never mind."

"He was an American icon, an actor, silly girl," Kofi said. "You can't be serious. You've never watched him on the old hologram archive TV in your neural library?"

I smirked, shaking my head. "Nope."

"Fascinating," Dad said, and laughed, Kofi joining him on the private joke.

I glanced up, catching a glimpse of another orbital drone zipping by overhead. "Why do I feel like my every move is being recorded?"

"They're not though," Kofi said. "No one can see us, I made sure of that when I hacked into the close-captioned security headquarters, down here."

"You can't do that?" I asked.

"Sure I can," Kofi said. "I used the infrared technology in our neural implants and sent out a LED signal."

"That's genius," I said. "Dad, what's this underground city called?"

"This is Ala," Dad said, and placed his hand on Lamp's shoulder. "A secret underground city for the rich but famously unfortunate people of Ghana. Sibaya contracted Lamp's father to build this when the war started a few decades, ago, Samora. His architectural firm was one of the most innovative companies in the world."

"That's why he could travel so often," I said.

"Yep," Kofi said. The light from the street lamp post made his face look spectral.

Kofi said, "Sir, I believe this is the spot."

"Yes," my father said, and gazing up at the flashing purple neon sign. *Kings' Shelter Bar & Spa.*

"Wait," I said. "This is Kings' Shelter?"

"Yes, why so surprised?" Dad asked.

"This is where we'll find the killer."

20

The place seemed like it was ripped off from a design of the Mos Eisley Cantina. There were men and women sitting at tables, drinking and laughing like they'd all heard the funniest thing in their lives, but each and every one of them had a deformity of some kind in their faces, their necks or some part of their body. Many of the women wore dreads or had their braids flowing over their shoulders, but over a dozen girls had colored their hair in bright colors of pink, green and even white.

There were men and women in various colors of complete facial makeup: blue, red and many women wore white face paint like geisha entertainers. Waitresses in tight purple yoga pants, white hi-top sneakers, and matching midriff tees, serviced the patrons. In fancy purple letters, *KINGS' SHELTER*, ran across their chests.

"FYI, this is not a spa, Dad!" I said, speaking over Apala music blasting from speakers throughout the bar.

Yoruban talking drums, a sekere, and thumb piano played while the sweet voice of a Nigerian singer crooned over the percussive rhythms.

"When I think of a spa," I said, continuing, "I think of a place to spoil myself in the luxuries of self-indulgence and relaxation."

"Wait for it," Kofi said, in a playful cadence, and moved on ahead of us.

We walked through the crowded room. People were drinking, dancing and carrying on like they spent their whole existence in that bar. Maybe they did, considering that the world above ground was, for the most part, a wasteland.

"So what do you have in mind?" I asked Dad.

He pointed to the bartender. Kofi dug into a bowl of roasted peanuts and went down to the other end of the bar counter to order, flirting with a waitress who walked by him.

"What do I have in mind?" Dad said. "We feed our palates and then we save the world!" He erupted in laughter and squeezed his large frame in between two patrons.

Kofi came back down our way with a quarter of his blut already gone and burped. It was a pinkish concoction of gin and blood.

"You couldn't wait one second more to come and have a drink of blut with us?" Dad asked.

Kofi balked. "Why would I do a thing like that?" He laughed. "Just joshing. Of course, I ordered blood beer for everyone," Kofi said.

A waitress came over to us, and handed Dad and me, a tall sudsy glass of blut."

Kofi held up his near-empty glass of blut to us. "Cheers to the bratty teens and their potbellied leader!" he said, and swallowed the last bit, slamming his glass on the bar counter.

"I told you I don't have a potbelly. I'm just bloated, right now," Dad said.

"For like, three months in a row?" Kofi asked. "Anyway, children. It's time for you to meet the others. I wanted to have more time to hone and develop your potential, but after tonight's attack, we have to act now."

"Dad, what if the killer of Lamp's sister and the person who created the retcon virus that struck Liati Wote are the same?" I asked.

"Little by little, as we drink, we make plans," Kofi said, quoting an old Twi proverb.

"And we will start soon enough," Dad said.

"Watch me hold my breath," Kofi said, and took a deep breath, only to spray out hundreds of tiny chewed pretzel bits a second later. "Not."

"Douche bag!" I said, stepping back and bumping a person behind her. "Sorry," I said, to the woman I nearly toppled.

It's Frankie!

"Hey!" I said, and started to go after her, but Kofi grabbed my arm.

"Where are you going?" he asked. "I'm about to make a toast!"

"You're such a jerk," I said, wiping a speck of pretzel from my cheek. "That was Frankie."

"You're mistaken," he said. "Don't you think I would've noticed her, being that I interviewed the weirdo, earlier today."

I took a step into the crowd, craning my neck. "I'm telling you that was her."

Dad laughed. "Seems like all it took was a sip of blut and you're already hallucinating."

The two of them laughed, but I didn't protest. Especially after what happened the other night when I drank too much. There was nothing to be proud about in regard to a contest of seeing who could last longer before becoming inebriated. I scanned the crowd, searching for Frankie.

Great. She's gone. Did I scare her off and blow my chance of catching her tonight?

I had no proof that she was the terrorist, and with only her tirades of accusations, that was hardly concrete evidence. All I hoped to do was speak to her. It wasn't a coincidence that she was in the city of Ala. I didn't think she was following us, but I sure as hell didn't think she was there for a girl's night out.

Where were her friends, anyway?

A tall gray-haired white man with a ratty beard, dressed in a green apron said to my father, "You're done there? What's your pleasure, mate?"

"Three shots of Tembo, Aussie," Dad said, pounding his fist on the bar counter. "The good stuff, dear sir!"

Kofi swallowed the last of his blut. "You're giving your green-behind-the-ears daughter Yoruban elephant blood?" Kofi asked.

"Damn, straight," Dad said, tapping Kofi on his arm. "I had my first drink of blut when I was seventeen."

Kofi said, "You told me your father was an alcoholic."

"And your father was a blood addict," Dad said, "But they were both brilliant. We would not have been the men we are had it not been for them."

"Yeah, scarred for life for being on the receiving end of his fists, each time he got high off blood smack."

Dad shoved him in the shoulder. "Let bygones be bygones. Him acting like an ass drove you to stay inside and tinker with computers. Now, look at you. No one can touch you." Dad spoke over his shoulder to the bartender. "Top shelf, my good man. Top shelf for children who are about to change our future!"

"ID?" the bartender asked, not amused by my father's joyful blabbering.

"Sending you a neural ID, as we speak," Kofi said.

"You can do that?" the bartender asked. "So you're one of those government guys. A scanner."

"That I am," Kofi said.

Really? I thought. My brother's connections were getting more and more impressive. It just goes to show that you can live with someone for years and still not know everything about that person.

Kofi continued, "What? You've never seen any government personnel in this dive with confidential level clearance?"

"Actually, no," the bartender said. "I haven't. Only low-level guys who always complain about their pay grade." He blinked his eyes and nodded. "Hey! You sent that straight to my corneal streamer. Running their credentials...And, um, okay. There you have it. The kid checks out. She sure doesn't look twenty-one, though."

"Looks can be deceiving," Kofi said. "For example, that Australian accent you try so hard to use is a cover for your real dialect."

"Which is?"

"American."

The bartender's face told us all that Kofi was right. You'd think a bartender would have mastered the art of the poker face, being the solicitous listener to everyone's problems. He just turned toward a patron seeking to order and went to him, saying nothing more to us.

Dad laughed. "What'd you go and embarrass the guy like that for? I might not ever get the good stuff, again because of you."

"You will always get the good stuff because of me," Kofi said. "There is nothing I can't hack into and manipulate."

"Hey Dad," I said. "I'm going to the ladies' room, be right back."

"Okay, Otsoo," he said. "Hurry back. I want you to meet the others and then there's a matter of utmost importance I must discuss with you all."

I spotted the sign designating the bathrooms, and headed in that direction, looking for a waitress there with Cadence on her name tag.

How many girls do you think work in this joint? No more than a dozen. At least, not on this shift.

I frowned.

If she's working, tonight.

The first waitress that came my way, I stopped. She was cute, short hair, purple lips, and glitter makeup.

I said, "Hey, sorry to bother you."

She said, "No, what's up, hon?"

"I was wondering if a girl named Cadence worked here? She was a good friend of my boyfriend, and I wanted to tell her that he recently passed away."

Her face showed empathy. "Oh, I'm so sorry. Um, Cadence? No, there's no girl that works here by that name."

The bartender barked, "Hey Toots! Don't you see that table in your area waiting to order?"

"Okay, Ham," she said. "He's such a penis. But, like I said, No Cadence works here. I would know."

"Okay," I said, and placed my hand on her arm. "Thanks so much for your time."

"Sure thing." She looked over to the bartender. "I'm going, Ham! You can stop staring, now!"

I was about to ask the bouncer I saw, walking around the club, pointing his flashlight at people blocking access to the bar when Kofi came up behind me.

"I thought you had to go to the bathroom," he said.

He caught me off guard. "Oh my God!" I said. "I thought you were a perv about to whisper in my ear." I placed my hand to my heart and exhaled. "No, I thought I did. It was a false alarm. I was just checking out the bar."

"Uh-huh," he said. "Sure."

"You know how much I like to people watch."

"Yeah, it's one of the few things we share in common."

I didn't say anything.

Damn! Why did he have to follow me? He gets on my nerves.

"You know," he said. "What each person wears, combined with their facial expressions and their gestures, tell a story."

"I know, I know, Kofi," I said. "Shouldn't you be with Dad?"

"He's a big boy. He can handle himself. I bet you were surprised, huh? Your father coming back from the grave and all."

"Yeah, he let me think all these years that he was dead. I could've saved a fortune on flowers at his and Mom's gravesite."

"Damn, that's kind of cold, even for you."

I forced a laugh. "I'm just playing. Actually, I'm not. Seriously. All I'm saying is that he's kept me in the dark for so long. What kind of father doesn't want to see his daughter after she's gone through such a tragedy?"

"Maybe it wasn't safe for you to know he was alive."

"You don't really believe that load of bull, do you?

Maybe he's been lying to us the whole time. That's a better scenario."

"I can't believe you're calling your father a liar. Everything he's sacrificed was for you."

"I'm just worried that you hanging with my dad is clouding your judgment. How long have you known him, anyway? You two look like you've been chums, forever."

Kofi cleared his throat and said, "He contacted me the first day you came to live with us."

"I've known you practically all of my life, and I thought we've always been straight with each other, and now I hear it's all been a lie?"

"Aw, come on. It's not like—"

I didn't have the patience to stand there and talk to him any longer. Bubbling out a heavy sigh, I walked away.

"Feeni?" Kofi called out.

I headed back to where I'd last seen Dad. Of course, Kofi followed me back to Dad.

My father looked at me, and then Kofi. "Uh-oh, sibling fight. You guys stop that, right now?"

"I'm cool," I said. "He's just annoying."

"Said the pot to the kettle," Kofi said.

I shook my head. "That doesn't even make any sense."

"Hah!" Dad said. "Look at that drunk couple playing quarters. My bit-credits are on the girl. I say she drinks her boyfriend under the table."

"I'll be right back," Kofi said, and shouldered through the crowd, eyeing a girl who I caught staring at him, several times.

"What's the matter with you, two?" Dad asked. "I know you guys were talking about me behind my back?"

"Of course not, Dad," I said.

"Here," he said, and handed me a drink.

I took a sip. "Thanks," I said, grinning.

"Look at my Otsoo's pretty smile," Dad said. He looked over to Kofi and with hands signals gestured for him to come back our way. "It's time we discussed something."

"What?" I asked.

21

01010100 01100001 01110100 01110101

"And you met Kofi as soon as Auntie Yajna took me in?" I asked.

"That's right, Otsoo," he said. "He was very reluctant, at first. And God, after you were there for nearly a year, he fought with me tooth-and-nail, said he felt like he was betraying you by spying on you, and for a whole six months, he wouldn't answer or return my calls."

I looked at Kofi. "For real?"

He nodded.

"I had to try a different tactic," Dad said. "I knew he wanted to get into the GAF, but he'd had a hard time passing the psychological part of the tests, so, I got some dirt on one of his senior officers."

"Grunt!" I said.

"You got it. Seems like Grunt had his own little racket going on the dark web."

"He was buying and selling bio-weapon software called Z3," Kofi said.

"Z3?" I asked. "I've heard of that, before. What is it?" I asked.

"I don't know all of the specifics," Dad said. "But from the gist of it, it's a mind-controlling software that turns off neural pathways in your brain responsible for fear and amps up emotions that create rage."

"Yeah," Kofi said. "Z standing for how zombie-like the host becomes and three being the third prototype."

"You see," Dad said. "When defense contractors pitched

it to President Mbutu, he flat out threw the designers out of the base right on their asses."

"Why?" I asked.

"The side effects were too harmful," Dad said. "Memory loss, suicidal tendencies, unstable mood swings, strokes, and the list goes on. But enough of that, it's time we discuss something very important."

"What?"

"You and your team."

"Team?" I said, chuckling with disbelief in his confidence.

"See there," he said, pointing at a couple of girls, both around my age, sitting at a table not far from the bar counter.

"Those two," he said, "are of the Sahelian tribe from Nigeria."

One had fiery red long hair that fell in waves over her shoulders. Her eyebrows were thick and furrowed over droopy eyelids. Tribal marks covered her neck. The other girl had reddish-brown skin. She looked middle-eastern, no, better yet, her heritage looked to be borne of India.

Why do they look so familiar?

Dad continued, "They are short-tempered war-mongers who seek out battle and destruction in every essence of their being. It's always best to ignore them as the fight is never worth it with them because they're so relentless. Those two, in particular, are perhaps the most brilliant in all of Ala."

"Above their ears," Kofi said.

They both had hummingbird-sized brown wings, just above their ears. Each of them had three-inch claws for nails, painted black.

"That's due to the radiation poisoning, huh?" I asked.

"Yes," Dad said, and took a sip of his drink. "They were born that way and instead of wallowing in self-pity of their defects, they united in solidarity and developed a sub-culture."

"You mean there's a whole, I don't know, race of bat wing-eared people?"

"Obviously," Kofi said, nodding. "The Sahelian tribe."

"Affirmative," Dad said.

Kofi took a sip of his blut and smacked his lips. "They wear their emotions in their ears."

"Huh?"

"If the wings caress over their earlobes, they're calm," Kofi said. "If it stands erect, they're offended, if the wings hide behind the ear, they're cautious—not fearful because I don't believe they know what fear is, but cautious, which means that they're suspicious—and that is usually not a good thing."

"Hmph," I sounded, looking at the swords protruding from their backs.

They both caught me looking at them, and their eyes sparkled with the kind of recognition one had experiencing a déjà vu. They nodded hello and raised their beer mugs to me. I looked behind me to see if that was meant for someone else. When I turned back around, they were knocking giant mugs of drink together in a toast, laughing heartily spilling suds onto the floor from their blut like children splashing water on the bathroom floor, playing in a bubble bath.

"Why do they look so familiar?" Lamp asked.

"Because you've played with them in the House of Oware game," Dad said.

"Wait," I said. "I thought I knew them! That's—that's Shaw with the red hair and her assistant. What was her name?"

"Durga," Dad said. "They look very similar to their avatars in the game.

Kofi said, "I mean, Shaw appears like a seventeen-year-old version of her but, that's them all right."

"You've played the House of Oware game, too?" I asked Kofi.

"No," he said. "But I, you know, have profiles on everyone, even their avatars."

Dad sounded out a humming grunt of approval after

he took another sip of his blut. "I swear they serve the best blood beer in all of Ghana, here. Now, where was I. Oh, yes. When you speak to them, never look at their ears, at least not right on."

"Besides the fact that it is rude in any culture to stare at a birth defect," I said. "I wouldn't do that anyway."

"Be aware of their emotions," Kofi said, continuing after a sip of his drink, "but never let their wings telegraph your own emotions. That could mean your death, or at the very least, the most pain you've ever felt in your life."

"I don't think killing your teammate is proper etiquette in any game," a voice said, behind us.

Her face was geisha white beneath a red satin Minang headdress. The headdress sat atop her head; two cones protruded from it that resembled ram horns. She wore a rose gold ankh around her neck, and a red dragon-printed robe over what looked like a black top and matching yoga pants.

My father turned around, spoke to her in Japanese, to which she replied, and bowed. He returned the gesture.

"She's wearing Versace black palazzo Jordan sneakers," Kofi said, in an almost inaudible tone. "Who wears that with a kimono?"

"So you've been preparing us to do what?" she asked in English. "Fight for your cause?"

"Not my cause," Dad said, "but rather for the welfare of our planet. It's not just rebels we want to train. This is not a revolution or a coup."

"Then what is it?" I asked.

"Survival," Kofi said.

The geisha girl stepped forward and extended her hand. "My name is Reiki. Reiki Tanaka."

"Tanaka?" I asked.

"You know me as Lt. Tanaka," she said.

"The big dude I met at the virtual version of this bar?" I asked. "You look nothing like your avatar."

"For good reason," she said. "Who would be intimidated

by a petite female whose skills sets include singing, playing classical flute and well, I guess knowing anything that has to do with computers and statistical probability."

"That sounds badass to me," I said.

"This is why you all met at the bar in the game," Dad said.

"I'm beginning to think that everything in the game was real," I said.

"It is," Dad said. "The virtual construct is actually an augmented reality."

"So a bunch of teenagers is doing the police work for you?" Tanaka asked.

"Teenagers in no danger of being corrupted by the vices we adults cling on to," Kofi said.

"Boy, you barely know how to wash your coconuts," I said.

"Do I sense a tinge of jealousy?" he asked.

"Not one bit," I said.

"The things a man would do to keep his daughter safe, or his family together have no price tag on them," Dad said. "But they are the kinds of things that a powerful man can use against him to do the most deplorable things."

"That sounds like a deeply personal confession," Kofi said.

"It is just an observation, or more so, a philosophy," Dad said. He started walking toward the table that Shaw and Durga sat. "Come! It's time you all officially meet each other."

We shouldered through the crowd toward them. I kept my eye on them the whole time. Shaw and Durga each wore a harness and back scabbard holding dual swords; crossed blades of death. They wore lime green baju melayu outfits, silk long-sleeve shirts, and trousers. On Shaw's head sat a pine-tree green songkok hat, and a kain sarung wrapped around her waist full of tiny razor-sharp shuriken. Like in the game, Durga's head and neck were covered with a black snood.

"Look at them," Kofi said. "They are always ready for a fight."

"They encourage it," Dad said.

"Sounds like my kind of people," I said. "They're like ninjas."

Kofi nodded. "Yes, and believe me, there's not a ninja in any tribe or from any land that would want to face a female Sahelian with purpose in her eyes."

"Their nails have a toxin in them," Dad said. "Which can paralyze an elephant in seconds, so never let them scratch you."

"Ironically, it seems to have become quite a fetish in the bedroom," Kofi said.

I shook my head and sighed. "Do you have any filter?"

Kofi chuckled. "None."

"Why did you recruit them?" I asked. "They don't seem like they play well with others."

Dad took a swig of his drink and said, "Because a Sahelian as an ally is the most honorable and unconditionally loyal friend any warrior could dare hope to have in their wildest dreams."

"Honor is not just a word to them but a lifestyle," Tanaka said. "Like my people."

"Just don't have them for enemies," Kofi said.

I finished my blut, stifled a burp with the back of my hand, and shot a glance at Tanaka. "Like my people."

22

01010100 01100001 01110100 01110101

"Where's your homegirl, Lamp?" Durga asked.

I inhaled deeply, glanced at my father and then said to her, "She'll catch up with us, soon. She had a family thing."

"Before we get started," Dad said, holding up his large mug of blut, "I'd like to make a toast!"

Seated around the square table, the seven of us raised our drinks in the air. The table was stained with spilled beer, wet napkins and soggy pretzels sitting in a damp basket.

I was still on my second blood beer, Kofi was on his third, and the others, who knows how many they had, but I was sure by their slurred speech and insatiable laughter, it was more than a few.

Dad cleared his throat and said, "Paying honor, glory, thanksgiving, praise, and homage to our ancestors, we ask that they guide us to finding a source of the virus so that we can cut its head like a snake that crawled into the wrong garden."

"Damn straight!" Shaw said.

"I watched each one of you grow up." Dad said, his eyes welling up, "I've seen all the horrors that you've all endured—my God, some of you have gone through so much and yet, you managed to keep a level head on your shoulders. And, well, I—I believe that you ladies are the key to our future."

Seeing him get emotional made us all get teary eyed. This meant a lot to him, and as we all looked at each other around the table, there was no doubt that each one of us felt compelled to recognize that we were all in this together. I knew then that these girls were my tribal sisters.

Dad bellowed, "To our future!"

We all responded, "To our future!"

Tanaka began singing a song I'd learned through the House of Oware game. If one of us lost a life, upon restart, our avatars attended the Funeral of the Fallen before continuing our case at whatever level we last played.

Tanaka sang in a beautiful operatic tone, "*So lift your voice*,"

Shaw and Durga replied, "*Ghana!*"

I grinned and sung the next line. "*It's the year of jubilee.*"

We all replied in unison, "Ghana!"

Lamp chuckled and sung, "*Out of Tonga Hills, Ghana!*"

And together in harmony, we all said, "*Salvation comes to those who bleed.*"

Dad began beating a rhythm on the table with his massive hands, and I complimented his beat with a more percussive beat. It was wonderful being with my father, again. I don't remember the last time I had so much fun before that. Looking at his bloodshot eyes, and the wrinkles in his face, I knew that he, too, had probably not had this much fun in a while. His work always came first, and he never took breaks. That night, he took time to celebrate life with me, and I enjoyed every moment of it.

Tanaka led a song we all knew well from childhood, "*Kaafo, Kaafo!*"

"I was just thinking about that song," I said, and joined in, singing, "*Kaafo ni moko!*"

Dad repeated the lyric in English, "*Don't cry, don't cry!*"

We echoed him, and while still drumming Dad sung, "*Ghana will survive!*"

"*Ghana will survive!*" we all said, almost in perfect synchronization, commanding small applause from the tables around us.

Dad lifted his blut to his mouth and guzzled and we

all followed suit, laughing and spilling blood beer all over ourselves.

"You're going to make them all too wasted to do anything but stumble around like buffoons," Kofi said, standing in exasperation. "Look at you all!"

"We are enhumans," Dad said. "There is no challenge that we cannot overcome. Even inebriation! Nor hunger!"

"No more hunger!" I said.

"Nor oppression!" Durga said, holding her glass high.

"We will regain the Ghanaian life!" Shaw said, clinking her glass against Durga's. Kofi sat back down. "All right, already. You're all giving me a big fat headache."

I stood and gestured my blut toward Kofi. "To the greatest eco-warrior! Kofi!"

Everyone cheered. Dad gave him a loving shove. Kofi reluctantly laughed, turned to the side, and crossed his bony legs, placing his elbow on his thigh and his chin in his palm. He reached for a pretzel, recoiling when he realized they were all soggy.

"Now, children," Dad said. "Kofi is right. It's time."

Dad and Kofi pushed back from the table and stood.

"I want all of you to come along with me," Dad said. "There is something that I need to show you."

Dad did a beeline through the club, toward the back.

"Where in the world are we going, now?" Shaw asked.

My father said, "To the spa."

"Spa?" I said, snickering. "Dad, this is so not a spa!"

"Wait for it," Kofi said, holding up his finger. "Wait for it."

Tanaka threw a shrug my way, and I tossed one back. Shaw and Durga brought up the rear, their faces, written in determination. We continued behind Dad and Kofi toward the back of the room. A bald caramel-skinned behemoth of a man stood in front of a closed door that was covered in purple velvet.

"Good to see you," Mr. Xo," he said, grinning.

"Baba Lemur," Dad said. "They're with me."

He looked us over like if we'd moved wrong in any way, he'd snap our necks without losing a single night of sleep. After eyeing Kofi with an even stronger gaze of suspicion, he nodded.

"Sure, Xo," he said. "Keep a low profile. You know what happened the last time you were here?"

Dad narrowed his eyes at Kofi. "I assure you nothing like that will happen, again, Baba Lemur, will it, Kofi?"

"I only had a few drinks, so you can rest assure that I will not upset the bar staff, tonight," Kofi said.

"Hope not," Baba said. "I have two unruly teenage girls to feed at home and need this job. It's just me, you know, to take care of them?"

"Ah, Akua and Afusa," Dad said. "They're both fifteen, now, eh?"

"Fifteen going on forty," he said, shaking his head. "They think they know everything, and they question every word that comes out of my mouth."

"I know the feeling," Dad said, and looked down at me.

"What?" I said.

He gently shoved me forward, and Baba Lemur knocked two hard times on the door. It opened and we were showered with neon pink light.

I glanced up at Baba Lemur, one more time before walking through the door. His face bore tribal marks that looked like a tiger clawed him precisely from the top of his cheekbone to the fore of his ear lobe.

"Move along," Shaw said, poking me in the back with her long nails.

"Hey!" I said. "Be careful where you stick that deadly manicure. I heard about you two."

"Don't worry," she said. "Durga and I have been living with these nails longer than you. I know very well how to use them. Now, chop-chop!"

"She's a little pushy," Tanaka said.

While passing Baba Lemur, I smiled. He wore humongous gauges in his ears and looked like his muscles were about to burst through his black suit with the slightest over-extension of movement. I was seventeen, and in my mind, an adult, but when I touched his arm to say thanks, he recoiled like I was jail bait.

When the door closed behind us, we were met with soft relaxing Benga music. The scent of peppermint sat in the air and smelled so good; hunger pangs jumped around in my stomach. I thought about Lamp and wondered if she was okay. God, she had just turned into an enhanced human.

Tanaka closed her eyes and inhaled. She was experiencing the Scent Effect. Since fragrance left a lasting imprint on the brain, it triggered emotions and memories. Like a memory chip, her olfactory bulb was recording and processing her new sensations for later recall. Yeah, she was loving it. I could tell. It was like we had stepped into a fascinating museum. The other girls' eyes sparkled at everything their gazes fell upon.

We were standing in an oval room that had smooth black marble walls, and dark-tinted double glass doors to our left. Cones of pink illumination shone down on us like we were caught in a spaceship's tractor beam. A stream of air blew from the ceiling vents and cooled my skin.

When the wellness concierge came through the glass double doors, it didn't matter that her name tag had KENYA on it. I knew exactly who she was: Cadence.

I sent a neural text message to Lamp: "Found Cadence. Will find a way to speak to her in private."

Lamp didn't respond.

Cadence was a voluptuous girl with blonde hair and skin like she had bathed in goat's milk all of her life, she walked behind a semi-circle desk that came up to her waist. A slither of her was also caught in the cone of light and the flamingo color illuminated the glitter makeup on her skin.

How did I know it was her? Holograms of baby purple dragons fluttered around her like butterflies dancing on the wind. I had heard of visual-romas before but had never known anyone who bought them. When Thomas mentioned that Frankie said she likes dragons to hang around her, it all made sense. The dragons weren't a youth gang, they were visual-romas.

Like those who wore perfume or cologne to accent their natural odors, some people wore visual-aromas to accent their auras. There were all kinds of visual-roma avatars: flowers, animals, or whatever one could dream of to enhance their physical appearances.

Inside a glass tank sitting in the wall behind the desk, a curvy nude woman with gold-painted skin and long blonde dreads stretched out on her stomach across a white twin bed. She was reading a magazine that rested on her pillow. Kofi seemed to have difficulty taking his eyes off of the chick. Dad discreetly elbowed him to get him to stop staring but that didn't stop the rest of us from doing the same.

"Hello Tribe! Welcome to the HoloDeck Spa," she said, grinning. "Hello. Mr. Xo." Cadence, or rather, Kenya, had dimples the sizes of dwarf planets. If she was the same age as Frankie, she was thirteen. Although she was a fully developed girl, I wondered how someone so young got a job there.

"Ete sen, Kenya?" Dad asked.

She replied, "Eye pa," which meant she was doing great.

Dad turned to us. "This is my daughter and her friends."

I glanced up at Dad and then back at her.

"And of course," my father continued, "You know my associate, Kofi."

"Hello Kenya," Kofi said. "I hope that you can forgive me for the last time I—"

"Good evening, everyone," she said, cutting him off, and keeping her gaze on my father.

"I called in advance for special preparations," Dad said, shaking his head at Kofi.

Kenya nodded, and tapped away on a virtual keyboard on the counter of her desk.

"Are you almost finished with your studies in virology?" Dad asked her.

Virology? To hear Thomas Benja tell it. Kenya, or rather, Cadence, was a delinquent, sucking his daughter into all kind of darkness like a black hole.

She smiled, still typing away. "Yes! I have two more classes left, a science morality class and rapid antigen testing practicum to complete my clinical training."

"My daughter, Xo, loves pathology," Dad said, and gave me a big proud smile.

"Yeah," I said, grinning. "I've been studying it since before I could ride a bike. Can I ask you a question?"

"Uh, yeah," she said. "Shoot!"

"What were you and Frankie doing at the water plant, yesterday? And if you could, would you be able to finger the persons you saw at the plant in a neural photo? The one who killed that girl in front of you two?"

"What?" she said. "I don't know what you're talking about."

"Whoa, whoa," Dad said. "What the heck is going on here?"

Kenya leaned forward and whispered, "Are you trying to get me killed? Please don't bring that up, again. The cameras are always on."

Shaw caught on, and said, "She was just joking. We're playing a prank game where we see which one of us can ask the craziest questions. For example, what do you think about downloading a person's consciousness onto a retcon, and then inputting that memory orb into a clone?"

Kenya didn't hesitate to answer that, although I could tell she was shaken. "If clones allow man to bypass death, immortality will be humanity's greatest downfall."

"SCNT is the next step in sentient beings' revolution," Shaw said. "The advantages far outweigh the disadvantages."

"I agree," I said.

"Eh, I'm not so sure about that," Tanaka said.

Dad said. "That is quite a bold statement, Kenya."

Kenya said, "As you know, my parents lost their

consciousness in the early stages of the retcon technology to a vicious neural implant virus, the same one that affected quite a few of our world leaders, so I've had a lot of time to loathe the entire process, even wrote my last term paper on it."

"Your parents were two of the most brilliant scientists I'd ever worked with," Dad said. "I wish they had chosen to work with me, instead of IGP Bete Sibaya's research and development lab."

"I do, too. They probably would have, had they known you were still alive."

"They knew. I'd sent cryptic messages to them that only your father would've been able to decode. He and I had invented—"

"The House of Oware," she said, interrupting with a chuckle. "Baba spoke of it often enough for me to know it was a grand accomplishment."

Shaw, Tanaka, and Durga glanced at each other with surprise.

"You invented the game, Mr. Xo?" Tanaka asked.

"I didn't know you were the creator," Durga said. "That's dope!"

Dad chuckled. "So he's shown you, Kenya?"

Kenya nodded. "Ever since I could crawl into his lap."

"Yes. I'm sure he did. He adored you."

"They both spoke highly of you, and Dad always said you were the best shot he's ever gone game hunting with."

Dad chuckled. "Yeah, well, I think he was just being modest. No one was better than your father. Kenya, sweetheart, you just make sure you find me when you complete your studies. I think you will be pleasantly surprised at what my team can offer you."

"I will!" she said, typing on the virtual keyboard. "And, um, okay. You're all set." Kenya walked from behind the desk, bringing her harem of dancing dragons along. She gestured to the dark-tinted glass doors. "This way, Tribe!" She glared at me.

I quickly found her business email under spa wellness concierge and sent her a quick mind-text to contact me. I also told her that we spoke to Frankie's father and he was very worried about his daughter.

I hadn't noticed how thick the glass doors were until I stepped closer. They were like bank vault doors and slid back into each side when we stepped in front of them. The corridor was arched, and a blue neon sign proclaimed VIRTUAL SPA. The peppermint aroma was stronger than ever, and the temperature rose as if we were about to walk on beds of hot coals.

Once we walked into the corridor, glass walls encased us, and plum floors made of marble were waxed to a spotless shine. Loud yells, instigating chants, and furniture collided in chorus like we were in a crowded cowboy saloon and patrons were jeering as two gunslingers who were in an angry dispute over poker hands.

"What's going on?" I asked.

"Yeah," Tanaka said. "What is this place?"

"As the sign reveals," Kenya said. "This is a virtual spa. The most transformative and therapeutic spa in Africa. People come from all over the world to fulfill their dreams, train for missions, or even relive traumatic events in this state-of-the-art holographic treatment center."

"Why would someone want to experience something that was obviously painful?" I asked.

"Imagine, for a moment," Kofi said. "Being able to go back in time and relive an experience when an alcoholic step-father, for example, was abusive?"

I shrugged, shaking my head. "Like I said, why go over that again? Once is enough!"

"You didn't let me finish," Kofi said.

"What Mr. Five-finger Freddie is trying to say," Kenya said, "is that, here, you can not only relive a painful experience but change the outcome of that experience."

"Ah," Tanaka said.

"So, let me get this straight," Durga said. "I can go back

and chop off the nuts of a bully in sixth grade that groped me in the lunch line every day?"

Kenya's mouth stretched into an evil grimace, and her eyes averted to Kofi. "Exactly, girlfriend! I actually did that twice last week."

"Sign me up," Durga said. "I'm down with that."

A sinking sensation moved in my stomach. All these years, on every case in the House of Oware game, Lamp had been by my side. Now that I was on a real case and discovering clues that possibly led to an arrest, I'd pissed off the one person who I needed the most.

23

My mind delved into a deep shame as I berated myself for all the terrible things I'd done over the last twenty-four hours or so. If I could go back, I would not have never gone out that night. How could I have been so stupid to drink and drive? The guilt weighed on me heavy, and for the first time, I thought of turning myself in and facing my punishment. Even though Jinni was dead, it was still a hit and run, and I should've reported it. That had to have been a crime.

Kenya walked ahead of the group and allowed us to absorb what we encountered passing each room, on either side. Some rooms were like peering into a person's nightmares, others, their fantasies. I couldn't tell what was real, and what wasn't. It reminded me of something Mom told me a long time ago. She said, "the subconscious mind can't tell the difference between something that is real and something that is imagined. It was why the heart rate increased in dreams that were adrenaline-filled or terrifying."

In one room to our left, an old man in a red checked cloth wrapped around his body, sat on a bench in a flower garden while boys from ages of five-to-ten played hide and go seek. The man laughed with boisterous energy, watching the children run around like playful rabbits.

Kenya said. "That is a Maasai warrior who pushed his boys hard all of their lives, like his father once did, and never allowed them to just be children and play."

"And his boys are deceased?" I asked.

She nodded. "They died game hunting when they encountered a pack of rabid hyena's that lived in the forbidden zone. Two of his brave boys fought off the pack who had attacked their younger sibling, but they all were bitten and died a slow miserable death from those radiation-deformed beasts."

On our right, a group of men stood in a forest and cheered as a woman climbed a rope up a tree. She had many cuts and abrasions on her legs and arms but was almost to the top. Below her, were scattered pieces of wood that may have come from a cart or wheel barrel, I assumed from the four small wheels spread out on the ground. I'd found the source of the furniture crash sounds and cheering.

"It looks like a narrow little forest in there," Tanaka said.

"You should see how it looks from the inside," Kenya said. "In there, the forest seems to be endless in every direction."

"So how do you not get lost?" Durga asked.

"Everyone is monitored," Dad said. "The spa can communicate to all through their neural implants."

"And they can't see us?" Shaw asked.

Kenya shook her head. "Nope."

Shaw scratched her head. "So, um. I get how interacting in the game works, yeah. Like a dream, our subconsciousness doesn't discriminate from reality and the game, so we think what we touch and smell and feel is real because our brain creates the sensations based on memories of real-life interactions but..."

Kenya smiled. "I get this question at least once a day. You want to know if the persons in the holoroom are for lack of a better word, interacting with ghosts, virtual projections that lack matter."

"I was kind of wondering that myself," Durga said.

"Several decades ago," Kenya said, continuing, "there was a popular television show who creators were so imaginative that many of the fictitious ideas they invented have become an everyday part of our life."

"I know which show you're speaking of," Dad said. "Although the name of the program is on the tip of my tongue. It used to be one of my favorites growing up, back when corneal streaming wasn't invented yet, and we sat in front of computers to watch TV. Dammit, I was just talking about one of the main characters to my daughter."

"Yes, well, thanks to Ghana's governmental R&D lab, the technology called holomatter was invented, just a little under a decade ago."

"That's one thing Sibaya got right," Kofi said.

"Holomatter?" I asked. "You don't mean that you've somehow integrated virtual reality with real matter?"

"That's exactly what I'm implying," Kenya said.

"You're shitting us," Durga said.

Kenya chuckled. "No, I'm dead serious. In our transformative spa rooms, objects and people are simulated via a synthesis of matter, virtual projections, odors, and temperature amalgamations to give you reality in its most imaginative form."

"That's incredible," Shaw said.

On our right, an older woman danced with two other women that were slightly younger than her.

"Hey!" I said. "They're doing the Kpanlogo dance!"

"That's correct," Dad said. "For the Homowo Festival. I've known that woman in the Kente cloth for a long time. She is dancing with her sisters who died, decades ago, when Russia bombed Ghana in the war before the Final Event."

"So this-this is a spa!" I said. "It's how people escape the horrors of the day by delving into a fantasy world made by their liking."

"Now you get it," Dad said.

Kenya smiled. "Our goal is that everyone has shed the weight of the world off of their shoulders, if only for a few wonderful moments while they're here."

"Moments?" Durga said.

"Yes, in the transformative room, you can program the

length of time you want to spend in there, from one minute up to six months. The entire experience will only be brief in real time. No longer than an hour, or two."

"That's great," I said. "But what if I wanted more time to solve a case, you know, review the clues, and such?"

"Many detectives come here to do just that," Kenya said.

"I'm moving in here," Tanaka said, "I'll be in a tank beside the gold girl."

Everyone except Kenya laughed. I believed she was still shaken up about the questions I asked her.

Kenya stopped in front of a door to our left. "The GACC, as you requested."

"This is it?" I asked.

It didn't look like a military installation. Before us, stood a vast garden of peppermint plants and white roses in an area about the size of a cricket field. Hundreds of white butterflies fluttered from flower-to-flower. The statue of a white elephant sat in the midst of the garden. Mom used to always tell me that when I saw a Pieris Brassicae, a white butterfly, that an angel came to watch over me and bring me good luck. She said the souls of my ancestors resided in the one that would land on my finger, to be my guide into the next world.

"In there?" I asked.

Kenya said, "Okay, folks. You've got it from here. Once you all enter and the door closes, give it about one minute and the program will begin."

We all stepped inside the glass door, and as soon as it closed, Dad was all over me.

"What kind of stunt was that you pulled?" He asked.

"Dad, we've been investigating this case, for the past few hours, before we knew you were alive?"

"I know you've been investigating the case," he said. "I'm the one who monitors the game."

"No, you don't understand," I said. "Lamp and I have been following real leads, and Kenya was one of them."

Dad looked stunned. "She was?"

"Her real name's Cadence," I said. "Cadence Baroudi."

"That's one of the victims who escaped being abducted the night of the murder at the water plant," Kofi said.

"How did you know that?" I asked Kofi.

He opened his mouth to answer but Dad cut him off.

"Whoa-whoa-whoa-whoa," Dad said, shaking his head. "Let's sit down and go over everything we know. Let's start from the beginning. You all need to understand why you are so significant. When we go in, we'll be in a war room of the Ghana Alternate Control Center, the GACC. This is where IGP Sibaya hid his strategic military base after he gained control of Ghana and neighboring territories."

Kofi said, "but just in case his defense department head monitors all interactions with the base, real or virtual, I'm going to tap into all of your brains and create an open source project, a process of onion routing."

Tanaka gasped. "Ah, that's genius. You give us access to the darknet so that no one detects we're there."

Durga said, "Cool. We can go anywhere, and literally be untraceable."

"That is exactly the point," Kofi said. "As an enhanced human, you already have acute senses but unless you're trained in how to optimize those senses, they're truly being wasted."

"Optimize them?" I asked.

Dad said. "It's new. It's fresh to Tanaka, who got turned, recently."

I turned to her. "You, too?"

She bowed and said, "Shi!" which meant yes, in Mandarin Chinese.

Dad continued, "So I expect all the ladies in the group to excel."

"If I get this right," Kofi said.

"You better get this right," Dad said.

"I was trying a go at being humble," Kofi said. "It didn't work. So anyway, what I meant to say was that you all will be able to gain access into anyone's neural implant."

"And see what they see, through their eyes," Shaw said.

"Sort of be a fly on the wall," Dad said. "Hear their conversations."

Durga grinned. "Shit, dude. This is better than any surveillance technology because it's undetectable."

"Let me be clear, though," Dad said. "I don't expect that to happen tonight. That will take quite some time and guidance, but in the future, trust me, you'll be able to optimize your senses."

"What exactly is about to happen, Dad?" I asked. "This is ridiculous. We can't pull this off. We're—we're...teenagers. Why are we even doing this?"

That must have pushed a button because Dad snapped at me. "We're doing this because our people are being exterminated. If you don't have it in you to stand up to genocide, then you can leave, right now."

I didn't say a word.

He continued, leaning in closer to me. "And you're not the brave daughter I fell in love with time-and-time again, like when you brought home that pink fairy armadillo or the countless days you rescued injured baby aye-ayes and begged me to help you nurture them back to health."

"Dad, you remember that?"

"Of course, I remember that," he said. "They're memories that kept me going when I was in that bed dying and feeling alone. It taught me to see past science and believe in something even when I didn't have the facts to base any investment of thought toward a positive outcome."

"Trust me," Kofi said. "You are all far better than we ever could imagine. It took years and years of placing impossible obstacles in front of you in the House of Oware game."

"Right," I said. "They were games. No fear of death or having a diaspora of people either gaining or losing on a single decision we may or may not make. This is real life!"

"You need to relax, Xo," Durga said. "You're killing my high. I think we're about to experience hacker history in the making. Mr. Xo! Whatever you throw at us, we're going to slice that bitch up like a butcher in a meat shop."

That relieved the tension in the air, and we all laughed, even I let out a chuckle. Dad didn't utter a sound, but his eyes spoke to me in a way that a parent communicates to his child, disappointment and hope, simultaneously.

"Dude," Tanaka said, "What's taking so long?"

As if on cue, the white elephant, butterflies and beautiful gardens disappeared, reshaping into the inside of a military installation war room, six hundred and ten meters below Mount Afadja. Like a big corporation's conference room, there was a long oval table with leather conference chairs encircling it. Glasses of bubbling carbonated blood, along with pitchers of ice sat on the table. There were note pads and pens in front of each chair.

We all found a place at the table. Dad stood at the end of it in front of a hovering digi-board. Seated around the table were Tanaka, Shaw, Durga and me.

"Hey," Tanaka said. "Why am I not in my avatar form?"

"Kofi disabled those forms," Dad said. "Now that you have all been formally introduced in the real world, there's no need for deception regarding your physical appearances."

"Okay, first things first," Dad said.

"Is there anyone else who started investigating the case in real life besides my daughter and Samora?"

All of the other girls shook their heads.

"Okay," Dad said. "Feeni, send me a memory link of everything you've encountered from the time you and Samora met each other until the time you met me."

"You can leave out any personal memories like taking a wee, or anything that might make us vomit on sight," Kofi said.

"I don't know how to filter memory links," I said.

"Send them to me," Durga said. "I can do it in no time, and then pass it on to your father."

"Uh, okay," I said. "Searching...and...sending."

"Got 'em," Durga said. "I'll have them to you in a jiffy, sir."

Dad nodded and said, "Terrific!'

"Done!" Durga said.

"Done with what?" Kofi asked.

"Filtering the memory links, dude. Sending them you, now, Mr. Xo."

Dad smiled. "I love your tenacity, my child. Annnnd I have them. Great! Scanning...and information received... Just like in the Oware game, I did my damnedest to replicate everything in our real world so that the spa could upload it into this VR world. How else do we expect to catch up to the African Crime Network who have made their modus operandi to be one step ahead of authorities at every turn?"

"The House of Oware game is not perfect," I said, "I admit because I don't have full acccess to all of the GAF's database, a lot of things are programmed on best possible sources of information I can get. Yes, sometimes I get genders mixed up, or ethnic backgrounds because I can only go on public sketches, and you know that isn't always accurate, but for the most part, it allows for us to find the clues we need based on the data input into the software."

"It's perfect to me," Dad said. "I've prepared all of you masterfully. Now it's time for you all to understand why I have so much confidence in you all."

He walked around the table, stopping behind each one of us. As he gestured to each person, he complemented his argument with a hologram via corneal stream transmission of the subject discussed. Each was in action, performing their duties. I must admit, I was impressed, having only seen Lamp in action and not the others. We were, more or less, a dream team. For the first time, I had confidence that I could actually do something in the world, something important.

"My daughter is arguably one of the best investigative pathologists in Ghana," Dad said, allowing us to absorb the holographic images displaying over the center of the conference table before moving to the next person. The hologram showed me performing autopsies. I'd been doing that via the game since I was six years old, for a little under eleven years.

"For that matter," Dad said. "I couldn't ask for a better actuary and computer geek than Durga."

Durga's avatar was shown compiling impossible statistics and making a tense decision to pinpoint a location out of many that allowed Ghana Allied Forces to find a missing girl held captive before the trafficker returned to make of his promise to kill her because authorities clapped back on his ransom demands. I remembered reading about that case in a newspaper clipping while trying to solve a case in the game. I remember thinking how brave and invaluable someone like that was to the police force. From the corneal stream, however, I didn't see the girl's face.

Dad tapped his hand on Reiki's chair. "No one is a better con that this woman."

Reiki was shown singing in geisha form, distracting a group of men with her seductive dancing, while stealing their wallets.

"Shaw does not only have the knowledge of a medical doctor but is the best damn driver and pilot on the planet."

The hologram of Shaw was like watching a movie trailer from an action film. First, we saw her treating Ebola patients in Sierra Leone before we saw her skimboarding on the waves of Hawaii, downhill mountain biking in Colorado and snowkiting on Norway's most northern Varanger peninsula.

"What are you?" Durga asked. "A fucking female James Bond?"

"Chikuso!" Tanaka said. "You're my WCW and today is only Tuesday!"

That made us all erupt in laughter.

"Well," I said, "since you put it that way, I stand corrected."

Dad waved his hand in front of the digi-board which was neurally-activated and worked incongruent with the controller's corneal streaming and neural transmissions.

"Okay, so here we go," Dad said, and got up. It's time."

"Whoa-ho!" I said. "Are we finally going to get out of this boring conference room and make a difference in this world."

Dad pointed at me. "And that's the kind of spirit that I love to see!"

He went to the door and opened it. The hallway that we came down was gone. In its place, was a police station, bustling with GAF officers going about their business.

"Follow me, ladies. Kofi is going to stay put in the conference room. He shouldn't be moving around much."

"He's our cloaking device," Tanaka said. "He has to concentrate."

"Affirmative," Dad said, and rushed through the large holding area.

There were suspects getting processed, women shooting the breeze with fellow officers by the water cooler, a couple of loud-mouth scantily clad prostitutes complaining to the chief about their pimp, and a gang of teenagers dressed alike, handcuffed in the holding area.

"This is spectacular," I said. "And all of these people are real?"

I tapped an officer filing a report at his desk on the shoulder, and he turned around and said, "You got a problem, miss?"

"Sorry," I said. "I thought you were someone else."

"Well, I ain't," he said. "So keep your hands to yourself."

Dad headed toward the front entrance of the station, and we followed behind, keeping up with his brisk pace.

"Mr. Xo," Tanaka said. "How is this possible?"

"This," he said, holding his hand up in the air, "Is nothing more than the program. But this upgrade, this amalgamation of the House of Oware game and the holoroom," he said, and he walked outside, "Is something I call the Oware Mosaic."

24

01010100 01100001 01110100 01110101

We went through the doors of the police station and walked outside to a beautiful sunny day in Ghana.

"So what, the night turned into day," I said. "We just saw a white elephant morph into a conference room. This is the virtual spa. We get it, they've figured out a way to create matter to make the experience real."

"Ah," Dad said, holding up his finger. "The difference is, with the help of Kofi, I've built software that piggybacks on real programs."

"Like the way a malicious virus replicates itself to spreads to other machines, wreaking all kind of havoc for the host?" Durga asked.

"In a way," Dad said. "But this," he said and snapped his fingers. "Gets in the mind of neural implants, any person we want to target, and bring them into our world."

Suddenly, we were on a hillside overlooking Bete Sibaya's massive complex. Next to each one of us was an Uno one-wheeled motorcycle.

"You've got to be pulling my freaking leg," Durga said.

"Oh, wow," Tanaka said. "Very nice! But I don't ride."

"You do now," Dad said. "We're in the Oware Mosaic. All I have to do is program your features and abilities and it's a done deal."

"Yo, look at our duds," Durga said.

I hadn't even notice, flabbergasted with my father's brilliance. "We all look like badasses."

Shaw said, "Long leather coats, black clothes. All we need is a pair of..."

"Look inside your jacket," Dad said.

We all did and pulled out a pair of shades.

"Okay, guys," I said. "I hate to rain on the party but we're not here to have fun. Real people have died, tonight, and from the looks of it, more may die."

"So why are we here?" Shaw said.

Dad said, "I'm glad you asked. This is the—"

"Dad," I said, interrupting.

"Hold on, Otsoo, let me finish."

"No, Dad, listen. I gave Kenya my number and told her to call me if she had any information."

"Yes, I know," Dad said. "I remember seeing that when I skimmed the memory links you just sent."

"Well, she just wrote me back."

"And?" Shaw said.

"Okay, first, for the rest of you girls, here's what we know," I said. "We spoke to Frankie's father a few hours ago."

"Frankie is the girl who played hooky at the water plant the day of Jinni's murder, right?" Durga asked.

I pointed at her. "Correct! So when after we spoke to the father, his name is Thomas, he called Lamp back and told her that Frankie and Cadence, who goes by the name of Kenya now, were together in the water plant, skipping school."

"They were lovers?" Tanaka asked.

I shook my head. "I don't know that if in eighth grade they were technically dating, but yes, they were a couple."

"So cut to the chase," Durga said.

"Anyway," I said. "Thomas said that he was worried about his daughter, and after the pandemic, the alleged terrorist attack on his village, he's worried that somehow, Kenya had something to do with it."

"Why would he say that?" Dad asked.

I said, "He said Kenya was always mixed up in trouble, and always got him stuck in the middle of her craziness, tried to arrange a meeting with a man heading the fishing slave ring." I stopped talking, my corneal stream flashing, alert me of incoming data. "Ooh, you have to hear this," I said. "She's sending me a lot of messages."

"Well, that's what we're waiting on, Xo," Shaw said. "Spit it out, girl!"

"Okay, so the first thing she hit me with is that, yes, she and Frankie were there at the water plant cutting class together, but that she hadn't seen her after that day."

"What?" Tanaka said.

"Yeah, you sure?" Shaw said.

"According to what she's saying. Kenya says that she saw a man kill Jinni, that she and Frankie had seen her only once or twice in the street over where a lot of the GAF officers drove by and paid for sex, over in the Nkonya village."

"That's the Volta Region," Shaw said. "Where a lot of human and anti-species trafficking is high, especially, slave trade for the fishing industry."

"What else?" Dad said.

"Well, here is the kicker," I said. "After that day, she received a lot of anonymous threats that she better keep her mouth shut or she and her parents would be killed. That's why she changed her name, and moved away, so that her parents would be safe."

"How did you say her parents died?" Shaw asked.

"I didn't," Dad said. "But they died in a..." His mouth dropped agape.

"Hold up. Don't tell me a house fire," Durga said.

"Yes," Dad said, and rubbed behind his neck.

"Hold on," I said. "Dad, you and Mom died in a boat fire..."

It hit me what dad was implying earlier. *I fought with your mother on many occasions, he told us. Had I known it wasn't safe for you to be in contact with us, Otsoo, I would've put you in foster care myself. But I was too naive to believe anyone would go to the lengths they did to stop our progress on gene coding and recombinant*

DNA technology. There are many people who didn't like the work we were doing.

"The killer likes to get rid of people with arson," I said.

Auntie Yajna was in an alleged arson incident, I thought, but the thought dissipated before I gave it a second thought. She was too loving and kind to be a killer.

"Are you saying that you're a clone?" Tanaka asked.

"Yes," Dad said. "Is there anything else Kenya wrote you?"

"No," Kenya said, surprising us all when she came up behind us, from behind a tree. "Frankie is here! The guard won't let her back here, into the spa, but she's here. She's here, and she says she going to make me pay for betraying her. I'm scared. I didn't call the police because I don't know what she can do! She's such a great hacker. She could tap into our electrical systems and make this place burn down or something!"

"You're safe, Kenya," Dad said. "You're safe with us. Frankie won't be able to hack our defenses because Kofi is creating an impenetrable firewall. It's probably why, if you tried, you couldn't see what we were doing."

She nodded and swallowed hard. "Now, I get it. Okay, well, there's one last thing, and it didn't bother me until just now."

"What's that, hon?" Shaw asked.

"When I moved here, I just wanted to leave the past behind. I was doing amazing in neuroschool, and developed new friendships, here, and even had a nice girlfriend for a while, but Frankie just wouldn't let me go."

"You guys kept seeing each other?" I asked.

"God, no!" Kenya said. "But that didn't stop Frankie from mind-texting me fifty-sixty times a day. And the more I ignored the messages, the more threatening they got."

"But you never responded?" Kofi asked.

"No, never! I swear," she said. "And then she went through this phase, or at least I thought it was a phase."

"What kind of phase?" Tanaka asked.

"A suicidal one," Kenya said. "Going on and on about not being able to live without me, and then she said that if I didn't come back, she was going to kill herself. After a while, it all stopped. And I know that this sounds really cruel, but even though I thought she might have actually gone through with it, I was relieved."

"You were relieved because you could move on with your life," Tanaka said.

Kenya shook her head. "No. I was relieved because I thought that she had finally found peace. Always being troubled, learning about being an illegitimate child, and I'm sure you met her parents, Thomas and Meredith. They're no walk in the park."

"That they are not," I said. "So why the change of heart? Why tell us all this now?"

"Well, after about six months of not getting any more messages, I started getting this weird visitor."

"Who?" Dad said.

"Well, funny you should ask, Mr. Xo," Kenya said. "Because she said she knows that big guy you came in here one time. The one with the hieroglyphic tats on his neck."

"Major Grunt?" I said.

"Yes," she said. "That was his name."

"That's how I finally met her because she said her friend knew someone in the government, and if I ever needed protection, he would be that guy. Major Grunt was the kind of person I should know."

"What's the girl's name who told you all of this?" I asked.

Kenya's lips trembled. She glanced down at the ground and took a deep breath. When she gazed back into my eyes, hers had a thin film of tears in them.

She said, "Jinni."

"That's preposterous," Dad said. "That would mean that Major Grunt was—"

"Dating an under-aged girl," I said.

Dad was in shock. "And the government official would be—"

"Kofi," I said.

The entire holoroom shut down, and when the real-life holoroom materialized, Tanaka, Durga, and Shaw were at my feet, dead. Silver fluid drained from their ears, and their eyes were caught in an expression of disbelief. I spun, looking for Dad's body, my heart pounding.

Kenya screamed from outside, and I hurried out of the holoroom in time to see Kofi dragging her through the tinted double doors to the Spa reception area. I ran down the corridor, and in my peripheral, saw that the people in the holorooms were sprawled on the floor, dead.

"Omigod," I said, pushing myself to run faster.

Another series of screams came from Kenya, and I went through the door and ran back into the bar. What I saw hurt my heart. It was a wake-up call, a slap in the face that this was no longer a game I was playing but a real-life tragedy. The floor was a sea of death. Not one body stirred. All with the same symptoms of the retcon supervirus. Kenya was right. Frankie was there. She was on the ground, at my feet. She'd died with her eyes open just like her mother. Thomas would be devastated. He no longer had any family left.

My family made sure of that.

Kofi got to the front entrance and stopped. He had Kenya by the neck and his shoulder pressing against the front door, cracking it open.

"You had to call the damn GAF, Sis?" he asked.

The only thing that came out of my mouth was, "Why?"

"Grunt told his little girlfriend, Feeni. Told Jinni what we did. He left me no choice!"

I stood there, speechless.

"Don't look at me like that!"

"Kof...I love you."

"Then stop looking at me like that!"

"Let me go," Kenya said, she wildly reached for a bottle on the bar counter, smashed it, and jabbed Kofi in the side with it.

For a long moment, he stared at Kenya with disbelief, and then he looked down at his wound, and his lips trembled watching his own blood drip onto the floor. He looked at me as if to say he was sorry. Kofi's eyes turned to fire and he yelled. He grabbed Kenya by the hair.

"No, no, no, no, no," he said, and ran back toward me, and grabbed Kenya's neck tightly in a headlock.

"What are you going to do, Kofi? Hack into my brain. Kill me, too?"

He did something to me, and the pain struck me so bluntly, I dropped to my hands and knees. "Who's next? The twins?"

"Shut up!" he said, and ran back into the Virtual Spa area.

I climbed to my feet, mad as hell at him. Angry that he was so pitiful. Pissed that I loved him. Enraged that I had to be the one to stop him. I screamed with every fiber of my being. "What are you going to do, big brother, huh? You gonna kill Auntie Yajna, next?"

"You come through that door, Feeni, and it'll be you!"

"Oh yeah?" I said and picked myself up. Pushing through the door, I yelled, "You think you have the balls to kill me? You want to hack up my brains? Kill me, then, brother! I dare you!"

25

01010100 01100001 01110100 01110101

I had Kofi cornered, he had nowhere left to go. With one arm around Kenya's neck, his other hand stabbed the jagged edge of a broken beer bottle against her jugular vein. Blood trickled down his hostage's neck from a razor-thin cut. They stood to the side of the reception desk. Kofi's tattered tee shirt exposed that he was losing a lot of blood. The end was near.

"One more step," Kofi said. "And I swear to my ancestors, cursing me from hell, that I'll do it!"

"Kofi," Kenya said, squirming. "No. Please. Don't do this."

I had my gun trained on the sick sonofabitch's temple. With just a little more pressure on the trigger, I had the chance to hand deliver a bullet with his name on it. But I promised myself to take my brother in alive.

Promises, promises.

"Kofi," I said, trying to talk myself out of killing this murderous maniac. "Let's end this before anyone else gets hurt."

Kofi's eyes blinked hard, while the blood-drenched more and more into his clothes. He pressed the glass deeper into Kenya's neck, making her shriek, and released his choke hold.

"Make a wrong move, Kenya, and I'll be forced to kill you," he said.

Kofi typed something onto the virtual keyboard of the holographic programmer.

"We'll get you some help," I said. "This doesn't have to end badly."

"My thoughts exactly," Kofi said. "I still have one more hack up my sleeve."

He shoved Kenya toward me. I raised my gun toward the ceiling so as not to accidentally fire the gun at Kenya. She fell into my embrace, and the force of the impact threw me into a backward stumble. When I recovered my balance, the double glass doors to the Virtual Spa shut.

I bolted through the doors, spotting Kofi just as he entered into one of the holorooms.

"It's over!" I said. "The room takes up to a minute to materialize. You're out of options."

I was a few steps away from apprehending this monster, but when I went through the door, was hundreds of meters above ground, freefalling out of a plane toward a snowy mountain. Somehow, he had overridden the safety precaution and had us skysurfing within seconds of entering the holoroom.

"You still underestimate my hacking abilities," he said, twirling with his arms outward like two leaves attached to a twig, falling from heaven.

With the initial shock of stumbling out of a plane, I dropped my gun and cursed while it spiraled down toward the arctic landscape. God, he was amazing. Gliding through the skies with the board on his feet made him look like he was surfing on air. He brought his arms close to his body and began spinning, cutting through the winds like a knife.

I bent my knees and brought them up to my chest and threw my arms out like a bird. We soared down toward the top of the mountain. Kofi put his head down and extended his legs upward to the sky. I did the same thing, trying to increase the speed of my fall-rate. It was working, but Kofi didn't care. With his body diving head first, he bent his legs and grabbed his ankles, and twisted his body so that he started twirling in a flawless aerial.

That allowed me to catch up to him, and I reached for

his legs. Managing to grab his board, I pulled myself closer to him and got a hand on his ankle before he smacked me in the side of my helmet, making me release him. The hit made me see stars among the blue skies for several seconds.

When I could see straight again, I ducked my head and dived toward Kofi. Like a graceful ice skater, he did a flawless layback spin.

"You think this is a joke!" I said, yelling.

"No, it's freedom! And it feels freakishly amazing!"

"There's nowhere you can escape!"

"The difference between you and me, Feeni Xo, is I embrace life...I'm not trying to escape life, but you are!"

He laughed like a child feeling the wind in his face, enjoying his first encounter on a swing set. The holomatter system provided diving equipment for us both, and like Kofi, I had a surf cutaway system built into a backpack on my back. He deployed his first chute, and after freefalling a little more, released the second one.

I deployed the main parachute from the harness-container case, allowing the chute to jettison out, and like him, dropped more before releasing the reserve. Kofi hit the packed powdered mountain with a yell, released the harness and skied downhill. Snow kicked up in his wake. He sped down and was several meters ahead of me by the time I hit the piste.

Dad called me on my temporal transmitter, and I answered, "Dad! You're alive!"

"Of course, I am."

"I have some hacking tricks myself. Made myself invisible in the program. Kofi couldn't find me."

"Tell me you can override the program."

"I'm working on it," he said. "It's important that you realize that you, too, can control what happens in this game."

Kofi picked up speed and was distancing himself from me.

"What do you mean?"

"You have the House of Oware game in your neural implant. With the upgrade I designed, you have the ability to manipulate the program as much as he does."

"Why didn't you say that in the first place?"

"You're the know-it-all, I figured you knew, smart ass."

"I'd rather be a smart ass—"

"Than a dumb ass," Kofi said, finishing my statement. "Make me proud, sister!"

I ended the transmission and smiled, then focused on making the holoroom create an environment I was more comfortable with: the GAF headquarters. The celestial snow mountains faded away, and we were back on solid ground. The streets of Accra. Kofi tripped over a curb and fell hard onto the ground. I, of course, was pursuing him on an Uno motorcycle. I raced toward him, jumped off, and tumbled into him. The bike ran into the side of a faded pink abandoned building.

Kofi elbowed me, and my head snapped back.

He rolled away from me and ran toward the entrance of the GAF headquarters.

Kofi said, "I see you have some tricks up your sleeve, too. But you're no match for me, Feeni!"

That's what he thinks.

I stood up, and looked down, and saw that I'd had long curved kukri knives holstered in scabbards on each side of my waist. The diving gear was gone. I now had on a black tank, black leather pants, and knee-high boots. A revolver was resting impatiently in a thigh holster on my left leg, and my devilish little Chucky sat in a back holster.

"Come and get me, bitch," he said, yelling from inside.

"Not a problem," I said, and dashed inside of the building.

Inside, it had already changed from something I imagined, into something Kofi hacked up. There were hundreds of dog kennels on the first floor. The stench of animal hair and waste was strong. The cages were all opened, and empty.

I hope Dad hurries up and finds a way to end this. I'm not in the mood for another dog fight.

I saw Kofi's head bobbing as he ran up a wide stairwell, and I followed him up two flights. Candle sconces illuminated grandiose baroque paintings that were twice my size and hung high in the corners of the stairwells. My kukri knives tapped against my thighs as I took two steps-at-a-time and reached the next floor. It was a dimly lit area, and like a scene from a British thriller, fog drifted down the hallway cloaking what nightmares Kofi orchestrated, down the long hallway. The floors were dark like ripe wine, and Elizabethan furniture cradled the walls while eighteenth-century mirrors carved in an oak frame, displayed winged gargoyles in ornate wall hangings.

Footsteps echoed from the stairwell. It sounded like an army of students rushing up steps to see a well-advertised fight. They weren't stealth-like like ninjas, that's for sure. Kofi meant for the growing noise to intimidate me. It worked. Just a little.

They were now only a stairwell below me, whomever or whatever they were, moving at a steady pace to meet their end. I didn't care if they outnumbered me, I had already made up my mind that only I was to leave that building with Kofi, by any means necessary. I stood in a kata stance, awaiting their death with utmost confidence.

That was before I finally saw one.

I hadn't expected fear to creep under my focus and unnerve me. However frightening their appearance seemed to be, I thought that the holoroom would not allow the hosts to die, so that imagining alone, gave me the courage to face the demons that Kofi summoned from the depths of the darkness within him.

The first of the horde reached the top of the stairs and spotted me, I bounced back on both feet like a boxer avoiding a jab. They were Maasai warriors, but their skin was translucent, and their eyes were jaundiced. The first one that made it to the top of the stairs had eyelids that were burned with a sickness like a child dying from Ebola. Beneath that invisible skin, blood spewed through his body. His purplish spidery veins made a network all throughout his skeletal frame, up and around his crooked teeth. His over-sized skull could not hide beneath the semi-transparent skin over his bald head.

The warrior's body was bulging with sinewy grayish muscles, but bare of clothes besides an oxblood kilt he wore that was made with leather strips. In his hand was a small lotus stick.

At first glance, I determined that they had Ehlers–Danlos syndrome, but that was my pathologic mind, the one that had empathy. There was no room for that nonsense.

Just from pure instincts and adrenaline, my feet started moving toward the African warrior. I ran toward him and did a one-handed cartwheel kick, bringing my heel down into the top of his cranium. Beast or not, he could be knocked unconscious. He fell toward the ground in silence.

Just as my feet hit the ground, two more came up the steps. I unsheathed my kukri knives and was about to slice into their necks when Lamp came up beside me.

Paow! Paow!

She blew holes in their heads. Dead center. They tumbled backward into a few others that marched up the steps, sending a domino effect of several of them toppling downstairs.

I turned to her, not knowing what to say. Like me, she was dressed in black with knives on her hips, but she had a pair of guns on each thigh holster, and a sword in a back scabbard.

She said, "I guess this means I forgive you."

With a smirk, I said, "You wanna wait for me to be out the way before you shoot, next time?"

"Affirmative," Lamp said, and holstered her guns. "Is this better?"

Shinnnt! Shiiinck!

She unsheathed her machetes, and I nodded.

"Hells, yeah," I said. "It's slasher time!"

I spun just as three Maasai warriors met me at the top of the steps. I side-kicked into one, sending him down the steps, shot an uppercut with the palm of my hand to one on my left, and grabbed the arm of the other, and slung him over my back.

Lamp stabbed her machete into the head of the one I slammed into the ground.

"Move out of the way, Examiner!" she said, "Why fight with blades when you have bullets?"

Lamp sheathed her machetes and took out her Glock 17's. I ducked and rolled over on the floor, and ended up by her side, while she let it rain bullets in the stairwell. After seventeen rounds in each mag, they were still coming.

While she reloaded, I clutched her arm and pulled her down the foggy hallway, into a two-floor library. I'd never seen one before, equipped with real hardcover books. Lamp closed the door behind us, and we moved toward the center of the room. High above us, hung a sparkling crystal chandelier. On each side of us, stood massive dragon-head statues with necks that stretched down from the second floor. The horrific beasts faced each other baring marble teeth the size of elephant tusks.

"We don't have time for this," I said, sheathing my knives. "We need to find Kofi. Forget about these creatures."

"Can't we just wish them away and replace them with something harmless like aye-ayes?"

"I've been trying," and pulled the gun from my back holster. "Kofi must have written a code that won't allow me to change it."

"There's always a cheat," she said, shoving the second mag into her gun. "Maybe we can find a backdoor in."

We were now on the twelfth floor of the building. Kofi had full control to do whatever he wanted and there was nothing I could do about it. Window walls encased the massive area, revealing that the moon fought its way in the room and past the dozen rows of book stacks and shelves. Outside, heavy storm clouds hung over the night sky. The vantage point from being that high gave us a depressing 360-degree view of an abandoned metropolis. In the distance, I thought I saw a pack of dholes dash behind a dilapidated shack, disappearing out of sight.

I sent a neural text to Kofi to give himself up just as two translucent-skinned warriors crashed through the double doors of the library, smashing them into pieces.

"They seem a little pissed," I said.

Both of them were carrying lotus sticks. I ran up the stairs to my left and Lamp took the opposite side. We opened fire on them. The two coming after me got too close for comfort until I blasted them in the face point-blank range, and both plunged over the top railing.

"I don't care what you see again and again in movies, hitting a moving target is a bitch!" I said.

"Will you shut up, and shoot?"

Lamp shot one, hitting it in the shoulder, but the warrior kept coming. I blasted half of his ear off, and he tumbled into one of the book stacks, knocking down several hardcover books. No more came through the door. We'd defeated them all.

"That's it?" I asked.

"There is nothing I can't do in this program!" Kofi said, coming up my rear.

I turned, prepared to block a punch if he threw one. Kofi stepped from behind the book stack and stood at the end, releasing a wicked grin. He had on a white martial arts gi. His feet were bare, but his face was covered in yellow warpaint. Beneath each eye were four scarred lines like crooked carvings on a wooden prison bedpost. He held a lotus stick in each hand.

I chuckled. "You don't think that you're a match for me, do you?"

He swung at me, I blocked his punch and he struck me in my wrist with the lotus stick. I cried out in agony.

That was my ulnar nerve pressure point!

He followed that with a quick strike with his other hand, smacking the wooden rod to my brachial plexus, a network of nerves near my neck and shoulder.

Another pressure point!

I fell backward, assessing his style. He stepped forward. I kicked him in the chin. He countered with a strike, slapping the stick to my ankle before I could snap my leg back. I thought that for a second, he actually lit my ankle on fire, it burned with such intensity.

He brought a foot up and stepped on my thigh. He threw his other leg around my waist, climbed over and around my shoulder, and thrust his knee into my back. I grimaced and yelled. His elbow crushed into the nape of my neck.

While I saw stars, stumbling forward in pain, another strike hit me in the stomach. I fell onto one knee and was about to black out until an arm caught me, snatching me to my feet.

"Come on, sister," Lamp said. "He can't defeat us both!"

Lamp ran and slid in an attempt to leg sweep him, but Kofi leaped in the air. I ran and clotheslined his ankles mid-air, with a mighty blow from my forearm.

He flipped forward and landed on his feet like a cat. Lamp had gotten to her feet and struck Kofi hard in his left side with a decisive kidney blow. He bent over favoring that side. I leaped in the air and did a side somersault. When I landed to the right of him, I spun and did an axe kick to the side of his head.

It was a kick that normally knocked my opponent out, but Kofi hit the ground and bounced right back up. Lamp charged him and shot her boot so hard in his knee, she snapped it. Lamp brought her other foot up and snapped her heel into his jaw. Kofi's teeth shattered, and he dropped like a brick. She knocked him out cold.

We both stood there, out of breath, and doubled over. Lamp had one hand on the wall and was half bent over, and I had an arm on my abs, feeling an excruciating burn in my ribs.

I plopped down in the chair, and it rolled back a little. "I thought this program was a simulation of reality."

Lamp pushed off of the wall and stumbled toward me. "This pain feels real to me. It's a good thing I'm an enhuman, now, or I wouldn't have been any help."

"When did he learn how to fight like that?" I asked.

"Who knows? Maybe he learned the same way you learned pathology or how I learned criminal justice."

"Neural school," we said, in chorus.

I stood up straight. "Well, guess we didn't need Dad after all. Let's end this holo-program and get Kofi processed." Limping a little, I turned around to get Kofi. "I don't know how to break this to Auntie..."

Lamp looked up. "What?"

"Where is he?"

That made us both stand up. We traded glances and then slowly looked at the door. I fully expected him to come walking through that door. Now that we were spent from one helluva fight, he would easily wipe the floor with our butts.

The lights in the library shut off. The moonlight easing in from the window wall provided a small semblance of lighting. A dark shape rose slowly from the floor like a disfigured warp cone being pushed from the underworld. The moon created a silhouette around it and the crinkled triangular shape rose higher and higher.

A witches hat?

It grew from the floor, forming elongated disfigured shapes of something that could have been human or beast. When it stood about my height, I stepped back. Things started scuffling on the blood-wine carpet. Ticking sounds like gravel being shifted in a tin pan filled the air with an ominous stirring of fear. The moonlight sprayed a cone across the floor in front of the figure cloaked in darkness.

Kofi!

He stepped forward into the cone of light.

"There's not just one of him," Lamp said.

"There's two," I said.

Two bodies melded together like warped melted plastic. I gasped, remembered that creepy painting called Sisters.

Had he hacked into my mind, tapped into my nightmares?

Kofi and his twin were dressed in identical pantsuits, reminding me of the twin girls in that ghoulish painting. A witches' hat sat upon his head. Their skin was ashen like death. At their feet were thousands of cockroaches, running across his feet and up his body.

"Okay," I said. "This is where I get off."

Lamp said, "Old Man, now would be a good time to bail us out of here!"

Until that point, Kofi and his twin's eyes were closed. Lightning struck outside and it began to rain hard, and when the skies flashed again, thunder boomed, shaking the entire library. Kofi and his Siamese twin opened his eyes. They were no longer pretty and green but amber like a wolf.

Lamp, not being one for patience, pulled out her Glocks and started firing. She lit Kofi's ass up and was charging at him with full speed. She rammed her shoulder into him and sent him flying across the room. The Glocks went flying out of her hands in different directions and she fell on her back hard, hitting her head. I didn't have the chance to see if she was unconscious or not.

It seemed like Kofi had summoned every cockroach that ever existed and sent them motherbuggers right at me. My breath was labored. I was tired as hell and had a kick-ass pain in my ribs that was probably broken, but there was no way in hell I was going to win any battle with cockroaches.

"Shoot at the window, Lamp!" I said, and started shooting at the glass. "Trust me, we can escape this way!"

Lamp got the idea and started blasting at the window,

too. She got up and ran toward the window. I awkwardly skipped and hopped over those damned bugs like I was barefoot, running over hot lava coals. The glass finally shattered and both of us leaped toward the window.

"Well if we're going to do this, Lamp, we may as well do it with a bang," I said, crashing through the window.

26

01010100 01100001 01110100 01110101

Rain greeted me, soaking my clothes immediately. I let out a hearty yell, soaring midair while shards of glass spun around me, shooting piercing twinklings of moonlight reflections in a blinding strobe-light fashion. The wind grabbed my hair and tugged it back toward the building like a savage Neanderthal. My heart shot up to my throat like a lump of hot coals, and my stomach was drowned in a concoction of panic and adrenaline. Not even the rain cooled the blood boiling throughout my veins.

Because the side of the building was at a seventy-degree incline, within what seemed like an eternity but was only a matter of three-to-four seconds, my boots clinked into the glass and slipped on the wet surface. My butt smacked on the outside of the building's window hard, and down I descended. It was like sliding down one of those amusement park waterslides, except I was sure that our deaths were inevitable at the bottom of our ride.

The pain in my ribs pretty much guaranteed that whatever I initially thought about not being able to die in this virtual reality-holomatter construct, was absolutely grade-A wrong. It took a few seconds for my equilibrium to balance my bearings.

Lamp had managed with extraordinary flexibility to turn onto her side. She was below me, sliding headfirst toward the ground.

I'd put Lamp through so much in the past twenty-four hours, I didn't want her death to be on me, as well.

What is she doing?

The rain flushed into my eyes, making it hard to see, but that didn't stop me from seeing that she had her guns in her hand, and was pointing them at me. I was convinced that she had declared herself a death doctor and was aiming to end my life with some semblance of honorable revenge.

Lamp fired her gun, and my reflexes autonomously made me blink, thinking I was in for a painful jolt. The velocity of sliding down the slippery side of the building continued to increase.

Between the wind and the rain, my eyes fluttered madly. The hyper-draft from our fall roared in my ears, but it was not enough to stifle the sound of the Masaai terror who was, unbeknownst to me until I glanced up, right above.

Many of the warriors had followed suit and were slipping, sauntering and veering uncontrollably down the side of the glass, their faces determined, sans fear.

Lamp managed to hit the big guy in the face.

The ground was approaching at a rate that I calculated would consummate our impact within the next thirty seconds.

The big guy was gaining on me. He was trying to scissor my neck with his legs, and when I slapped them away, it sent my body spinning so that I was now falling head-first, too.

I could've taken that opportunity to lose my shit altogether, but instead, I started shooting at the translucent-skinned warrior.

Trust me, it wasn't intentional, but my first shot went right into the groin. The second caught the bottom of his foot. The third, yes, that was the kicker; hit that bastard right in his chin, and then another caught him in the head.

I didn't stop there, either. By the time I emptied both mags, they were all dead, and just when I wondered how much longer it would before my cranium was split open from the impact of hitting the ground, I heard Lamp crash into something that sounded more like she fell into a table of poker chips.

Three seconds later, my head caved into a mountain that stood nearly three stories high; a mound of skeletal remains. I burrowed at least two meters deep into the mountain of bones before stopping, pieces of osseous matter punctured my shoulder, arms and side. It hurt to bloody hell.

Skissh! Slossh! Twack! Frummp!

The lifeless bodies of the Maasai warriors smashed into the mound around me.

Lamp punched her hand through the pile of bones and clutched my arm, snatching me out.

"You all right?" she asked.

"Not at all," I said.

We both tumbled over and fell to the ground. It reminded me of the time I was playing tag on the hill behind one of my foster parent's house in Accra with one of my cousins. We had both tripped and rolled some nine-odd meters to the bottom. Even with all the scrapes and bruises we accumulated, we laughed until we both wet our shorts.

This is no laughing matter.

A nauseating smell lingered in the air. The ground was prickly. We both knew what layered the earth.

Human skeletons!

Lamp and I were on the ground moaning, trying to absorb our wounds.

She said, "There is no way we survive this."

I sat up. Behind the building, there were dozens of mounds. Skeletal remains of thousands of people. My heart was still racing from the fall, but this, this was something that the human mind could not ever be prepared for; the residue of carnage.

She and I picked ourselves up and stood there observing the corpses of the warriors we'd terminated.

I couldn't believe the decimation that surrounded us.

Even though the world had a history of wars, some religious, most political, all brutal, there was nothing like standing in a cesspool of death. There was nothing that hurt my heart more than knowing that every one of these people had mothers, or fathers, wives, husbands, someone who loved them. Even though it was just a hologram, the subconscious mind did not discern between reality and fantasy. I was a pathologist and had done many autopsies, albeit, in the House of Oware game, but still, it was a bit overwhelming.

To our left were three rows of rusted rundown cars, ten, maybe twelve vehicles. In front of those, old motorcycles stood on their kickstands. There were two gas pumps and a small mechanic shop in front of the motorcycles. Not even a hundred meters from the edge of the building stood part of a man-made lake that wrapped around the front of the building.

Behind us were more kennels. All of the gates had holes in them large enough for a healthy German Shepherd to come through. There were skeletons inside some of the kennels that looked canine.

A breeze did us the honor of sweeping that vile, decayed smell under our noses. It was one that I'd grown to know over the past few days. I didn't have to warn Lamp. She knew when we heard the growling.

I let out a hard sigh, and said, "I hate these bitches."

"Now what?" Lamp said, and turned.

I shook my head, and withdrew my machetes. "You have to ask?" I said, and turned around.

There were several dozen dholes facing us, each snarling, all drooling with hunger. Most of them had misshapen heads. A couple of them had deformed torsos, and one had a tumorous neck.

I backed away slowly, and then I yelled, "RUN!"

Hoping that one of those police vehicles were opened, I dashed for the car door, hearing the pitter-pattering of a mob of wet paws giving chase. The dholes barked with an angry hunger that autonomously made me run faster than I ever thought my feet could go. And Lamp, hell, she passed right by me like the hare racing the tortoise. She leaped over one of the vehicles and her butt slid across the hood.

I tried the driver's door to the first vehicle I got to, and sonofabitch if the damn thing wasn't locked. I turned just as a dhole leaped in the air for my throat.

I ducked and elbowed the driver's window.

The dog went flying on top of the wet roof, his feet clumsily skidded over toward Lamp.

Two other wild dogs leaped at me, and I shifted out of the way just in time for them to soar through the broken window into the car. One of them yelped, as I imagined its ribs snagged into a broken shard of glass jutting from the broken window.

I withdrew the 9mm from the front of my drenched holster. And fired at a few of the dogs approaching while I kept moving toward the row of motorcycles.

They fell and slid in the wet earth. One dhole tripped over an injured dhole, but the others leaped over the dead dogs, while most of them ran around the fallen. Glass broke and I figured either Lamp got into a vehicle or shoved a dhole so hard it smashed into the window.

Gunshots came from Lamp's direction, as well as yelps from injured wild canines. I made it to a bike and saw that most of them had keys in them.

"Lamp, the bikes have keys!" I said, running for it, the rain slapping me hard in my face. "Get to the bikes!"

"Got it!"

A few of the dholes must've had the same idea. They flanked around and were at the bikes before I got there. One nipped at my ankle and down I went in pain. A few bones on the ground pierced my side.

Two of the dholes tore into my arms and legs. I fought them as best as I could, screaming bloody murder, never having had experienced that insane amount of agony before.

Suddenly, they stopped biting.

For a few seconds, I was too busy grimacing with excruciating pain to realize that all of the dholes had stopped barking, too. I sat up, rain sending my blood to the earth laden with human skeletons. My jaw fell agape.

Lamp stood on top of one of the police cars with her arms spread wide, her palms up like a teenager in love with the joy of a downpour of rain. Her eyes were closed, and there were two dholes at each side of her feet. Her own blood spilled from both hands onto the dholes. But that wasn't the shocking part.

Every single dhole stood still like obedient trained dogs waiting for a command from their master. Their heads were up, facing Lamp. Their eyes were blue, glowing. None of them moved, the rain pelting their fur. The rain tapped against the hoods and ceilings of the police vehicles like rhythmic drumming of a tribe summoning the spirits.

"Xo," she said. "Find Kofi, and make sure he never takes another life again."

Standing up, I yelled, "You choose the worst times to say goodbye!"

Ffffffffwhapppp!

The loud startling noise came from where we first landed, and by the time I turned, several Maasai warriors had landed onto the ground.

Kofi and his Siamese twin, stood in front of them all, grimacing like a bully on the school playground. I glanced up and saw more than twenty of them sliding ferociously down toward us.

Great!

To be honest, there was no way in hell I was in any condition to fight any more African masters of martial arts.

Lamp screamed and I turned. She jumped down from the roof of the police vehicle and stood in the midst of all those dholes. Kofi disabled her control over the dholes, and they started after her. She leaped over the hood of the vehicle and took off. They gave chase. Lamp hopped onto another vehicle and started hopping from the hood of car-to-car. The wild dogs gave chase but kept clumsily sliding off of the wet cars. t.

Kofi and his ghouls charged toward me.

I let out a war cry and withdrew my guns, blasting at them. "Let's do this, boneheads!"

A bolt of lightning struck the ground between Kofi and me, a black wisp of smoke rose from the ground and the rain stopped. Another bolt of lightning struck the ground near Lamp and hundreds of tiny webs of electricity zapped the dholes to ashes.

Something stirred in the lake behind us like a tsunami was about to rise.

A giant arm the size of a tros-tros bus emerged from the lake and stretched out toward us like an elastic band. It grabbed Kofi and lifted him up in the air.

As if our bodies were metallic, and the body of water was the magnet, we started sliding toward the lake. Lamp went for her guns, but dropped them as soon as she touched them.

"Hey, they just burned my hands," she said, and shook her hands in pain.

I went for my machetes. "Christ!" I said, and dropped the scorching weapons. I placed my hand on my 9mm and snatched them away when the kukri knives singed my hands.

Our bodies were being pulled toward the lake.

"What's happening?" Lamp said, trying to ground her feet.

"I don't know how he's doing that."

Both Lamp and I tried grabbing hold of one of the police vehicles, but they were too slippery. Our bodies slithered to the ground. We squirmed, and fought, and even tried to grab the earth, coming up with a handful of skeletal remains but some invisible force continued pulling us toward the body of water.

"Let go of me!" Kofi yelled.

"Stop this!" I said. Our bodies were pulled into the lake. My legs delved deeper into the frigid water. I tried to swim, but it was like being sucked into a whirlpool. My efforts were useless.

Lamp went under and struggled to get to the surface.

When I heard her cough one last time and didn't see her, I screamed, "Lamp!"

Water flushed into my lungs, and I coughed. My eyes stung as my head bobbed under the water. I lifted my head to the sky. Buildings seemed to bounce before my eyes. And like some surreal dream, the buildings melted away, and only the sky was left. There wasn't a cloud in sight. It was beautiful, like a vast flower garden. There were so many rich hues and luminous shades of blue.

I coughed once more and found myself on my knees, naked and cold. The floor was marble, white as snow, and a body fell into me.

It was Lamp.

"You're alive," I said, and hugged her naked body.

She pushed me and we both fell to the floor, laughing.

"He did it!" I said. "Dad did it!"

In the distance, someone sniggered, and I sat up on my elbows and searched for the source of the sound. The entire area was one giant space of nothingness that stretched for infinity. Like a tiny stain on a brand-new cotton sheet, Kofi sat on the floor, his knees pulled up to his chin.

He was grinning and mumbling to himself.

"I made everyone pay," he said and laughed. "I made everyone pay!"

An oversized shirt draped across my body, and I glanced up. It was Dad, shirtless. He was grinning like a young boy who had just passed his rites of passage. I wrapped part of Dad's humongous shirt around Lamp and helped her up.

"Thank you, sis," she said.

"No, thank you, sister," Lamp said.

"So what's wrong with Kofi?" I asked.

"He's stuck in the game," Dad said. "It was the only way

I could defeat him by rewriting the entire program. He was a very formidable hacker."

"I couldn't have solved the case without you, Lamp." I said.

"Why would you ever try, Examiner?" Lamp said, pushing me in the head.

I acted like I was going to hit her. She dodged my swing, making me laugh.

Kenya stepped in the room, with two GAF officers, and gestured to Kofi. They nodded and went to him, placing him in handcuffs.

"Call his mother," I said to the officers. "Tell Auntie Yajna, he's coming home."

"Home?" Lamp said.

"Yeah, home," I said. "He'll be under house arrest. But I'm sure he'll be no problem for anyone, anymore. I'll make sure of that."

"We'll see what IGP Sibaya Bete says about that," Dad said.

Lamp smiled at me, and said, "Because taking care of your family is one of the most important things we beings could ever do in life."

I hugged her and kissed her cheek. "So right, sister. So right."

ABOUT THE AUTHOR

Nzondi (Ace Antonio Hall) is an American urban fantasy and horror writer. He is best known as the creator of *Sylva Slasher*, a teenage zombie slasher who also raises the dead for police investigations. His non-fiction book, *Lord of the Flies: Fitness for Writers* was published by Omnium Gatherum.

Among his many short stories published in anthologies and print magazines, Hall's short story, "Raising Mary: Frankenstein," was nominated for 2016 horror story of the year for the 19th Annual Editors and Preditors Readers Poll. A former Director of Education for NYC schools and the Sylvan Learning Center, the award-winning educator earned a BFA from Long Island University. Hall currently lives in Los Angeles with his bonsai named Bonnie.

Made in the USA
Coppell, TX
17 July 2020

30996252R10133